THE WAY OF GENTLENESS

This story arose out of the tragic accident which shook the world on the morning of 31 August 1997. However, the characters, feelings and reactions here described, as well as the ensuing events, are purely the constructs of the author's imagination.

ELIZABETH VICKERS

The Way of Gentleness

HarperCollins*Publishers*

HarperCollins*Publishers*
77-85 Fulham Palace Road,
Hammersmith, London W6 8JB

Published by HarperCollins*Publishers* 1998
1 3 5 7 9 8 6 4 2

Copyright © Elizabeth Vickers 1998

Elizabeth Vickers asserts the moral right to
be identified as the author of this work

A catalogue record for this book
is available from the British Library

ISBN 0 00 225788 2

Set in Fairfield Light

Printed and bound in Great Britain by
Caledonian International Book Manufacturing Ltd, Glasgow

To the other Mary
With Much Thanks

ACKNOWLEDGEMENT

Grateful acknowledgement is made to J.M. Dent for lines from 'Fern Hill' in *The Poems* by Dylan Thomas.

CONTENTS

I VOW TO THEE MY COUNTRY

Hymn chosen to be sung at the funeral
of Diana, Princess of Wales 6.9.97

I vow to thee, my country, all earthly things above,
Entire and whole and perfect, the service of my love;
The love that asks no question, the love that stands the test,
That lays upon the altar the dearest and the best;
The love that never falters, the love that pays the price,
The love that makes undaunted the final sacrifice.

And there's another country, I've heard of long ago,
Most dear to them that love her, most great to them that know;
We may not count her armies, we may not see her King;
Her fortress is a faithful heart, her pride is suffering;
And soul by soul and silently her shining bounds increase,
And her ways are ways of gentleness and all her paths are peace.

GUSTAV HOLST (1874–1934)
CECIL SPRING-RICE (1859–1918)

I

SACRIFICE

I

'Daddy took us to a play.'

'Did he, darling? Was it awfully boring?'

The boy looked at the young woman, trying to assess her mood. She was zigzagged across an armchair reading *Harper's* – her long legs draped over the blue brocade arm. Elegantly cropped hair gleamed, halo-like, in the light of the tall rose-shaded reading lamp.

The boy thought, 'She's like Dad's new horse.'

Artemis was a dark bay with a white blaze on her nose and Edwin loved her almost as much as he loved his mother. Artemis was temperamental too.

'No, it was OK, actually.'

He knew his mother would prefer that he was bored by his father's choice of entertainment and he didn't want to hurt her – hadn't she been hurt enough? Pleasing her, letting her see how much he cared, was about the only thing he could do to help. But he was fond of his father and sorry for him, too. It wasn't

3

Dad's fault he was awkward with him and his brother, Hugh. Dad had been brought up that way.

Edwin cleared his throat. 'It was a Greek play.'

Sometimes his mother liked to hear what he and Hugh had done on their visits to their father. So long as Jessica was never mentioned. Jessica was Dad's girlfriend. Edwin did not know how long before his parents parted Jessica and Dad had been, well, friends but he knew that she was someone his mother must never hear about when he discussed his and his brother's visits to Dad.

'Fetch me a Purdey's, Edkins, there's a duck.' She smiled her extraordinary smile which stopped hearts. 'Greek, huh! Like Grandpa?'

Edwin didn't know yet that he had inherited that smile and that hearts might also stop when he let it slide across his face. 'Well, yes, I s'pose – ancient, too, like Grandpa!'

Now they both laughed, conspirators. Mum might, if she wasn't Dad's girlfriend, have liked Jessica, who was OK when you got to know her, but she would never in a million years like Grandpa. Grandpa had been nice to them when they were little. He made rabbits out of his hankies which jumped up his arm and had taken pound coins out of his and Hugh's ears. But Grandpa was not so good when you were no longer a kid or had views of your own. And he was hopeless with Mum. Not even Edwin, who tried to please everyone, liked his grandfather when he got at Mum – although he tried to laugh at Grandpa's abysmal jokes even when they were sexist or racist or some other 'ist'. Mum, who had tons of friends who were black, as well as tons of friends who were gay or crippled, really hated that sneery way Grandpa had about people who weren't like them. Of course now Mum wasn't 'them', which made it tricky for Edwin when he visited his grandparents. Mind you, Edwin didn't think Granny approved much either of Grandpa's jokes although she would never say so in front of him and Hugh. She just sort of turned her face away from Grandpa when he started laughing and looked as if she was thinking about something else, like her horses, until it was over. Granny was a famous horsewoman.

Edwin did like his grandmother, even though she had called his mother 'that impossible girl'. Granny was a bit distant, and she could be irritable at times, but she was generally fair. She had also been known privately to refer to his mother as 'a corker' and Edwin knew she meant it – it wasn't intended to be snide. Granny wasn't envious or jealous of Mum's looks, like some people were. It was just that she was a believer in what she called 'turning a blind eye'. She expected Mum not to mind about Jessica – which was stupid if you knew the first thing about Mum. She was all or nothing, Mum was. Edwin tried again. 'Shall I tell you the story?'

The young woman patted the chair, indicating that her son should come and sit beside her. His legs, longer even than hers, stretched out sideways as he leaned against her, perching companionably on the chair's arm and drinking from the can of Purdey's he had fetched from the fridge hidden in the French walnut sideboard.

'You might have liked it – it's kind of about Helen, your namesake,' – and then as she looked a question – 'you know, Helen of Troy. The one who launched a thousand ships. You must have been called after her, Mum. She was a stunner too!'

His mother made a gesture of dismissal but Edwin knew she was pleased – which was good because he wanted to tell her the story. Dad liked ancient things. He and Mum used to have a joke about that which made Edwin sad when he remembered it. When Mum used to worry about getting lines on her face and stretchmarks and that sort of stuff, Dad would say, 'Never mind, old girl, I'll only like you better – I like ancient things!'

That was in the days when they all lived together – him, Hugh, Mum and Dad. When Mum and Dad still got on.

'So, what happened to my namesake, then?'

She was up from the chair now and stretching out her lean form. Edwin watched her. She had remained the same weight now for some time, but he still monitored his mother's body carefully. During the bad years, when she used to make herself sick, he had often got up in the night to see if she was all right. Once, although he tried to push the memory away, he had watched her, through the bathroom door, take a lot of pills out of the medicine cabinet. He had been thinking he was going to have to rush in and take them away from her when she put them back. That was during the time she had got so thin he had bruised his hip against her when she had hugged him hard after a photographer chased her down the M4. Bad times.

'Well, do you know the story of Troy?'

He had to be careful: Mum wasn't clued up on these things like Dad but she resented it if she was treated as if she were just a bimbo. It was clear to anyone with a brain that Mum was a million times more than that, but even with him she could be touchy. Still, she seemed in a good mood tonight.

'Not really, chicken, only what I remember from your Ladybird book. Tell me!'

It was a command as imperious as anything given by Granny but as unlike his grandmother's delivery as could be imagined. Uttered in the low sweet voice which made you want to go to the ends of the earth for her, you understood how, when people had met her they wanted to be Mum's friend for ever.

'It takes a bit of time . . . ?'

'Well, haven't we got time, sweetheart?'

Helena walked around the high-ceilinged room, arranging cushions, adjusting the photographs of her two sons: Hugh in nappies; Eds learning to walk; both boys under the mulberry tree at her father's estate; all four of them on a Scottish moor, her husband stiff-faced in his kilt; then the endless photographs of just the three of them, her boys and herself – by a lake in Vermont, on the beach in the Caribbean, skiing, on a water chute – laughing, always laughing, although her heart had so often been in tatters. She watched her tall, grave son who had inherited her eyes as he began to recite to her the old tale of Troy.

'You see, it all started with these goddesses – they all wanted to be thought the most beautiful so they asked Paris –' She stopped him at that.

'Paris? Edkins, I was meaning to tell you – I'm probably going to be in Paris just before I pick you two up, before school starts again. Is there anything deliciously French you want?'

Helena looked towards the photographs again. Concealed behind one of the pictures – a shot of her kneeling alongside a woman in a wheelchair, whose hand was reaching out to touch her face – there was another. Briefly she imaged it in her mind's eye.

The snapshot was of a man, dark-faced in early middle age – a man with a bit of a tummy on him it was true but nevertheless you could tell he was attractive to women. Too attractive sometimes. Helena sighed. She was not sure she could take betrayal again. But Milu swore he loved her – swore by all the stars of Egypt – swore that all the other women with whom he had been entangled were nothing to him. He had simply been waiting – waiting, through eternity (he had such a pretty way with words) for her. She sighed again, pleasurably this time, and turned back to her grave-eyed son.

'. . . so they had to go and fight, to get her back, d'you see?'

'Yes, darling.'

He knew she hadn't been listening. But she seemed happy – it wasn't that terrifying distraction that meant she was thinking

7

about when she could make herself sick. Thank God – Edwin believed in God and often consulted Him – the bulimia seemed to have stopped. She wasn't really engaged in the story, but he finished it anyway.

'The Greeks needed this wind, you see, to blow them to Troy to get Helen back. So the head of the Greek army, King Agamemnon, who was the brother of Helen's husband, actually sacrificed his daughter, Iphigenia, to get the gods to send them a wind.'

'And she let him?'

'Who?'

'Iphi– what's her name? She let them sacrifice her?'

'Iphigenia. They tricked her. She thought she was coming to be married – married to Achilles, the greatest warrior in the Greek army – so, this was really sad, Mum, she turned up with all her wedding gear on and then they grabbed her and tied her down on a rock and her father cut her throat.'

Now she was interested. 'God, I know how she must have felt.' People called her the most glamorous woman in the world but it wasn't Helen of Troy she was like; it was this unknown Greek princess – Iphigenia. She, too, had gone in joy to what she thought was a wedding and had ended up as a sacrificial victim to the ruling powers.

'But, Mum,' the boy was excited now and his remarkable eyes grew wide with emotion, 'in *this* play, the one Daddy took us to, she doesn't –'

The phone rang, making them both jump. Helena moved so rapidly towards it she knocked her ankle on the walnut sideboard. 'Damn! Eds, love, be a sweetheart and put this down for me – I'm going to take it in my room.'

Later, the boy couldn't remember if he had finished the story. In the sleepless nights which followed, endlessly, endlessly he

8

would go over in his mind that last talk he had with his mother: the extraordinary, the beautiful, the magnetic and much-pursued Princess Helena.

2

Helena stepped outside on to the balcony and looked out over the Paris skyline. Lights shone out like fairy decorations of gold and white, as the Parisians took their late evening ambulations. She breathed in the night air freighted with the unmistakable smell which is France.

The door opened behind her and he came out, walking quietly like a cat – or a burglar, she half thought. He placed a hand on the small of her back and began, with his other hand, gently to massage her shoulder. Smiling, she turned her body to enjoy the sensation more. Milu seemed to know just where it hurt.

'Are you OK, my pearl?' He spoke softly into her left ear and she wriggled a shoulder in response.

'Oh, yes! Happier than, I think, ever. If you knew the torture it has all been for me . . .'

He stopped her mouth with his finger and then held her face off, a hand against her cheek.

'You are a princess whatever happens. But will you mind?'

'Mind?' She knew what he referred to but she wanted time

to frame her answer. Would she, after all, mind giving up the name which had caused her so much misery? And there were the boys to think of. What about Edwin and Hugh? Would they mind if their mother surrendered the title which linked her to their royal destiny? And what would they say to having Milu as a stepfather? Hugh, she was sure – sunny, good-natured Hugh – would accept anyone, especially if it made his mother happy. But her elder son had his father's serious nature as well as his mother's intuition. She wasn't sure Edwin had quite liked Milu when she took the boys to meet him.

Thinking of her two boys brought on a fizz of excitement. Tomorrow she would see them again after a whole month. It was the first time since the divorce that she had not ached with missing them every morning she awoke without them. To see them again was always heaven. Not even what she was beginning to feel for Milu could replace the love she felt for her boys. The 'terrible trio', she called them, herself and the boys – oftentimes, they seemed like a small gang against the world of pomp and circumstance that she had left when she left their father. Their poor father! She must be in love because she was able to think quite sympathetically of James and his uptight life.

'I've devised a scheme to get the paparazzi off our backs.'

'Oh, Milu, you have no idea how fiendishly difficult that is!' She spoke fondly but even in the unclear light she detected his expression cloud.

'Do you think I'm not up to it?' There was an aggressive edge to his voice and Helena felt herself shrink back. Once or twice she had noticed he took a kind of fit of pique, which bothered her.

'Of course, darling.' She patted his hand reassuringly. 'It's just that I'm such a frightfully old hand at this. Heavens, don't I wish I weren't!'

'Well, they won't see through this one.' The man spoke less

aggressively. He was confident about his plan. Two decoy drivers had been arranged: one in Helena's Mercedes, one in his own car. The hotel chauffeur his father used on all important occasions was going to pick them up by the back door. Jean-Claude was a thoroughly reliable driver with military experience.

This was what Helena needed, Milu thought. Someone like himself, who knew the world, to give her guidance and support – help her get away from this ghastly life she had been living. Perhaps then she would settle down and give up the good works. He shivered at the thought of touching her lovely skin after it had been pawed by lepers and gays with Aids. Luckily she didn't seem that keen on bed yet so they could keep a hold on that department until he'd got her to promise to give up the more hideous aspects of her 'work'. It wasn't appropriate that his wife should work.

Helena doubted Milu would have managed to put off many of the paparazzi but the last thing she wanted was a scene on this night of all nights. On her finger was the diamond ring she had chosen with him only days earlier. She turned it to the inside of her hand, instinctively preparing to protect its view from the brutal flash of the cameras.

'Come on, bitch, open yer legs. Give us one, Helen!' She hadn't dared to tell him what it was like – the horrifying coarseness of their insults designed to make her cry. Pictures of Princess Helena in tears, in today's market, were worth millions.

'Come on, show us yer tits, love. How you keeping the spare tyre down?'

'See over 'ere, Helena! Who's getting up you now? How's the cellulite? Give us a break!'

What would Milu make of it? Was he going to be equal to the terrible onslaught, the constant hectoring, the relentless harassment, the cameras right in your face, the lies, the jibes, the obscenities, the complete and overwhelming invasiveness so total that you longed to set about them with some sharp instrument, a hatchet or a knife, and cut them all to ribbons? Could he, could any man, take her if such a gross entourage came with her, like the terrifying creatures that chased the Greek prince across the sea in the story Eds was telling her just before she left?

Dear Eds! For a moment she imagined the imminent reunion with her boys. Hugh, still a child, would hug her tight and want to know all about Paris, but Eds, Eds would hang back watching, waiting to see how she was. Her 'first advisor', she called him – the person in the world who had best known her through the dog days – amazing to think that one day he would be crowned king of England.

The man beside her stirred, detecting that her thoughts were away from him. 'Darling?'

'Yes, darling?'

'I'm going to make the final arrangements. Will you be all right here?'

He placed a protective arm round her waist and squeezed. How lovely it was to have a man protect her at last. No one since Daddy had been able to make her feel so safe.

'I'll be fine. I'll watch the stars.' As she spoke, a star shot across the sky and a fizzle ran down her spine. 'Milu, did you see that?'

'No – what?' Already he had turned away, anxious to tie up the final details of the planned getaway.

'A star – a shooting star.' She was filled with an excited apprehension. 'We should wish. Let's wish, Milu.'

She caught his hand but he merely patted her with the other, disentangling himself. 'No, Princess, you wish. It was you who saw the star. I'll go and arrange the coach before it turns into a pumpkin!'

He was gone, his dark form in the white suit fading from her like an old negative into the blackness. She looked over towards Notre Dame. The cathedral stood in its surrounding spotlights like a vast wedding cake. It reminded her of the day – almost sixteen years earlier – when she had married. Another life.

'Notre Dame,' Helena spoke within herself, 'Notre Dame – Our Lady – help me to wish well.' For a minute she stood, her head bowed, then she knelt down on the balcony and spoke aloud into the dark.

'I wish that I could be free from the public gaze, that never again would I be pursued by the press. And I wish . . .' What was it she really wished?

She touched the ring on the little finger of her right hand; a modest-seeming ring with a single pearl in it. Her father's gift – she had treasured it more than the legendary jewels which marriage to James had brought her. Until now, her father's big, shy presence had been her only protection against the demons which pursued her. But tonight she felt another source of protection.

'Daddy?' His name was like a farewell.

The resonant words of the marriage ceremony, conducted under the great dome of England's most triumphant cathedral sounded in her head. She had walked up that long aisle on her beloved father's arm and neither of them had known who was the more scared. 'And shall you, Helena, forsaking all others . . .' But her husband, the man she had adored with the devotion of her nineteen-year-old heart, had not followed the exigent command of the marriage service. He had not forsaken all others. The pain and shame of it had dogged and haunted her – but tonight she felt all that could change and she might be free. Another way was possible now.

She stood looking out over the city cradling the pearl ring in hands which she had cupped to form a protective sphere around it. Then, on a strange impulse, she kissed the ring, leant over the wrought-iron rail, and flung it as far as she could out into the streets of Paris. 'A sacrifice to make the wish come true.' It seemed only the night air heard her before she descended into the lobby of the hotel.

Milu came to greet her, dabbing at his nose with one of his cream silk handkerchiefs. His eyes were bright as he looked adoringly into hers.

'Everything is ready – the two cars have gone ahead and ours is ready and waiting.' He squeezed her forearm.

'And our destination? Where are you taking me?'

He had kept even from her his design for where they were to spend the night. And this she had allowed, wanting him to feel he had some choice in the life they were about to lead together. How little real choice she could give him he had yet to discover.

'My apartment, my darling one.' He clapped his hands in enjoyment and for a moment he seemed to her almost like a little child – one of her own when they had planned a terrific game. 'I have something waiting for you there. Something I want you to read tonight.'

It was the only time he had ever managed to get the words out of his head and on to paper – the poem he had written for her and had transcribed on to the silver tablet which lay under the pillow in the room he now called hers. Often, when he smoked, he had these really potent ideas – but they disappeared when the light of reality penetrated the incandescent interior of his mind. He had written songs before but never a poem. And this was how he knew that he loved Helena: he had sat up all night and fought with the temptation to hit the sack, in order to finish what he had started and follow the impulse through. Tonight of all nights, while the world was still ignorant of their great plan, he wanted her, before she slept, to find it, his poem, well, almost his – he had got the idea from an old Arab love song – so that she would know how much he was willing to do for her. Tonight she would see the extent of his care.

Jean-Claude had spent the latter part of the evening playing patience downstairs with the wine waiter. Between them, they had split a bottle of Margaux '83 which a customer had sent back and another of Lynch '79. Jean-Claude never drank when he was on duty – except wine, which hardly counted and was a matter of helping the wine waiter out. He was careful, of course he was. The medication he took for his nerves since he'd got into debt said, on the label, that he shouldn't drink while taking it. Jean-Claude prided himself on his abstemiousness when he was driving.

Tonight he was driving the boss's son and the new dame he had picked up, so he had to be doubly careful. Not that any affair the boss's son had was likely to last.

Jean-Claude was unprepared, however, for the identity of the young woman whom he found himself helping into the back of the big Mercedes. Looked like young Milu had struck lucky at last. No wonder there was a five thousand franc bonus on the job tonight. Great legs, too, and a smile that made you want to walk on your knees for her.

Helena had never had much faith in Milu's plan. She had lived so long with this particular enemy that, at best, she had stopped expecting anything more than a degree of civility in their attacks. But she couldn't help hoping that the wish which she had solemnized with the pearl ring had somehow worked. Her heart sank more than usual, therefore, when the great roar of bikes thrummed up beside them.

'Come on, Helen, baby, where's he going to take them off?'

'What are they saying?' Milu, slightly deaf, was frowning.

How dare they! How dare they despoil the magical evening, her chance of happiness ever before it had even begun. Years of having her nerves ragged had frayed her natural manners. Dropping the window she shouted, 'OK, you bastards, catch us if you dare!' And as the car purred away she said to Milu, 'He *must* lose them, Milu. Make it come true – please, make it OK for us, darling?'

The ride was the strangest Jean-Claude had ever known. The boss's son's offer to multiply his bonus by twenty – a sum which would almost wipe out his debts – should he lose the paparazzi who drove like demons, weaved through his thoughts as the bikes, in turn, wove in front of their eyes: beside them, at their rear – always calling, calling and gesturing for the young woman who sat in the back seat urging him:

'That's it lose them, lose them, the vultures.'

For Helena, caught up in some powerful sense of destiny, swore there and then to herself that if they escaped, this once, from the rapacious attentions of the paparazzi, then that was a sign – a sign that she should marry Milu. She sat, white-knuckled, as the car gathered speed, dodging the tenacious presence of the men on bikes who rode faster than the hounds of hell to torment her peace. This was more than any race. It was the race that would determine her whole future. If there was a destiny which she could influence, then from this night on she would be free for ever; or, if fate decreed otherwise, if they caught her, then she would know that, for her, love would always be a matter only of brief episodes of brightness within an ever-closing circle of lonely doom.

3

They said later that the sound of the car hitting the central wall of the tunnel was like an explosion. Several people, walking late in the Paris evening, heard it and thought 'Terrorists!' and ran for cover. In the tunnel itself vehicles came to a screaming halt as drivers and passengers hurriedly left their cars and ran to the scene.

But the first there, as everyone agreed, were the paparazzi: crouching, kneeling, flashing, crawling all over the car with its grim harvest. The ambulance had been called and the shocked young doctor who had attempted to help the only two survivors had already exhausted his efforts when the identity of one of them, the young woman with the blonde hair who sat huddled between the seats waving her hands and faintly wailing (like a kitten, he later explained to his wife), was at first incredulously suggested.

'C'est Helena – c'est la Princess!'

Afterwards, it was acknowledged that the ambulance staff, the doctors, the nurses at the public hospital to which the still-conscious body of Princess Helena was taken, acted with exemplary skill and dedication. For three hours they struggled to sustain the erratic pulse of life in the damaged body of the world's most famous and sought-after woman before, exhausted in the early hours of the French morning, the doctor ceased his steady pumping of her heart to pronounce,

'Elle est morte.'

Silence fell upon the theatre; even the Paris street noises seemed suddenly to cease. Into the soundless moment a young male nurse broke down. The surgeon, his own mask dampening discreetly, ordered that they all keep 'très, très calme'. Accustomed to crisis and tragedy, nevertheless no one knew quite what they should do next in so grave an event. The body was wheeled out and into an antechamber while the operating team scrubbed down and changed. During the course of this it was decided by M. Charnet, the hospital administrator, that he should telephone the British ambassador. It was an English tragedy – the English would know what was to be done next. Meantime, the press were to be told that Princess Helena was still undergoing surgery following the disaster.

When Angela Claire was six years old her father had walked out of the Ealing flat where he had lived with her mother and returned by ferry to his native France. Ten years later his English wife died of a thrombosis in her leg, following an operation on her varicose veins, and his daughter had sought him out at his Paris address. Now training as a theatre sister at the Hospital Notre-Dame, Angela had just been thrown out of her father's flat in Montmartre by his third wife, Jacqueline.

She was wondering where she was going to stay when at 4 a.m., walking down the corridor to report for duty, Angela saw a woman coming towards her. At first she thought it was a man, mistaking the tall frame. Closer up though it seemed to be the

Chief of Nursing Staff, who stopped and fixed Angela with a level gaze.

'Angela, do you hear me?'

At the time Angela did not think it was at all odd that the head nurse seemed changed. Angela had had little to do with her superior previously but now she felt herself transfixed by the wide grey stare.

Whispering so as not to disturb the serious operation taking place behind her, Angela answered, 'I do.'

'Then listen to me.' The head nurse inclined her face and Angela noticed a smell of violets; she had given her mother eau de violettes the Christmas before she had died. A kind of heat flooded over her and she felt her face and chest grow warm.

'You must wait until the operation is over. Then . . .' The head nurse spoke carefully in Angela's ear.

'But must I tell no one?' Angela, afraid, looked up into the other's eyes and feared still more. A smell of pine seemed to be filling the hospital corridor. Angela felt her legs begin to tremble.

'Do as I say and you will be doing no wrong.' The head nurse smiled and Angela felt reassured. 'You will be rewarded.'

Suddenly the other was gone. No sound of feet along the corridor which stretched some distance until it curved on either side round to the elevators. Angela, her heart beating violently, moved along towards the operating room. She put her head to the door and listened.

At first Helena could not believe they were going to leave her there. From her vantage point above she watched them as one by one they discarded instruments, slipped down their masks. Some of them were in tears. Almost all of them reached out and touched her. A young male nurse dropped a kiss on her hand and she felt his beard rough against it – but as if her hand were far away from her, as though she had grown into a giant. The surgeon who had opened her chest stood longest, looking into her closed eyes. It was odd but she could see from her present perspective that her eyes were closed. Then he too gently pressed her cheek and left the room.

From the same vantage point she watched her body being covered in a white cloth and wheeled into an adjacent room. Then they left her. She tried to call out, 'Listen, listen to me! There's been a mistake. Look up, I'm here, here,' but no sound issued from her mouth.

She could not move her hands under the sheet. The hole in her chest did not hurt, which was odd because she could see, from where she was, that it was wide enough to be dangerous.

She was alone. Quite alone. But she didn't feel lonely. She couldn't remember at first who she had been with. Then she wondered where Milu was and what had happened to him? Nothing too awful she hoped, because if it had it would all be because of her – not her fault exactly, but thanks, once again, to the press pursuing her. She couldn't be sure why she was here in this hospital – for that was obviously what it was. Where was it? She hoped that Edwin and Hugh wouldn't worry too much. But she would be able to talk to them soon. The hospital had probably rung them all already. Poor James!

Thinking of her boys, Helena tried to stir again but could make no movement. She tried to do her yoga breathing, watching herself extend her spine along the high trolley-like bed she was lying on.

The door opened and a young woman with red hair came in. She looked terribly scared. Helena wanted to reassure her but her lips simply would not move so she lay back as the young woman, moving very quietly, began to wheel her body out of the room.

The victim of the crash which occurred in the tunnel along the left bank of the Seine was not the only casualty dealt with at the Hospital Notre-Dame that night. Alicia Fenton-Kirk, of no fixed address, crossing the road after too many drinks at the Bar Nemo, had lurched in front of a battalion of bikes racing at over 100 mph. One sent her ricocheting across the road, fracturing her spine. By the time the emergency services reached her she was clean dead.

Alicia too was left in a side room covered with a white cloth. The following day the hospital bureaucracy should commence the search for her next of kin. But for the moment all was taken up with the crisis of a more famous casualty. That night, at least, unhounded any more by debt, heroin-longing, drunken dreams or the persecutory thoughts of her parents, Alicia Fenton-Kirk lay undisturbed; granted, by the grace of the Princess Helena, an anonymous peace.

James was dreaming he was walking over the moors with his sister when a black sheep crashed down the mountainside and banged into him, hurting his shoulder.

'Sir, sir!' He woke to feel his shoulder urgently jolted.

'What?' He was awake in seconds. The clock said it was 4.15 a.m. 'What the bloody hell?'

'Your Royal Highness, James –' It was Helena's brother-in-law, Richard. Wild-eyed in a dressing-gown, he stared at the future monarch. James observed Richard was holding the back of his head with both hands.

'What is it?'

'There has been an accident . . .'

For a second James thought, 'Oh my God, not the boys!' and was relieved, almost, when the words came: '. . . Helena. Oh, sir, Helena – I am so sorry. I am afraid, sir, Helena has been killed.'

For the rest of his life he never forgot the moment when relief turned to guilt and guilt turned to despair. It was days, weeks even, before he felt the full impact of what he later came to understand as the most meaningful event in his life: the death of his former wife, the woman whom he had married to be his queen and from whom he had parted only a year previously. But at the time he could only sit up in bed and hold his face.

'Dear Mother of God, how?'

'We don't know, sir . . . The Prime Minister is on the phone . . . Oh, dear . . . Would you like to . . . ?'

It was not from the Prime Minister but from the surgeon himself, Dr Denot, that James heard how his former wife had died from internal injuries following an accident that morning in Paris. He learned that the driver and his wife's friend had been killed outright but his wife had been taken to the Hospital Notre-Dame where Dr Denot and his team had battled for three hours to repair a pulmonary vein, mortally damaged in the crash. Princess Helena had finally given up the ghost at 4 a.m. that morning.

James asked few questions. 'And the press? Were they there?'

'Mais bien sûr,' the doctor had replied. 'They were of course there. Where Princess Helena goes . . .' his voice died away. Across the Channel there was silence.

Dr Denot cleared his throat. 'She was, please, can I say this – forgive me if it is an intrusion – but the Princess, before she left us, she was . . . we all noticed this . . . she was extraordinarily serene.'

Another silence. A faint curlew-call of a Paris siren filtered across the space between the two men. Then, 'Thank you for helping her,' James said. 'I shall be with you shortly and I would like then to thank you personally, if I may.'

Edwin was awake when his father came into his room. A dream had woken him – not a nightmare, as he sometimes had, but rather a comforting dream about a strange, tall lady who smelt of the flowers Mum used to pick when they visited their other grandfather in the country. The tall lady had had a message for him from someone, but Edwin couldn't remember either the message or who it was from when he woke up.

He knew there must be something wrong 'cos Dad never came into his room like that – let alone at 5 o'clock in the morning. He looked all white and peculiar, and for a second Edwin wondered if his father was having a heart attack. He was almost out of bed to get a doctor when his father knelt beside the bed and took his hand. This was scary. Edwin sat, half in and half out of the bed, his leg twisted uncomfortably under him.

'Edwin, old son, you're going to have to be very brave – I've got some dreadfully shocking news.'

Edwin knew at once that it was his mother. His reaction, too, was an odd sort of relief because his first thought was that Dad was going to tell him that Mum had killed herself and somehow, he didn't know why, that would have been worse – if anything could be worse than this. He sat, still half in and half out of the bed and let Dad squeeze his hand till Edwin thought Dad would break the bones. Not that Edwin would mind having his bones broken. In fact it might help stop the pain in his chest.

The pain was so bad, as Dad was talking, that Edwin was afraid he might cry out. He knew whatever he did he must not do that, for if he did the tears would come and then they would never stop. And now Dad was twisting his hands and asking him, Edwin, how they were going to tell Hugh. So Dad needed him and Edwin could see that, for the time being, that was going to help.

'D'you want me to?'

The boy's mother's eyes looked out at James.

'No, Eds, I must tell Hugh. But would you be there too? He might . . . I don't know . . . He, I, we'll both need you.'

*   *   *

24

Even later, when they had all heard the news, Edwin himself did not cry – not even in the fastness of his own room. Instead he stared, dry-eyed, into the dark, willing and willing his mother back.

4

James had not spoken to Jessica since Sunday. He thought about her now as the plane passed over the clouds which piled thickly above the Channel. Helena's two sisters sat mutely across the aisle.

The three were travelling together, sorry ambassadors in a journey to bring back the body of the woman to whom each was connected intimately – two by ties of blood, the third through the solemn vows which they had taken together before the nation's delighted view. Vows which each had broken since, and, he now recognized, separately in guilt and pain.

For James it had always been Jessica – even, heaven help him, when he had gone to tell her about the wedding which all the world watched in rapture. Jessica had not cried then, and he had assured her that it would make no difference to them. She was not technically free – it was unthinkable that a divorced woman should ascend the throne of England, and he had a duty to perform. This marriage, he assured her, was something that must be done for the sake of the country. More likely for the sake of his parents, she had said, uncharacteristically waspish. One of the points about Jessica was that she understood about the protocol he was obliged to observe. And his parents. She understood about his parents as his just-twenty, easily embarrassed bride had not.

Had his marriage made a difference, he wondered now as they began to descend, through cloud, into the Paris outskirts. For his part it had probably only served to quicken his interest in Jessica. Capable and calm, she was always there, waiting for him without reproach, able to mop up his anxiety, to comfort him and make him laugh as no one else ever had.

Certainly not the shy young woman he had married, he reflected now. But then how could a twenty-year-old virgin, damaged by years of parental squabbles and by temperament unfitted for the aloof restraint which was the hallmark of his family, understand what he might need from a relationship? Who among them, anyway, had helped her? Of them all, only his sister, Mary, had made the effort and she had such a bluff and breezy style that to begin with, at least, it had put Helena right off. They had been better friends recently, since the divorce. Quite pally, in fact. Mary was a good sort and Helena, older now, more worldly wise, was better at taking the rough side of Mary's tongue – better at seeing that it wasn't personal but was dealt out, in true democratic style, to everyone. Of them all, Mary was the one best suited to democracy. And Mary's 'horse sense', as he privately called it, ensured that when Edwin and Hugh visited their aunt they were treated in the like-it-or-lump-it style with which she had raised her own children – pretty damn successfully, as James was the first to admit. Matthew and Zoe might have come from any decent comprehensive school in the Home Counties.

The car that drove them to the hospital was a Mercedes uncomfortably like Helena's own armour-plated one. Who, in the name of God, had allowed her to drive in anything else? For the wreck that had been so horrifically and graphically described to him could never have occurred had his wife been travelling in her official car.

James sat close to Henrietta wanting to put his arm round her but not quite able to touch her. They were like her, the sisters. So like her that meeting them that morning had almost provoked a loss of control. But neither Henrietta nor Pamela had that extra quality, that 'edge'. He had witnessed it often enough in his wife in its more neurotic manifestations but that same knife-edge produced the other effect too: a gleam which came reflecting back from the light that Helena evoked in others. Increasingly through the years that capacity she had had, of illuminating another's being, seemed to grace her own with a special aura. Sitting here between her two siblings, driving through the Paris morning, James realized that it was a gleam shared by others who had died in tragic circumstances: Kennedy, Marilyn Monroe, James Dean – an indefinable quality which seemed almost to predict their end. As if nature were subtly foreshadowing, in the charisma of such people, some clue which, if one could only interpret it in time, might have saved their lives.

Had he been envious of it, the charisma that attached to his former wife? People said so. His family had disliked it – felt it took something from the people's love of him – but had he really minded for himself? He thought not, but the older he got the more he recognized how little one knew about oneself. Pamela, weeping quietly in the far corner of the car, sneezed suddenly and he patted her hand. They drove silently towards the Hospital Notre-Dame.

It was not entirely surprising that the usually efficient hospital staff had failed to log the body of Alice Kirk, a.k.a. the Hon.

Alicia Fenton-Kirk. She had been brought in at 3.45 a.m., having been found at the kerbside, a little short of the scene of the night's more prominent tragedy. In the atmosphere of feverish excitement not even the scrupulous ambulance workers remembered the body of that other young woman, so involved did they become with the fate of the one whose life was a subject of global concern.

Alice Kirk was the subject of no one's concern, not even her family's, for they had long since washed their hands of her. In and out of various clinics, drug rehabilitation centres and the beds of a list of men too numerous even for Alice to tabulate, she had reached a new low on the night of 30 August after an unsatisfactory conversation on the phone with her latest lover, a sculptor. The lover, on the whole a tolerant man, had locked her out of his studio apartment some weeks earlier, after she had set fire to his bed. In the course of the episode she had also set fire to her passport, her identity card, her wallet and the few remaining photographs of her father (she had torn up those of her mother long ago). She had no photograph of her only son who had been adopted when his mother was just twenty years old.

She had lost her job, the only job she had been really happy with, when they discovered she was pregnant. She had thought that a nursery school, of all places, might not mind. And the kids loved her. But the mummies in their smart BMWs, their Jags and Daimlers had looked at the bump which grew so embarrassingly obvious on her twig-like frame and caused spiteful talk behind her back. Funny to think she had lost her job to the woman who had, in turn, then lost hers, as the future queen of England.

Alice, who believed in such things, liked to think there was a connection between herself and the woman who had taken her place – although, to be fair, Lady Helena had had no hand in Alice's sacking. People even said they looked alike – less so now – though for different reasons they were both slimmer. Alice had often felt like writing to her, especially during Lady Helena's troubles over the divorce, just to say she knew how Helena must be feeling.

Alice had given birth to her son almost exactly six weeks before the royal wedding. They'd all watched the preparations in the high-class nursing home where her parents had sent her. The day the social worker came to take the baby away for the last time was the day before the wedding. On the day the world watched Lady Helena Grey walk up the aisle of St Paul's, Alicia Fenton-Kirk tried heroin for the first time. She had felt as good as Lady Helena on that Wednesday.

It was the recollection of the adoption which had led, in fact, to the orgy of drink and heroin which in turn had occasioned the potentially serious fire and the end of yet another attempt on Alice's part to stay in a world which seemed unwilling to welcome her. For the past weeks she had been sleeping in the beds of men who picked her up as she walked by the Seine – always looking for the next drink, another fix of 'Horse'.

That late summer day, turning away from the river, she found herself alongside the Ritz Hotel. You could often pick up a good payer there, especially if you went round the back to the Rue Cambon. Waiting on the corner, smoking a Gitane, she had chanced to look up and had seen a star flash a fiery path down the heavens.

'Star!' Alice had said conversationally to a vagrant in a doorway. And then, 'Wish!'

Vaguely she remembered from childhood that if you saw a shooting star you made a wish. There seemed little to be lost in keeping up the practice now.

'I wish', pronounced Alicia Fenton-Kirk, 'that for once, for bloody once, I could be centre stage. Just the once, mind, I'm not greedy.' She wagged her finger at the vagrant who nodded back his agreement.

An image of her mother shutting the door in her face floated into her memory and she tugged at the locket at her throat. 'Please,' she said, 'let me be special, even if it's the last thing that happens.'

Out of the sky there fell something which made a light tinkling sound at her feet. Swaying on her stacked heels, Alice squatted down and picked up a small circular object. Dimly it gleamed under the light of the street lamp.

'A ring,' said Alice and perhaps because she was drunk she was not surprised. 'A ring. Someone up there heard.' And now she was no longer talking to the vagrant. 'Thank you, whoever you are up there.' And then, because she was essentially a well-mannered and generous woman: 'I hope you get your just deserts – I hope it breaks even for you, too! This means', she spoke confidently as she placed the ring on the little finger of her right hand, 'my wish is going to come true.'

He had to identify the body, of course. Henrietta and Pamela were too distressed and it was right that he should. James himself could barely look at the woman who had been his wife. It was some time since they had met; briefly just, at Edwin's speech day, where they had brushed cheeks for the waiting press. But even then she had tried to embrace him and had murmured, 'Darling!' and he had been embarrassed, pushing her away.

Now, risking only dabs of glances at her closed face – for each glance risked some inevitable retaliatory pain – James observed that she had lost weight again. All that wealth and care and she looked as skinny as a street cat. And her hair, usually so perfect, looked almost scruffy. She would hate that. The toll of the accident – and the hours on the operating table while they struggled to keep her alive – had left her barely recognizable.

But the fine bones were there, the blue veins over the eyelids speaking generations of breeding.

Perhaps most pathetic was the small ring on her right hand. They had removed her other jewellery, presumably for the operation – but had they forgotten, or maybe could not remove? – what Helena had called 'Daddy's ring', the ring the Earl had given his favourite daughter when she won the swimming cup at school. It was the one area in which she had been successful as a schoolgirl. Astonishing, James couldn't help thinking, when you considered her accomplishments since. He had been dismissive of the ring, advising her to leave it off: it was too insignificant for their state events. But she wouldn't. Later, he had seen this as the first sign of her stubbornness. The recollection of this particular piece of unkindness sprang back at him now like uncoiled barbed-wire.

He had asked for a few moments alone with the body of his dead wife and he found, when he was granted them, that he didn't at all know how to use the time. Alone with her he felt afraid. His heart had contracted to a small dense painful lump lodged inside his breastbone. Feeling he should pray, he couldn't get the words out of the lump that had become his heart and into his mouth.

Dropping to his knees he grasped the cold hand which wore the small pearl ring.

'Helena, wherever you are . . . be at peace now.' He knelt for moment longer then added, 'And Helena, for any wrong I have done you, please forgive me and help me and the boys in our life to come.'

5

An unknown thing had happened – unknown at least to Edwin. There had been a row between Dad and Granny. More than a row, a regular holocaust with Dad shouting at Granny and at Uncle Richard, Auntie Pamela's husband.

Dad wanted Mum to have a public funeral and Granny had tried to pretend that it was not what Mum would have wanted – but they all knew it was really that Granny didn't want it. Granny, who always seemed unerringly to know what to do, had been all to pieces.

Edwin had been almost glad about the row because it had at last allowed him to say, to insist, that he was going to walk behind Mum's coffin. He had planned that if they didn't let him he was going to steal Artemis and ride up into the middle of the funeral procession and let them try to stop him. After all, what could they do with all the TV cameras and everyone watching? Shoot him? But it turned out there was no need – which Edwin rather regretted – because Dad had just said, 'Of *course*,' as if there was no argument about it, and Granny had pulled her mouth down, as she did when she was annoyed. But she said nothing.

Grandpa had not been very pleased when Granny had declared that in that case Grandpa had better walk behind the coffin too, at which Hugh had insisted that he wanted to walk as well and had threatened all kinds of resistance when it looked as if there might be opposition to this idea. No one wanted to upset Hugh and, anyway, Dad seemed to be on their side, so Hugh was going to walk too.

Edwin had not really liked the idea of Grandpa walking along behind Mum. It was fine for Dad, of course, because after all Dad had been her husband, even if he hadn't always treated Mum the way she had wanted. But everyone knew that Grandpa hadn't liked Mum and wouldn't even talk to her when they were alone together, so it seemed wrong that he should be there with Mum's brother and the rest of them. Still, that was what Granny had decided when she had seen she wasn't going to be able to stop him and Hugh. Edwin was too tired to fight a cause he suspected he wouldn't win. Once Granny decided something you might as well argue with the Tower of London.

Edwin wrote to his mother every day in his journal – ordinary things that she would like to know about him or Hugh, or how the new fashions looked, or what he had been watching on TV. Which was mostly stuff about her. He told her about the people all round the world, people like the President of America and Nelson Mandela (whom Mum liked and said was sexy) all saying what a good sort she was and how much they were going to miss her. He also told her about all the flowers people had been bringing – which he and Hugh and Dad had helped to deliver – he had seen Dad almost in tears when a woman gave him some lilies and Dad had put one of the lilies away in his pocket, which Mum would have been pleased about – and all the messages and toys and the lines and lines and lines of people crying

34

in the streets and not bothering to cover it up and taking days off work to sign the books of condolences.

I wish you were here to see it, Mum, because it's quite amazing. No one has ever seen anything like it. They keep on saying how it's not really English – more like the Italians or the Greeks, which I guess will please you! Huge banks and banks and banks of flowers, all your favourites. Fantastic! When Hugh and I went out to meet them a woman gave me a bunch of those coloured ones that you said once were the 'lilies of the field' in the bible. You know, the ones like 'Solomon in all his glory' that don't toil or spin. I liked her. Another woman grabbed my hand and said, 'She was a good woman, your mum, she would have been proud of you.' I hope you are, Mum, where ever you are.

Not even Hugh knew about this journal which Edwin kept locked up with a small brass key. Aunt Mary had given it to him last Christmas and had winked when he opened it and muttered, 'So you learn how to get yourself some privacy.' He hadn't talked to Aunt Mary yet, but she was the one person he was looking forward to seeing at the funeral, if you could say he was 'looking forward' to anything about that day. And his cousins. He wanted to see his cousins.

Jessica Howes-Peters watched the funeral, like most of the nation, on television. She was surprised to find that she had a lump in her throat which seemed vaguely hypocritical in the circs.

She was old enough to remember Churchill's funeral to which she had been taken as a child. But an old man at the natural close of his life, albeit a life which had done the state much service, was not the emotional equivalent of a young woman cut off in her prime.

35

The procession with its dark bay horses and the lonely gun-carriage looked strangely small and stark. Jessica had expected the horses to have black plumes – like Queen Victoria's funeral. Bereft of any other adornment the three white wreaths appeared almost austere beside the massive citadels of floral tributes brought by the grieving public. Jessica squinnied at the television.

Helena's brother, the fiery Earl with the scowl, had sent lilies. Nothing from James. It looked as if the boys had sent tulips and rosebuds. A note with the plain inscription 'Mummy' became evident as the coffin drew out of the vicinity of Helena's royal quarters and the lump in Jessica's throat dissolved. The mistress of the future king joined the rest of the nation in astonished mourning for the woman for whom she had had least reason in the world to care.

As the moment to join the funeral procession arrived Edwin thought, 'I need to record all this as accurately as possible, to tell Mum *exactly* what it was like.'

The coffin had already passed Granny and Great Aunt Polly and all the others, Aunt Mary and the cousins, Auntie Zelda and her girls. And the other uncles. Now it was him and Dad and Hugh, and Grandpa, of course, who was out of step and kept on trying to talk which was nearly driving Edwin mad. And Mum's brother, Uncle Roland, whom he and Hugh hardly knew but what they did know was that he was very angry with Dad's side of the family and was going to give the funeral address. Edwin had gathered they were all a bit scared of Rollo because he was what Dad referred to as 'a wild card'. What did they expect? They were a wild family, Mum's. Wasn't she always being called 'a loose cannon'?

In the cool of the ancient Abbey, scene of generations of coronations, historic weddings and funeral parades, visitors were arriving: some grave-faced, some – mostly politicians – smiling for the cameras. The best politicians were those who remembered to smile while looking as if they had been doing some crying too. Disc jockeys sat side by side with judges, fashion designers, ballerinas, grooms, mediums, footballers, psychotherapists, pop stars and, of course, representatives of the multitudinous good and charitable causes that the Princess Helena had served and aided in her inimitable style.

At the end of the central aisle Angela Claire sat beside a Labour life peer.

'Did you meet her?' he asked. 'I met her once. Or was it twice? Unforgettable.'

'I met her once too,' Angela said.

'Oh, really. Charity work, was it?' The peer clocked the uniform but he didn't listen for an answer. He was busy looking to see who hadn't been invited whom he could telephone to impress that evening. Angela looked down at her feet. She didn't want to talk.

When the coffin passed she felt she herself might be going to die, so great was the influx of emotion: the collective feeling of those assembled in the Abbey flowed around her, bringing up a deep and primal source of grief. Outside, the crowd, hungry for a last sight of their Princess, sent out waves of love and pity to mingle in the extraordinary atmosphere. Even Angela's neighbour, the peer, seemed genuinely moved, and the woman on her right, who had two sticks to prop her and wore the shortest skirt Angela had ever seen, even in Paris, had tears dripping from her chin.

'Look, look, here they come.' The mini-skirted woman was murmuring in her ear.

Above the straining shoulders of eight red-faced, square-shouldered Welsh soldiers the lead-lined coffin was borne high – its contents the remains of a gentle life, too fragile and too doomed to reach its natural end.

Behind marched, still in steady step, the Princes James, Edwin and Hugh. The Queen's consort had fallen back as if abashed at the force with which the British public had refuted his view of the woman they mourned.

Angela looked carefully at Edwin. No changeling there – you could see his mother in him. She watched the young Prince as he passed with down-turned gaze and firm stride.

Afterwards it was the song and the tribute that they talked about, in the great aftermath of the greatest funeral England has known, perhaps since the burial of Nelson, perhaps ever. The friend and confidant of Helena – who had publicly revealed that he had lately quarrelled with her and had only made it up at her impress – turned his popular song dedicated to another lost myth into a contemporary lament for the Princess which outshone all the effects of the original. The song topped Verdi in its power to evoke and even those trained to avoid public displays of grief finally could not hold back tears.

But it was Roland's tribute which made the deepest impression. A sound, which began like the falling of soft but urgent rain and grew to a tidal wave of astonishing applause, rolled through from the crowd outside, up the crammed aisles of the old Abbey. It was then that Edwin understood how the crowd shared his uncle's emotion. Somehow it cheered him because it gave him something to hold on to. It meant that Mum was right when she told him and Hugh how the people wouldn't like it if they behaved as if they thought they were a cut above everybody. Obviously, if you are one of the Royal Family, you are a cut above others in some sense. But, as Mum used to say, it's important not to confuse the office with the person. Being king or queen didn't necessarily make you a better human being. You could be as good or better a person if you were dying of Aids, or homeless, or even a drug addict on heroin, Mum had said. It was when she said things like that Edwin knew Mum wasn't dim at all – as the papers sometimes tried to make out. About things like that she was one hundred per cent right. And, what's more, the people, who one day would be his people, knew she was right.

That day in the Abbey, before an audience of millions, the Princess's brother made a solemn pledge to his sister. No one, however, heard the pledge that his nephew made on the same occasion – for this was altogether a private matter. Taking his cue from the hymn he had made sure they sang (he knew it was his mother's favourite), silently Prince Edwin spoke.

'I vow to thee, my country, the service of my love. I will keep faith. I will try to be as Mum wanted me to become.'

6

It was some days before James allowed himself to see Jessica. They spoke of course. Each morning he rang her from his bed at the palace, sitting up in his blue silk pyjamas, which she would surely tease him about if she saw them. He would never now let her see them, for what he could not have told her if he had – because then the tease would have turned to a meaningful silence – was that the pyjamas were a gift from Helena, the last Christmas they had spent together.

'A silly extra gift', she had said, still, in spite of all her worldly knowledge, looking shy. 'I thought they would match your eyes.'

He had not troubled himself with it at the time but now he speculated whether it wasn't him, after all, who had made her shy. The pyjamas were a comfort now. James pulled the blanket round him. Helena had instituted duvets – 'healthier, darling,' – and James had, pettishly, as he saw it now, argued against her. He had reverted to sheets and blankets once they had started to sleep apart.

Stupid, the quarrels married couples got into. He wished he could go back into the past and unsay all the hurtful things he had said to her. Not that, even now, he could live with her. Whatever his present view of his late wife, and it was permutating constantly in these peculiar times, he knew that he could never have assuaged the feeling of loneliness that lay inside her like a dangerous chasm. His own loneliness was too significant not to be alarmed by it. Desperately she had needed, just as he needed, someone safe and solid, to be reassured and comforted by.

Which was where Jessica was so brilliant. Jessica's smile said, 'Don't worry – it will all be all right.' Helena's smile had said, 'Do you love me? *Please* love me?' James was too much in need of love himself to be able to respond to someone who needed love so nakedly. Odd how alike they had turned out to be in some ways.

When he and Jessica finally met, over a week after the funeral, it felt awkward, more awkward than it had ever done before – even counting the first meeting after the honeymoon when she had smiled wryly and said, 'I absolutely do *not* want to know – not now, not ever, please.'

About that they had been pretty good, he and Jessica. Neither had ever discussed the other's bedroom life – not that there was much to discuss from his side because once the two conceptions were over – 'one heir, one spare' – he and Helena had pretty well stopped doing anything like that. Helena always wanted a cuddle and he . . . Well, he wasn't too hot at that stuff.

He didn't mind, though, when Jessica cuddled him, although with Jess it was more of a hug than a cuddle. Sometimes she would grab his arm and say, 'Now, you have to pretend you like this,' and so, of course, he did like it. Helena had never got the point that with him you just had to bash on and *do* it – whatever *it* was – hugging or holding hands or kissing even, which he still didn't like that much.

41

Jessica tried to kiss him now and he half let her, but she knew him too well not to feel his pull away.

'What's wrong?' As the words formed she wished she could take them back. She'd never done that before – commented on his gestures of withdrawal. And now of all times, when the reasons for it were so obvious.

Trying to retract, she touched his shoulder briefly, 'Hey, kid, I'm sorry – as if I didn't know.'

'Kid' was their acknowledgement that she was a couple of years his senior.

But she didn't really 'know', that was part of the trouble. For the first time, ever, Jess couldn't understand how he was feeling. How could she, when what he was feeling was this sudden, this extraordinary emotion over his wife.

'She's good, being gone.' Who had said that? The words had come to him as he had stood, searching his heart for words, by the quiet body in Paris. It was not the first time James had wanted to be alone while in the company of a woman, but it was the first with Jessica.

Intuiting some of this she smiled and said, 'Look – I just wanted to clap eyes on you, see you were OK. There's no need for me to stay. Honestly.'

That made him feel a heel. She was a brick, was Jess, and now she was determinedly making no fuss. Appalled at the way he'd let one woman down, he felt suddenly fearful he was going to damage the other.

'I'm sorry, Maud, it's, well, things . . .'

'Maud' was his old pet name for her since long ago he'd famously asked her into the garden, at her father's home, and kissed her, passionately, under the tulip tree. By then she was already engaged to another man – a man whom they both still liked. James had been too unsure to ask her to break the engagement and she had been too decent to suggest it. A little less reserve on his part and a little less decency on hers and this appalling tragedy might never have had to happen. You take a decision or you don't take one – and other people get caught up in the consequences. Lady Helena Grey would never have been pursued into a Paris tunnel by the paparazzi if she had not, once, been the wife of the future king of England.

Jessica smiled again, more sincerely this time, warming to the pet name. 'Of course. It must have been bloody awful for you.'

Never for a second did she allow it to show that what she hoped might have been 'bloody awful' was the gap between the face he had to present to the world and the nature of the true feelings he held for his dead wife. She alone had heard him speak his mind about what he called 'Helena's monkey tricks'. Honest as she knew him to be, wouldn't it be a strain now to wear the badge of grief without also wearing the badge of hypocrisy?

Jessica was not unusual in judging a situation on past evidence. In scientific law that is a rational, indeed a desirable procedure. But the heart, as has been famously acknowledged, has its own logic and our past feelings about another human being have, in certain circumstances, little bearing on the present. Death alters things – not least our responses to those who have died. Jessica might have known the general truth of this but the very personal form in which it was about to affect her life was still a blank to her.

'It has been quite, quite *awful*!' It was a relief to speak the words and he felt some of the old comfort at her company ease back. At least with her he need not keep that upper lip so frightfully stiff, as he was alarmed to see Edwin was doing. For except for one moment of respite, his eldest son had retained an alabaster stoicism.

'Can I help?' They seemed to be back on keel again and as

43

she spoke he confirmed it by moving into her arms. 'It'll be all right, it'll be all right,' she said, but whether it was her lover or herself she was reassuring not even she really knew.

7

The sea had been quiet when they left Brindisi but it grew rougher as they entered the more open swell. Angela watched the cream-tipped waves making patterns on the water. Gulls wheeled and cried about the ship. She had heard people say they were supposed to be the souls of drowned sailors.

They had been two hours now at sea. Angela's mind, which had been pulled and stretched into so many new dimensions, filled with a vast calm.

In the calm, she began to assemble the events of the past seven days. The Chief of Nursing Staff, whom she had apparently met in the corridor of the hospital, had, it turned out, been confined to bed with gastric flu that weekend. So who was the tall woman who smelt of flowers and pine? The tall woman had briefly visited the side room where, following her instructions, Angela had wheeled the bed of the recovering patient. Angela had watched the strange woman (who looked so like the head nurse) touch the patient's forehead, then pass long hands over the length of her body and finally lay her finger on the patient's mouth.

The patient had moaned slightly as if in pain and afterwards she had lain stiffly, her complexion grey, almost like death.

But she had not been dead, for, as Angela sat with her, out of the young woman's mouth issued strange words which sounded foreign. Angela had heard from the hospital buzz as she came on duty that this was someone important. The hospital was agog with it – some had said it was Princess Caroline of Monaco or the English Princess Helena – but when Angela heard the funny words being spoken she thought maybe this was a foreign film star whose anonymity she had somehow been caught up in guarding. Princess Helena would surely never have been left alone in a recovery room like that.

The violet-smelling woman had gone away, but later a short, plump doctor had appeared. He was called Dr Asklepios, though Angela did not know how she had learned this because she had never seen him before and he wore no identity label. The doctor had examined the patient – Angela's patient, as Angela thought of her now – and had spoken back to her in the funny language. It was odd how, as you listened, you got an idea of what was being said even though it was Greek to you. The little doctor seemed to be saying that the patient needed to go to his special clinic where people were cured through their dreams. Kind of psychotherapy, Angela guessed, though it seemed an odd kind of treatment for someone who had been in a road accident. But maybe it was one of the new ways of dealing with trauma. Angela had briefly been involved in a post-traumatic stress clinic and had been impressed with the work done there.

The doctor had taken the patient down to the hospital basement and out through a side door, which Angela had not noticed before, and had supervised the patient while she was carried into a waiting van. It was a smart green van with an emblem on the side like a coiled snake, which Angela guessed was the logo for the doctor's special clinic. The little doctor had motioned her to get into the van too and when she did – she wouldn't have dared disobey him even if she had wanted to – she found the inside of the van was an incredibly sweet-smelling place – full of aroma-therapy oils, she supposed – with two comfy-looking beds within – a larger, whiter one for the patient and a smaller one for herself, she gathered, should she too need to lie down. So the clinic must be at least an overnight drive away.

Dr Asklepios, who was not Italian – she knew Italian – had held her hand, just for a second, and she had felt it grow hot in his grasp and her fingers had started to tingle. Then he had touched the patient again on her chest, and she must have been feeling better because she had, just a little, grinned back at him. After that he had closed the doors, ever so quietly; he did everything very quietly and not as if it was a matter of life and death like Dr Denot. Then the van had driven off.

Angela hadn't known where they were driving. From time to time she had wiped the face of her patient with a soft cloth she had found in a silver-coloured bowl, or given her some mineral water from the aquamarine bottles in the small refrigerator. Once she had dipped her finger into a jar of dark gold honey and her patient had sucked the honey from her finger like a small animal learning how to suckle. Mostly they sat in the cool dim interior of the van, moving noiselessly towards an unknown destination.

Maybe a day and a night later they stopped. Angela never saw who had driven them on the weird journey but the van doors opened unassisted and she had looked out on to a glass-blue sea. No one else was about. Whoever their mysterious driver was, he or she had vanished into the landscape.

They were parked at the edge of some sand dunes looking on to a deserted bay of white sand. Angela judged it must be about an hour after dawn. No road could be seen behind them. They had driven, it appeared, clean over the soft white sand hills which surrounded the bay.

In the absolute quiet a voice spoke.

'Please tell me your name.'

It was the young woman and she must have been feeling better because she was propping herself up and also looking out of the van at the wide sea.

'Oh,' Angela turned back to the bed, 'should you? I mean don't stretch yourself unnecessarily.'

'Thanks, but I think I feel OK.'

No trace of an accent. The foreign-sounding words that Angela had heard had been replaced by a quiet, thoroughly well-bred English voice.

'Can I get you anything?' Like feathers their words drifted into the quiet air.

'I seem to feel OK?' It was as if she was questioning herself, rather than replying to Angela's question.

Angela looked at her patient. She had fine blonde hair, beautifully cut, and a firm, rather beaky nose. But what you looked at were her eyes. It was not true to say that Angela had never seen eyes like them before. She had. In all the magazines, on the TV, in the newspapers.

'Excuse me, I know this might sound daft. But, do you . . . Can you tell me . . . I mean, I don't know . . . Can you possibly tell me who I am?'

Angela looked into the unmistakable eyes of England's Princess Helena. 'I don't know,' she had found herself saying.

Thinking back on it now, Angela wondered how the few clothes and trinkets from her Paris apartment had appeared that evening by her bed, in the house on the headland where they had been taken by boat.

The boat had been steered by a young man who said nothing. When they arrived and he helped them ashore, he opened his mouth and Angela saw that he had no tongue.

She did not understand how it had happened that she knew she was to attend the funeral. The small red plane that carried her from a tiny airport (it looked no more than a mown hayfield) had no one but herself aboard; nor did she ever see the pilot. The plane might have been flown by the same mute who had brought them to the house on the headland where Angela's patient had remained.

Before Angela had left she had gone to see her patient in the room with the wrought-iron balcony that looked out over the sea. (The same sea, Angela supposed now, that they were sailing on that very night to an unknown destination.)

'Angela?' The woman had grown stronger during the week they had stayed in the house on the headland, and was sitting out in a reclining chair watching seabirds skim the water. 'It is possible you may see my son.' So she had remembered something. Angela said nothing. 'I don't know what may occur, but if you had a chance . . .'

Angela had looked out to sea where a little fishing smack was ploughing back towards the sandy coast. She felt it was not her business to look at the other's face at this moment.

'Tell him,' the voice had hardly wavered, 'the elder, tell him that he must remember my hymn, the one he is going to have them play, the one he knows I love. And Angela,' – and then Angela had turned and looked straight into the sapphire eyes – 'tell him, "Mum says to look after your brother."'

Such strange recollections. A gull landed on the foredeck looking for food. Soon she must go below and see if her patient needed anything. Her wants were few now. Mostly what she needed was to talk.

Since the funeral Angela and she had started to talk more, though neither of them had broached the question of her name. Without anything being said it seemed as if they were both aware that whoever this woman was she was no longer Princess Helena, former wife of the future king of England. And yet – and neither of them ever commented on the logic – she was still the mother of the princes Edwin and Hugh, whom Angela had met and spoken with only two days before.

It was the day before the funeral and London had been in a state of nervous calm. The Royal Family had emerged, pale-faced and tensely affable, to walk among the people and observe the ranked floral tributes.

Propelled by that sense which had been growing stronger in her ever since the strange woman had accosted her in the Hospital Notre-Dame, Angela had gone straight to London when she landed, joining the crowds in the Mall. At the last minute, caught up in the general mood, she had purchased a bunch of scarlet, blue and white anemones.

It was her nurse's uniform which had done it. A man near the front of the lines of spectators had fainted in the crush and she had been pushed forward by a crowd who were keen that the charitable nature of their lost Princess should be apparent now in their own behaviour.

'There's a nurse!'

'She's a nurse!'

'You're a nurse, love, can you help?'

Angela, pushed to the front of the crowd, loosened the collar and wet the lips, with one of the many proffered bottles of mineral water, of the overcome spectator from New Zealand. When his wife finally led him away, Angela had remained in their vacated space.

A collective murmur caught her attention and she saw, approaching her stretch of the Mall, a small boy with red gold hair and an older, taller, blond boy with the eyes of the woman she had last seen looking out on an unknown sea.

'Edwin! Edwin!' 'Hugh! Hugh!' the crowd keened.

Instantly, the brimming sapphire gaze cut into her mind.

'Edwin.' Angela spoke quietly and, perhaps because hers was the lowest note in the surrounding clamour, he turned and looked directly at her, 'Edwin – I have something for you.'

The boy walked towards her and afterward she realized that she was smiling and that perhaps, in this way too, she had appeared singular amid the great press of people he saw that day. As he approached she pushed the posy of coloured flowers into his hands. He stood not knowing what to do with them. Angela noticed his hands were too large to hold the flowers easily. In the way of such unpredicted events, around them a momentary quiet welled up.

'I have a message for you.' He was close to her now and she could see the strain in his young face. 'It is from her.' She did not dare to be more explicit, but it seemed his attention was caught. 'She says to tell you, you must remember her hymn, and she said . . .' And here Angela lent across the barrier to whisper words too private to repeat aloud.

He was gone then, swept along to a further stretch of duty, and she did not know if he had heard. But she had done her own duty, that was the main thing. Now there was only the funeral to be endured.

8

The stars were exceptional that night. Angela's patient had joined her on deck and she stood, curved, like the serpent on Dr Asklepios's van, over the rail.

Angela felt an anxiety the long form might suddenly slide over the side but when you heard her speak you knew that was an unnecessary fear.

'It's OK. People who survive death do not easily succumb to it again.' The voice, still and clear, made an intimacy of the space between them.

Angela shivered. An eerie light made her think of a poem she had learned at her school in Ealing. That was about snakes too. Water snakes.

'It's *The Rime of the Ancient Mariner*, isn't it? He sees the snakes, the mariner does, when he is on the mend.'

That was twice she had plucked the words out of Angela's head and spoken to them. Earlier she had said, 'We're alike you and I, we lost a parent when we were young. That's probably why we try to help people,' just as Angela was thinking about her father.

Angela looked at the face beside her. It appeared sterner than the face she had first seen on the hospital bed ten days earlier. The nose more proud, the cheekbones sharper. And her patient seemed to have gained in height – or was that merely the effect of seeing her, at last, more or less upright?

A scent of pine blew in on the night air and Angela began to yawn.

'Would you mind if I . . . ?'

'No, my dear, you need your beauty sleep. I'll stay out here a while and then I'll bed down too.'

'Are you sure? Will you be OK?'

She inspired concern, this woman, although her demeanour was anything but pathetic. Angela allowed herself, as she prepared for bed in the wooden bunk-bedded room beside her patient's quarters, to ponder on what she had known about the young woman who had been the focus of the Western world: elegant, talked about, but always with that suggestion of the victim about her which had, they were saying now, resulted in her being 'hounded literally to death'.

Her brother's words – spoken in the wide Abbey but relayed to the wider fields of England's citizens beyond – a clarion call from the Red Earl for a halt on the hunt which, he angrily asserted, had slaughtered his sister. And, he made no bones about it, a hunt which looked like damaging, if left unchecked, the precious sons she had left behind.

Angela reflected on the boy who had stood before her on the eve of his mother's funeral, cradling the blooms she had bought in his big hands. Had she, she wondered, managed to convey to him his mother's message? Among so many messages of condolence could he have picked out the uniqueness of hers? She felt a sudden uprush of love for the boy with his mother's eyes and his red headed brother. The younger prince's hair was a bit like her own. Maybe she reminded his mother of her younger son?

Angela lay down on the white-sheeted bunk while the steady rhythm of the sea acted as nurse to her sleep.

The scent of pine, blown across the dark roll of the waters, increased and with it came the smell of violets – the sweet white violets that she used to find with her brother when, as children, they played their game of 'ordinary families' on their father's estate. She had always played 'mother' – and what was it that she wore? An apron one of the maids lent them. But there was something else, something funny? Of course, that old bath-cap their real mother had left behind.

Dear Rollo. Her small brother still. The thought of his sad, furious, loyal face hurt almost as much as the other thought – the one she could not even name to herself for fear the pain would do what the impact on reinforced concrete at 110 mph had been unable to do. She had willed herself to give the message to Angela. The news that Angela had spoken with Edwin was enough. Leave that alone for now.

And she had other matters to attend to. The pine-and-violets scent, which harbingered a more powerful presence, was now all about her as a tall form approached.

The figure spoke into her mind.

'Helena is dead. You are no longer she.'

'Who am I, then?' No need to speak the words aloud.

'You are my servant now. Your name will come to you. In serving me you will serve others.'

'Where are you taking me?' She was not afraid.

'To sanctuary, where no one will find you. There you will rest while you are instructed in the required arts. The girl who is called after my Christian colleagues will accompany you. Do not be afraid. You are safe now and under my protection.' The voice was remote but not unkind.

The aromatic smell gathered in intensity. The woman who had been Princess Helena and now had no name felt a spot of fire touch her forehead. Then both the hurt and the scent abated and she was left watching a path of light fade towards the horizon across the dark sea.

They had barely communed but it was enough. She knew that whatever life lay behind her, something greater than herself had intervened, had taken her up with swift wings from the jaws of the dogs of death, and that, whatever her life was now to be, it was no longer in her control.

9

Edwin had got used, over the years, to hearing the boys at school talk about his mother. He had been instructed by his father that whatever was said to him he must ignore. What he absolutely must not do, his father emphasized, was to answer back – or, worse, hit out. This last injunction was delivered, sorry-faced, after Edwin had thrashed a boy for calling his mother a bimbo.

Edwin's father had been naturally concerned when Arkwright minor's parents had requested a transfer for their son, following his stay in the school sanatorium with a broken cheekbone. But Aunt Mary had given Edwin one of her winks and, later, had banged him on the back and slipped him a twenty-pound note. It was generally assumed that the future king of England would be flush with money, but the truth was that both Edwin and Hugh were often worse off than most of their peers at school. What with their mother's anxiety that they not be thought too special and their father's fear of spoiling, they came off rather badly in financial matters.

But now Edwin wished that the others at school would mention Mum again. Everyone was so concerned not to upset him that they kept a kind of ghostly silence. Edwin missed talking about her. He couldn't talk to Hugh, in case he upset him, and Dad just went all solemn and looked as if he might start howling himself, which Edwin knew neither of them would know how to cope with. His grandparents, obviously, were not up for cosy chats about Mum. His grandmother was out of her depth at the way the country had responded to the loss of her former daughter-in-law, and his grandfather hadn't yet cottoned on that his opinion of her was in the minority.

Edwin had heard his grandfather refer to his mother as 'spoilt' and had eyeballed him over breakfast until his grandmother had asked him to leave the table. It certainly wasn't comfortable staying with them right now, specially with them getting on so badly with Dad.

But it was half-term he was really dreading. Usually they would have spent it with Mum. She would have taken them to some brilliant film, or to the Hard Rock Café or something. Edwin had actually been planning to ask if he could go to Haringey to watch the dog racing. He'd bet Mum would have said, 'Great, darling, that's a brilliant plan.' Now he and Hugh were going to have to spend half-term with their father, who would probably want them to go to some concert, Sibelius or Elgar or something.

Edwin quite liked Elgar but a kind of loyalty to his mother prevented him from wanting to admit this. Also, Dad might want to bring Jessica, which was tricky because they knew Mum wouldn't have liked that either – though lately Mum had stopped asking about her, maybe because Mum was happy with her new boyfriend.

Even to himself Edwin had not liked to admit that there was one aspect of the terrible accident that he did not regret. Edwin, who knew about these things, sensed that Milu was not at all a good bet for Mum. Quite the reverse. He'd watched her new boyfriend carefully when Mum had taken him and Hugh on holiday with Milu. In fact, one of the things he had been dreading was finding a way of telling Mum why he didn't like her latest, which he would have had to do if she had gone on with the guy. Now at least she was spared all that – wherever she was.

For Edwin had never quite allowed himself to think of his mother as permanently gone. There was something, he couldn't say what, that prevented his believing he would never see her again. And there was that woman. The nurse with red hair who had shoved the bunch of flowers into his hand and given him the message about Hugh and Mum's hymn. He had insisted they play it in the Abbey because, though he was the only one who remembered, it was very important to Mum. She used to sing it to him as she sat by his bed when he was little. Sometimes she and Dad would be going out and she would be wearing one of her dresses with shiny stuff on them. He always thought of those dresses when he thought of the 'other country' with the 'shining bounds'. It gave him a place now, in his mind, to imagine Mum in – a place where she would never be treated roughly again.

Edwin wished he could tell Hugh what he believed but he couldn't let Hugh believe Mum was OK until he, Edwin was surer. And Hugh might blab, which Edwin knew mustn't happen. If Mum was still around somewhere, however she had arranged it, she would know when to get in touch herself. Then he could tell Hugh. Meantime, though he didn't believe it was, it might just be one of those things he had read about that happen when you miss the dead person so much you don't believe they are dead.

*　　*　　*

Half-term turned out to be a nice surprise. It seemed that they were going to spend it with Aunt Mary and the cousins at their house in Berkshire. Which was good because it saved spending too much time with Dad, knowing that he'd rather have had Jessica along.

Edwin could not know this, but in James's mind there was no question of inviting his mistress to join in his children's half-term. The thought horrified him – especially when he remembered how he had fought his mother for the right to do just that.

'No, really,' she had said (in the same voice she had once said, 'Remember, James, I am your monarch before I am your mother' – a recollection which still depressed him), 'it is out of the question. Jessica is a nice gal, and I'm pleased to say your father likes her, which you know is quite a triumph, but we cannot have her mixing with the boys. Imagine what their mother would make of it when she got the press on to it. There is simply no argument about this: Jessica must stay strictly offside.'

Which is where, to his dismay, James found he too now wanted her. For Jessica – comforting, jovial, good-tempered Jessica – had become a source of embarrassment to him. Not to his exterior person, whose embarrassment he was accustomed to and had learned to manage, but to a much more significant part of himself. In his deeper self he had begun to question the liaison between himself and Jessica.

For years and years he and Jessica had been the best of pals, lovers, confidantes. He had wept in her arms, laughed in her arms, been tipsy, funny, bad-tempered, sentimental, pompous probably, and all of it she had taken with the greatest goodness of heart. And yet, since the death of Helena, he found he didn't want to see her – didn't enjoy her company, even – which was a terrible admission to make.

Because poor old Jess had done nothing to deserve this sudden reversal of feeling in him, other than not be the woman who had died, whose death he now found he was unable to excise from his mind.

'Oh, my dear, I can't,' he found himself saying yet again when she rang to suggest an evening with friends who had protected the relationship over the years and who, she said lightly, were keen to remind themselves of what he looked like. 'It's the boys' half-term.'

'But aren't they going to Mary's?'

She had begun to question him – press his reserve, so that there were times when she reminded him, almost, of Helena at her most suspicious (although heaven forbid that Jess would ever try to chuck herself downstairs).

'Yes, but I'm going too.'

'To *Mary's* . . . but you never –'

'Jess, I have to. They must still be grieving terribly.'

'You never minded before.'

'Jess, don't.'

'But you didn't. They had all kinds of needs and illnesses and you were able to leave them.'

'They had a mother then, Jess.'

For a moment he hoped she would put down the phone and give him the excuse he half wanted to avoid her further. Perhaps she sensed this, for her voice changed.

'God, I'm sorry. I'm such a cow. Really. I'm so sorry, darling.'

'It's OK,' he spoke dully, willing her to terminate the conversation.

'It's just that I miss you and . . .' She waited for him to say 'I miss you too' and when it didn't come she found her voice becoming bright. 'OK. Well, look, give us a ring when you can manage it. And remember, I love you.'

He could not find a way to say, 'I love you too', but he was too fond of her to leave her with her affection unmet. 'I know you do, Jess. Look, just give me a tad of time. I'll be fine. Time the great healer, you know?'

Aiming at jocularity, he merely managed to sound ridiculous, as too often he did to himself. And he had hurt her. She didn't show it but he knew he had.

'Tell you what, in a couple of weeks we'll take a short holiday somewhere, just us two. They've lightened up a lot of my engagements and I'll square it with my mother.'

Jessica liked his mother, who had not concealed her regret that Jessica had not encouraged James to behave dishonourably all those years ago. Years back, Jessica had gone on with the marriage to Michael instead of following her heart and leaving him for James. Lest she appear like one of the many frightful fortune hunters who plagued him at the time, Jessica hadn't dared suggest how much he mattered to her. She couldn't stand the idea that he should think of her as being in pursuit of his hand. Too much hung on it – his dear hand – which is why, she supposed, he was so reluctant to reach out and grab what he wanted. His hand had always, since he was a boy, been heavy with responsibility.

'How is she, your mama?' Jessica never referred to James's mother by her title. The only power she ever exerted was the power which declined to be in awe of his family. 'Send her my best, will you?'

'Surely. She's bearing up – still reeling rather over the fuss about Helena. I'm afraid we scrap a bit these days.'

Which is a pity, thought Jessica, because they are alike, James and his mother – both socially reserved people with a maverick humour concealed deep within. She put the phone down but the tears which had begun to form in her throat never emerged. She was too sensible for that. James would be king of England one day. She had long ago resigned herself to the fact that before that day came he might feel he must leave her. The process had to begin sometime. Perhaps it was starting now.

10

Henri Astaffort had, at first, been grateful for the non-reappearance of Alice Kirk. Affectionate and amusing as she was, she was also trouble and her recent act of setting fire to his bed had driven him beyond the limit of his tolerance. He was fond of her but he could do with a rest.

But as time went on he began first to miss her and then, vaguely, to worry. They had had rows before and he had chucked her out. Usually she went off on a bender and slept with God knew who. He didn't mind – it gave him licence to pursue his own proclivities. But she had always turned up again, 'like the bad penny' he used to say in his schoolboy English, and she had smiled her tolerant smile and asked to be forgiven.

Twice he had received calls to collect her from hospital – once from casualty and once from a psychiatric ward, which had bothered him, especially when he saw the faces of the other patients. 'Why do you let yourself get like this?' he had asked, but she had offered no reply other than that appeasing smile which sometimes made him want to hit her.

This time he had rung round various of the hospitals, even, steeling himself, the psychiatric hospital where he had found himself going to see if the amnesiac woman in her thirties was by any chance Alice. She was not, and he left the hideous concrete building in a mixture of relief and dismay.

The Hospital Notre-Dame was one of the first he tried and got nowhere. But passing it one day, on his way home from visiting an old friend on the Rue de Bec with an absent husband, he went in.

The woman at reception was of a certain age and build – a kind that generally responded to Henri.

'Excuse me, Madame. My sister, I have spoken before with your colleague but she is young . . .' he shrugged to indicate the inferior understanding of young women. 'My sister is a little bit alcoholic. Sometimes she lands up in hospital and she has not been home for a while.'

The woman adjusted her shoulders the better to reveal her excellent bust. 'I am so sorry – I am temporary here. But if you need some help . . .'

Her face invited him into the wood-and-glass cage where she showed him the computer which stored the names of patients past and present.

'I cannot allow you . . . my job, you see . . . But if you would like me to . . . Your sister's name?'

He gave her the various permutations which he had known Alice use, but nothing came up on screen.

'Thank you, madame, you have been most kind.'

On his way out towards the heavy swing doors which kept the Paris streets at bay, she called him back.

'Monsieur! When did you last see your sister?'

He smiled. 'It is like the English painting, "When did you last see your Papa?" I saw her . . .' he tried to think when he had actually last heard from Alice. She had rung, drunk, from a call

64

box and he had replaced the receiver on her. When was that? Then he remembered another event which would place it for them both. 'The precise date I forget, but I heard from her the day before the tragedy. The day Princess Hélène was killed.'

The woman had a daughter the same age as Princess Helena, who never spoke to her mother. 'The poor thing. That was the thirtieth. A catastrophe. And so happy at last.'

'They whom the gods love . . .' Henri was surprised to find himself moved. Not by the dead Princess – he was too much of a Republican to care about the British Royal Family and their goings-on – but the moistening eyes of this middle-aged woman reminded him, in their eagerness to please, of Alice.

'Ah yes, they die young,' she finished the quote, proud to be abreast of it. 'That morning there was a terrible confusion. Such a tragedy – maybe someone was slipshod.'

You could see this was a woman who would not know how to be slipshod; stripped naked and hosed down with water she would still be competent and precise. But she was right – there may have been confusion, in which case Alice could have been here after all. Trust Alice to get herself mixed up with royalty. He had an idea, from something she had muttered when drunk, that she was related to some of those English nobs, but later, when he joshed her about it, she had denied having said any such thing.

'Are there any other records?'

'There is the accident book. That we still write by hand. Would you like . . . ?'

She fetched an old-fashioned ledger with school-type squared paper. 'Let us see, Samedi 30 Août – nothing for you there.' A phone rang. 'Please, look yourself.' She went back into her cage to answer it.

Henri scanned the entries. No Alice Kirk. No Lisa Kirk or Peggy Church nor any of the other names he had known Alice use. The woman was still on the phone. A curiosity overtook him and he looked over the page to see if the name of Princess Helena was there.

Dimanche 31 Août. There it was. Suddenly, he was involved in the disaster – as if the possible connection with Alice gave it some kind of personal validity. It gave him a jolt to see the name of the currently most significant woman in the world recorded in this ordinary book in humble blue biro. It was like the book he used nowadays to keep a record of his work materials for his new accountant. But there was no reference, hand-written or otherwise, to Alice. Now the woman with the good breasts was turning back to him, smiling.

'You had luck?'

'No. Nothing.'

'Then, I am sorry . . .' She shrugged regret and then, unwilling to let this attractive stranger leave, she offered a confidence.

'It was strange that night, that morning. It was as if there was something cosmic, maybe Saturn? The computers went down. We lost all our records. Don't tell anyone,' – she moved closed so that he smelled her perfume, Trésor – 'but we do not even have the complete records of the Princess – only what you see there.' She looked excitedly at his blankness, enjoying her part in this larger mystery. 'It is a fact. All the information had to be, you know, put together afterwards. It is rumoured that they lost a body.' She wriggled her shoulders excitedly.

Alice. He stirred and she, misinterpreting his restlessness, dangled a final hook.

'The property box. Sometimes, you know, with no identification . . .' Her voice dropped. 'If there has been a death, I am sorry . . .' Her face apologized for the suggestion that the stranger's relative might be a corpse.

'No, no, please, a box?'

'Yes, we have a box – a safe, I should say – where unclaimed

66

possessions are placed. Sometimes if people are unidentified . . . although of course there are procedures . . . but if your sister . . . that night in particular . . .'

'Can I see it?'

'Of course.' She was smiling now and pulling her top to accentuate her figure. 'If you come back when my duty is over I can show you. I hope it is not the case, but something of your sister's might be there.

II

❦

Angela had seen no one for days. Her watch had disappeared. There were no clocks, no radio, no TV, no newspapers, nothing to give any sense of the world she had known or the passage of time. Only the sun and the moon for guides.

The woman who was no longer the Princess Helena break-fasted at dawn and went to bed as the moon rose. Her companion had to spend long hours alone. The island seemed to be quite uninhabited. Angela had tried to walk around it but a sudden sheer drop had left her vertiginously clinging to a wiry bush. Dissuaded from pursuing that particular plan of exploration (there appeared no way round the ravine) she turned back. Instead she walked over the scrubby hills behind the stone cottage where they slept at night.

The island was full of goats, brown and fawn and white with bells at their tufted throats, but no goatherds. Sometimes Angela could hear the bells clink-clinking as she lay on the edge of sleep on the stout mattress made of feathers on which she slept. The woman she looked after also slept on a feather mattress, on a high wooden bed built into the cottage wall. The high bed was the only mark of difference between them.

In all other matters they shared the daily tasks equally. Angela took charge of the food preparations. During the days, when her companion was off Angela wasn't sure where, she collected shellfish, cockles and winkles from the encrusted rocks or long razor-shells which she pulled out at low tide.

From time to time food was brought but Angela never saw who brought it to them. In the outhouse where she supposed the goats had sometimes been housed, bread, cheese, tomatoes, olives, oil, wine appeared with a mysterious and regular largesse. Angela spent two days watching the outhouse door to see if she could surprise the invisible donor. Then, when she went off to swim in the still-warm sea, she arrived back to find a basket with eggs and white cheese waiting – a kindly joke.

There was a black stove on which she boiled the razor-shellfish which they ate with their fingers, throwing the bladed shells to a crowd of shrieking gulls. Mostly they ate salads of tomato and sweet red onions with herbs she brought back from the nearby hills. Physically tired from the walking, and from the sea and the sun, Angela found she ate hungrily. Her companion ate more sparely, but both drank the dry red wine which arrived regularly in squat green glass bottles.

As she got to know the terrain better, Angela learned where she could collect figs from the trees by a cove a little distance from theirs, or, as the weeks went by, she gathered blackberries on her walks. In the evening they lit a fire – more for the look of the thing, because the evenings were still warm, even though the year had wheeled into autumn. Here the autumn was golden and dry – hotter than an English August.

They sat, in the evenings, in a quiet in which no speech was necessary, except for the exchange of simple information.

Then one evening Angela's mistress, poking at the fire, which had become her charge, said, 'Tell me, if you wouldn't mind, about the funeral.'

It was odd to be asked to describe a person's own funeral, but she sounded quite relaxed about it. Angela found she didn't feel awkward at all. But how – to her of all people – was she going to manage to describe what an extraordinary occasion it had been?

'The thing I noticed most was how well-behaved everybody was – not just on the day when, you know, everything happened – but the evening before too. We were all being extra nice to each other. I mean, nobody was pushing or getting angry – for instance, I didn't hear anyone swear.'

'Was it then you saw my son?'

Angela had thought a great deal about her meeting with the young prince when she had passed on to him his mother's message. It was as if he had become a familiar presence in her mind: more a part of herself than her own family.

'Yes, the evening I arrived.' It seemed like a dream now, the small red plane in which she had flown. 'I told him what you asked me to say. It was the greatest luck that I had the opportunity.' Was it 'luck', she wondered? 'And after that I went to, well, your house. It was full of people, the grounds in front of it, walking about, or sitting or camping there – children too, but so quiet – like a temple must have been.'

She had heard a groundsman saying that the grass was so trampled that they were going to have to re-seed it in the spring.

'They liked my house?'

The blue eyes were eager as if she really hoped the people had enjoyed themselves. There was a generosity in this woman's responses which Angela had heard talked of by those who gathered at the gates of the London palace where she had resided. 'She restored my faith in womankind,' Angela had heard one middle-aged man say to another. 'She was the only really feminine presence on the world stage.' An elderly lady sitting on a bench had said to her friend, 'She's the only one of them didn't wear gloves.' And the thousands of notes on the railings, pinned to trees, bushes: 'We miss you always', 'Good-bye our Beloved Princess', 'We will never forget you'.

'They loved it. It was a kind of shrine – you never saw so many flowers.'

'They knew I loved flowers.'

There were other messages, too, Angela recalled. She had seen more than one version of the placard which declared, 'I killed you – I read the tabloids.' Best to say nothing of that for now. 'After it was all over, or supposed to be, the ground in front of your house was full of candles, songs and candles spelling out your name.'

'I would have liked to hear the songs.'

Words were inadequate. The truth was that Angela had never experienced anything like those days. What she most wanted to convey was the quality of the silence: and that minute – a small eternity – when the whole of England had held itself in check, like a heart which had chosen to stop itself from beating.

'What I will always remember is the silence.'

Although Angela's father was a Catholic she did not believe in the Holy Ghost. But on that day she had watched a silver kite, loosed into the air, spinning, spinning towards the clouds. Looking back, it seemed to her now that the fragile silver shape was, in its ascendant flight, like some holy spirit or an image of a human soul.

'They knew I wanted silence.'

One day, when Angela walked down the steep path to the bay, she found a beached yacht with green sails. Later, when she returned to the cottage, the doctor from the hospital, Dr Asklepios, was sitting by the fireplace.

71

He grinned a recognition through grimy teeth. And when he spoke it was in a careful, rather old-fashioned English.

'Welcome to my little colleague. I trust our countryside entrances you?'

Angela had only speculated on the exact whereabouts of the island, but seeing Dr Asklepios there now she realized she had subconsciously determined it.

'Yes, I like Greece.'

'Ah!' he showed brown teeth, 'Hellas, Greece, whatever you wish. And so, my country 'likes' you, I perceive. You are touched by the god of the sun, full of colour. Not any more the pale little weasel I met in the Paris hospital.'

Nothing more had been spoken of Dr Asklepios's clinic.

'Have you come to take us to your sanatorium?'

He laughed at this – more brown teeth. 'But you are in it, do you not see? Here is where we conduct recovery. Have you not noticed?'

He nodded towards the doorway where her mistress, who had been collecting fuel, came in now from the goat-shed with some cut logs and pine cones to feed the fire. Angela thought, she's changing. The princess look had almost disappeared.

'Angela has been telling me about the funeral.'

The doctor took out a pipe. 'Would you mind if I smoked? Thank you.' Not waiting for a reply he extracted a branch from the fire. 'It is interesting, is it not, how you people tend to think a funeral is an ending, whereas of course it is merely a beginning.' He touched the glowing stick to his pipe and sucked vigorously.

The woman who had been Helena looked with blue-eyed decisiveness at Angela.

'Angela.'

'Ma'am?'

Angela had devised the 'ma'am' when she had not known how else to address her companion. She knew it was the usual term of address for royalty. But it also seemed congruent with the dignity and authority of this person.

'Tell the doctor about the young man.'

Angela, thinking about the young Prince, had recalled an incident she had been involved in that day. She had been telling the other woman about it. Such a different boy, but grieving the way a son might have grieved. It was in the Abbey. The service had ended and everyone had been making their way out – quite dazed – when a young man, a boy really, had fallen to his knees. She wasn't alone in going to help him but she was the first. The boy had been sobbing.

'He looked a bit, you know, rough. But he was crying so hard I was worried. So I said – I hope I didn't do wrong, but it was difficult you see, knowing what I knew – I said, "Don't be sad, she's still with us."'

The doctor made no response but went on sucking at his pipe. It looked as if he was having difficulty getting it to take.

Angela glanced to see if she should go on. 'I don't know if he heard me – he didn't say anything at first. Then he said this really moving thing. He said, "She", meaning, you know, the person in the coffin, "was like a mother to me." I guess he meant you, ma'am?'

'And this distressed young soul, did you learn his name?' The pipe was alight now and the doctor was puffing away like a contented dragon, cradling a high-instepped foot across a plump knee.

Angela thought back. She had asked him his name, thinking she might be able to help the boy who seemed to be weeping out his heart. What was it he had said?

'He said he was called George.'

'Yes,' the name seemed to strike a chord with the doctor, 'the English patron saint – a truly English name. So your young man mourns for Britain?'

73

'I should have found out who he was, where he lived. I would have liked . . . I don't suppose it would have been possible, but I would have liked to see him again.'

When Angela had retired to bed the other two sat looking through the open door at the salmon-and-gold streaked sky.

'Dr Asklepios, what Angela told us made me think of something. I've been trying to remember what it was like when . . . you know . . . before I came here.'

He looked enquiring but said nothing only puffing away.

'I don't remember anything clear at all about, you know, when it all happened. Mostly it feels as if I was in a kind of baggy transparent envelope. But when Angela told me about the boy, I remembered a dream I had.'

He made a gesture of invitation with his pipe.

'Well, there was a young woman. She seemed drunk, really, sort of falling over. She was talking and laughing in a bar – drinking, I guess – and then she was by a road. Then some bikes came by at speed and she stepped out in front of one of them . . .'

It was like a film she was watching on a screen in her mind.

'. . . and she sort of staggered and fell back and they roared on past. Then I saw her lying on a bed and a man came and knelt beside her. He was crying. Dr Asklepios, I think the man was my husband?'

'Indeed?' He looked interested. 'And the young woman, you know her?'

In reply she shook her head. 'No, but I thought I had seen the bikes . . . ?' No reaction from the doctor, so she continued. 'And this is the odd part: she was wearing my ring.' He raised his eyebrows at this. 'It was nothing really – an inexpensive little pearl ring Daddy gave me. But I loved it – I used always to wear it.'

She didn't tell him about the wish on the Paris balcony, but he seemed to know.

'Ah, yes, the wishing ring. Not inexpensive at all, I should say – a pearl of great price! And what was she like, this unfortunate?'

'Well, it's funny but I suppose she looked a bit like me.'

'To be sure.' The plump hand rubbed the plump instep. 'So, our island climate is clarifying your vision.'

'I don't understand. Who was she? Should I know her?'

From across the water they heard the unmistakable ghost cry of an owl. Dr Asklepios got up, walked over to the open door and looked out. 'Athena's hunting early. It promises a fine day tomorrow. Look –' he said, pointing at the rosy sky. 'Delighted shepherds – I think you refer to them still where you come from, as we have done for aeons here. But you asked, was she important – the woman in your dream?' He walked back towards the glowing fire. 'All lives have many possibilities. Sometimes, in extraordinary circumstances, when time and fate meet, a person encounters, in another's life, the fate which might have been their own. Sometimes one mortal bears that fate for another. Sometimes one mortal bears it for many.' He was knocking out his pipe on the stone fireplace but he spoke the words carefully. 'And while you were here with us, someone had to be at the funeral.'

12

Henri met Marie-Thérèse in the Bar Nemo, which was conveniently near the Hospital Notre-Dame. She asked for a Campari with lemonade – the kind of mixture which, in Henri's experience, often indicated a robust sexual appetite. She was a pleasant enough woman and he looked forward to seeing what she looked like without her clothes on. With those heavy breasts he guessed she might wear good brassieres.

He listened to her story about the daughter who had married a banker and no longer wanted to go shopping with her mother. Families! No point in saying it was all in the upbringing, as the fashionable shrinks did – you just couldn't predict. The women he dined and slept with told him tales of children for whom they had sacrificed their lives who thought it beneath them, or too boring, to visit their mothers now. He had adored his own mother who had left his dull but stable father to dance at the Crazy Horse. And Alice had been so traumatized she wouldn't even speak of her parents.

Thinking of Alice made him feel guilty.

'This is such a pleasure, my dear, but forgive me . . . My sister . . . I am still agitated.'

'Of course.' Marie-Thérèse was flustered. She had forgotten why she had come to meet the attractive enquirer. In her handbag she had the key to the safe which contained patients' valuable possessions or items which had been lost or became detached from their owners during the unsettling procedures of a hospital stay. Quite how she had managed to acquire the key made her neck flush even more because it had involved allowing herself to be held, more intimately than she would have wished, by M. Gautier, the aged clerk whose job it was to guard the safe. Nevertheless, permitting M. Gautier's advances had produced a result. This man, whom she had so luckily encountered at a moment when life seemed likely to remain very dull, would be grateful for her help.

'I have the key . . .' and as he didn't at first grasp the significance, she explained: 'to the safe. Where they keep anything that is not claimed . . .'

He cut across her. 'Heavens, I didn't expect such service. I must have pleased my guardian angel. Or perhaps *you* are my guardian angel . . .' And then he smiled with practised seductiveness.

'Would you like us to go and look? This is a good time. I can easily go back to the hospital as if I have forgotten something. The man who is in charge of the safe will have gone home. No one will check on us. I am too . . .' she tried for a word which would not diminish her in his eyes, '. . . too discreet.'

It was as well there were so few valuable items in the safe, Henri thought: the rape of it proved too easy. In fact there was very little in it at all. Some envelopes, sealed and marked with large amounts of francs – too many to risk in a bedside locker; a few worthless-looking brooches; a crucifix; and Alice's turquoise locket.

When he saw the distinctive turquoise-studded heart Henri was hit by a sharp pain just on the bridge of his nose; he felt as if he were about to have a nosebleed. Either Alice was there, in the hospital, or she was dead. And if he had to bet on it – and he was a man practised at betting – then Alice was dead, for he had never once seen her without the turquoise heart at her throat.

He was not the kind of man who pried but he was an artist; therefore neither was he incurious. He had tried once, when she was insensibly drunk, to turn the locket over and prise open the slim catch at the back. There was a secret stashed away there, he guessed, but she had groaned and turned away toward the wall, flinging a hand to her throat, as if, even in sleep, she would fiercely guard her privacy. And he was a man who respected privacy, so he left the locket alone.

Whether or not it was to protect the secret still, he instinctively now repressed his excitement.

'No. Nothing here. My poor sister.'

'What was your sister's name?'

He had to think for a moment before he produced his own sister's name, 'Ah, Bernadette. I guess she's just off on some *amour*.'

He was anxious to be away. The sight of the turquoise heart had disturbed him. The thought of anything sexual now with this woman made him feel queasy.

'You have been charming. May I express my gratitude by offering you dinner some evening? Soon,' he added hastily, seeing suspicion gather in her eyes.

As a precaution he gave her the card he kept with the wrong telephone number on it, which had been printed in fortuitous error. Henri, having pointed out the error, had kept the cards. 'For bookmarks,' he had explained to the surprised printer, who was puzzled that Monsieur, who had been so irate at the mistake, now wished to keep the falsely printed cards.

It was astonishing how useful it was to have one's phone number printed erroneously, Henri thought as he hurried away into the metro. People trust what they see in print, which is odd when you consider the amount of muck that is generated through the printed word. The subject made him think of the English princess who had died the night he had last heard from Alice. Alice had been incoherent with drink, but he wished now he had listened. The coincidence had created in him a strange affection for the dead princess. Poor creature: she had suffered from the printed word, all right. His instinct told him that Alice had died too, that night the press hounds pursued Princess Helena into the tunnel of death. And if, as he believed, Alice was dead, how was he to get back her turquoise locket?

Two days later, Violette de Sousa, old friend and mistress of Henri Astaffort, telephoned the Hospital Notre-Dame requesting that they search for her heart-shaped turquoise locket which she had perhaps lost – she had been so distracted – while visiting her dear friend who was in for an operation on his prostate. She expressed much relief when she was told by the lost-property clerk, M. Gautier, whose keys had been covertly returned by Marie-Thérèse under a pretence of massaging his frozen shoulder (she couldn't, she really couldn't, face anything else), that the locket was secure in the hospital safe. Violette expressed herself eloquently in other ways when Henri called to retrieve the locket and to offer his old lover his thanks. And Marie-Thérèse was pleased to receive a large bouquet thanking her for her help and a card announcing the happiness of the sender at his sister's return 'from an impromptu *vacance* – in Maroc, would you believe! I think, my dear madame, it was perhaps an affair of the heart!' The note concluded, 'À *bientôt* from your new friend', which permitted Marie-Thérèse the luxury of dreaming, for a week or two, about a future with the attractive stranger whose telephone seemed permanently out of order – until another fantasy arrived to take its place.

13

Edwin had had a reasonably good time with Aunt Mary and his cousins. His aunt had not treated him as if there was anything specially wrong. She had fussed a bit with Hugh, seeing he watched what he liked on TV and got all his favourite food, which was still hamburger and tomato ketchup with chips.

It was good for Hugh that Aunt Mary was so unlike Mum: tiny, where Mum was tall, and clipped in her speech and quite rude sometimes, really, where Mum was always ever so polite and sweet-spoken. What Aunt Mary really liked was horses and although Mum quite enjoyed riding, you couldn't say that horses were the be-all and end-all for her as they were with Aunt Mary. But surprisingly they had got on together lately. Mum had admired the way Aunt Mary had ridden for England in the Olympic team when she was younger. 'Good for her,' she had said, 'because she got into the team on her own merits. Nothing to do with *them!*' – which is how Mum had referred to Dad's family when she was really cheesed off with them.

But Aunt Mary, in spite of making no fuss about Mum –

which was a relief – had, nonetheless, knocked on his door on the last evening and sat at the end of his bed with her forehead all wrinkled up.

'You OK, Spiderman?'

'Spiderman' was her name for him because when he was small he had tried to frighten her by sticking a spider down her blouse and she had just fished it out, cool as a cucumber, and said, 'Don't be a bloody little idiot.' Then she had dropped the spider on to his head. It was after that they had become friends.

'Yup, I guess.'

'They treating you all right back at headquarters?' The Palace was not, Edwin guessed, her own favourite establishment.

'They try. Granny's upset and Dad seems to be angry with her over Mum, though it seems hard on Granny – getting stick from the papers as well.'

Edwin was very fair. It wasn't Granny's fault that Mum and Dad hadn't got on. And Granny had to stick up for Dad. After all, he was her son. Anyhow, Edwin had heard her ticking Dad off in private over Jessica. People were angry with Granny because the morning she was told Mum had been killed she didn't have Mum's name mentioned in church. But Edwin knew that was not to snub Mum – it was to spare his and Hugh's feelings in public. And no one had made him go to church either. In fact, Dad had been dead against it. Edwin had *wanted* to go – God was about the only person you could talk to when you got news like that – and Hugh wouldn't be left behind. So it was mean to blame Granny.

'Well, your Dad's probably feeling the pressure. But you're OK?'

He looked at his aunt. Her fair, slightly equine face expressed concern.

'I write to her.' She raised her fine eyebrows. 'To Mum. I write to her in your journal, the one you gave me for Christmas.'

'That's a great idea, Spiderman.'

She looked relieved until he added, 'So's she can read it.'

'How do you mean, love?' Princess Mary, although like her father in many ways, did not share his tendency to perceive madness in those unlike himself. But this sounded dicey.

Edwin took a gamble. 'You see, I don't think she's dead, I think . . .'

'Oh, Ed.' Uncharacteristically his aunt had clutched him and was hugging her nephew to her slight frame.

'No, really, I'm not bonkers. I know it sounds mad.' He had struggled out of her arms and was standing up now, very tall for his years, his cheeks pink and his eyes bright.

Princess Mary, who had scant time for appearances, looked at her favourite nephew. No doubt that he was a looker. He was going to carry off peoples' hearts every bit as much, maybe more, than his mother had.

'But, lovey . . .' This kind of stuff was not really her strong suit. She'd better talk to James. No wonder the boy hadn't seemed to be in distress. She'd been pleased at first, then puzzled and, lately, increasingly worried.

'No, really.'

Edwin tried again. It was important that he got her to understand or she'd go telling everyone and that might be a disaster for Mum. For Edwin had twigged. This was Mum's only hope of beating the press. The accident was a fix. Mum had had herself spirited away somewhere safe and she had sent the woman in the crowd to tell him. When Mum was ready she would send for him and Hugh. Meantime, at all costs, he must keep her secret.

Maybe, though, it was a mistake to have told Aunt Mary, although generally she was like the grave. And it was a strain not telling – especially with Dad grabbing him and Hugh all the time and kissing them, which he had certainly never done before.

And Granny and Dad so irritable with each other. Edwin sat down next to his aunt.

'Listen, I'm not nuts. There was this woman – she spoke to me.'

'Where?' Aunt Mary sounded sharp. Unlike her own children, the princes were closely guarded.

'No, it's OK, it wasn't anything wrong. In the crowd before the funeral.'

Funny how he'd almost said 'wedding'. Milu's family had sent a poem he had written for Mum to have buried with her. Edwin guessed they had hoped Mum would marry Milu. At least that couldn't happen now.

'But they said all kinds of things, didn't they?'

'This was different.' Edwin was sure. Again and again he'd rehearsed in his mind the words of the red-haired woman who had given him the bunch of anemones – flowers that Mum loved. 'She says you must remember her hymn. And tell him from me,' – and then she had whispered – 'Mum says to look after your brother.' He had tried.

'What did she say?'

But that he wasn't going to tell anyone. 'It's not what she said, it was the way that she said it. It was so obviously Mum speaking.' He smiled his devastating smile at his aunt who was agitatedly popping and unpopping the duvet cover.

'She, the woman, spoke like it was from her heart – right into mine. I was very, well, I suppose Mum would say "open", and everything that anyone said to me then I knew if it was true or not.'

Which is why he knew that Dad wasn't lying when he had said to them both that he was sorry. Edwin knew Dad was referring to the things he had said in the past about Mum. Edwin had loved Dad more than ever after he said that.

Princess Mary looked at her nephew. He had none of the

glittering look of the slightly mad. Mary had mistrusted the boys' mother initially, thinking her slightly dotty, until she had seen that Helena was rather a sane and decent woman behind the superficial nonsense. Maybe the boy needed to have this fantasy to get him through the ghastly aftermath of his mother's death. Mary's upbringing had not encouraged the development of the imagination, but that did not mean her upbringing had been correct. It had been fairly useless in other matters, after all.

'Guess it does no harm to hope. Best keep that diary locked, though. We don't want people thinking you've gone daft.'

'I'm not daft.' The future king of England looked at her with his mother's eyes and she recognized something. She respected him – and with her, respect was not a response that occurred easily, as her husband had often humorously reminded her.

'No, Spiderman. You're not daft. And listen, it's been great having you here. Come again, won't you. Come whenever you like.'

14

Henri was breathless when, after visiting Violette, he got himself back to the studio he rented off the Rue Serpente. It was a good location, commanding a, nowadays, fashionable Left Bank view of the Seine. Henri had rented it ever since his arrival in Paris forty years ago. The landlady then was a Parisienne divorcée, who had taken her young tenant to more than her metaphorical bosom and had sustained the fondness for him into her old age. The lease was up next year and Henri faced the challenge of having to create a relationship with his landlady's less than agreeable son — an envious-looking man who recently, late in life, had married.

His landlady's new daughter-in-law was a lawyer who, to Henri's unreconstructed eye, looked more like a lesbian than what he still referred to as a 'proper' woman. He had tried chatting up madame the lawyer, desisting only when it became apparent that she was more likely to slap a harassment order on him than invite him to renew, on favourable terms, his tenancy in her mother-in-law's house. For the time being, however, his landlady, aided by Bollinger and Chanel 22 which Henri took care to supply at Christmas, seemed set fair to make the century.

The studio was high and cool with a north window, though as a sculptor Henri had no need of the painter's traditional light. He was finishing a large construct in copper, an exciting commission for the Jardin Shakespeare in the Bois de Boulogne, and he now sat on the maternal curve of one of its surfaces to recover his equilibrium. He was shaking as if all the sugar had left his blood.

The turquoise heart had been returned to him by Violette only after he had paid her in the coin she best liked. He was fond of her, but the effort of raising the necessary parts to perform had involved an exercise which he privately referred to as 'scraping the barrel of the imagination'. On this occasion he had had to dig deep to dredge up a fantasy equal to the task. Henri liked sex and saw to it that he had it most days – on good days more than once. But this business of Alice had knocked the stuffing out of him. He didn't want to perform, not even for an old friend like Violette. The only desire that possessed him was to get back to the studio to penetrate the secret of the locket.

The locket had a gold hinge at the back. Some delicate work with his finest chisel slipped it open. Inside there was a sliver of paper. He remembered, suddenly, that he needed another prescription for his heart arrhythmia – and as the thought occurred, he felt, simultaneously, the familiar pain in his chest. Ignoring the palpitations he tweezered out the paper and gently unfolded it.

A whisper of soft dark hair tied with a blue silk thread and a thin strip of plastic with a name inside. The name was written in faded biro – Henri turned it towards the studio's northern light. It read – 'Baby Fenton-Kirk: 17.6.81.'

A child! He had guessed from Alice's nipples that there had been a child. Henri was a man who knew most of what there was to know about the female breast. He even knew the early symptoms of breast cancer and twice had been instrumental in getting women diagnosed before the doctors had picked up the signs. The aureole, the circle around the nipples of a woman, darkens irreversibly in childbearing. But he had not thought of a child as the secret.

Male egocentricity had presumed it was a lost lover whose image was sanctified in the core of Alice's turquoise heart. Fenton-Kirk. So he had been right. She was a nob. His artist's eye had picked out that aristocratic bone and gait. Also her manners. Even at her most *distraite* there was a kind of *noblesse oblige* about Alice.

The name suggested wealth. Henri Astaffort was not a mercenary man but he was curious. More curious now than when Alice had been with him and alive. What had caused her to so kick over the traces of her background? He was convinced that the turquoise heart which he had found through the offices of Marie-Thérèse was proof that Alice Fenton-Kirk had sidestepped out of life.

Perhaps it was for the best, Henri mused as he lit a Gitane and poured a strong coffee from the metal coffee-pot which bubbled on his stove. The hot, bitter coffee tasted good with the tobacco. She was fragile, that one, too highly strung perhaps to live in these stressful times. The Lord knew, he found it hard-going enough and he had his work.

Alice had nothing. Had had nothing. He knew so little about her, had never asked what had brought her to Paris in the first place, perhaps assuming that to live in the world's most evocative city required no explanation. Now he wondered. Had it been the birth of Baby Fenton-Kirk that brought her here? And did the child die, or was it adopted?

Henri, so far as he knew, had no children. He did not quite understand why, but somehow this matter of the turquoise heart with its secret seemed to touch him as personally as if the new-found Baby Fenton-Kirk were discovered to be his own flesh and blood. It was too late in the day for him to become a parent but a kind of natural law began to work in him. Instinct makes us want children. Once that instinct was necessary for the world's survival. Nowadays, who knew what purpose it served, but for the first time Henri Astaffort found himself questioning his desire to pass through life leaving no new life behind.

Lighting a second Gitane, he looked up at the higher coils of the copper image. It would be finished soon and he had promised himself a little holiday when it was off his hands. Delicately he held the remnant of Baby Fenton-Kirk's plastic wristband in the palm of his hand. Such a scrap of a thing to carry such a secret. Why shouldn't he – for who, after all, would know? – go to England and see if he couldn't find out more about the Fenton-Kirk family? Maybe this was all a needless scare and Alice had merely drifted back to her own country after their last spat. His sixth sense might be wrong. Anyway, it would give him a chance to look up a marquise who had once posed for him in return for bed and comforts. She must be about fifty now. He would like to see Christina again.

For the time being, he placed the turquoise heart in a cigar box he kept under his bed and with it he laid, respectfully – for he was a man aware of proprieties – the lock of hair and the plastic remnant. Then he turned back to the massy sculpture which winked copper lights at him.

'Very well, mademoiselle,' he said. 'I must to England. We'd better get you out of here and off to your nunnery.'

15

She hardly thought of Milu now. At first, when the girl had gone off back to England, she had thought of him all the time and the shock of losing him had felt unbearable. Only when they crossed the sea again and she had come to this other land, the island, did the shock begin to diminish. To find a man who loved her, and to lose him so soon, seemed part of some dim pattern. Like an old mosaic of the Tree of Life she had seen with her husband once, in the Middle East, under the sand.

And here, in this utterly peaceful place, the sun's warmth and the blessed privacy did, slowly, seem to be repairing something. She scarcely missed her former life, not even the clothes – nowadays she wore a simple yellow dress – nor the fine food – the food here was delicious and she found she wanted exactly enough to satisfy her hunger – and certainly not the never-ending round of public engagements. Here was simplicity and profound calm.

She missed the boys fiercely, but even this was made bearable because she met them so often in her dreams. She longed to hold them tight and kiss their dear faces and squeeze them and make them grin, but to be with them, if only while she and they slept, was a great blessing.

And what a place it was for dreaming! One day she spoke about this to Dr Asklepios, who had called that evening with a bottle of the dark wine suggesting he might eat with them.

'I am dreaming a lot,' she said.

Dr Asklepios was eating olives. 'Of course,' – he spoke as if it was to be expected – 'we are on the edge of things here, you know!' He spat out an olive stone. 'Dreams happen on the edges of things.'

'So, do you listen to them – dreams?'

'Most certainly I listen to them.'

She remembered something her husband had liked and spoke it aloud. '"We are such stuff as dreams are made of . . ."'

Dr Asklepios snorted. '"We are such stuff as dreams are made *on*" – always when people speak this line they forget the "on". They think Shakespeare wrote "of". We are not made *of* dreams. Imbeciles!'

'I'm sorry – my husband always hated it too when I got that sort of thing wrong.' She felt abashed.

The doctor looked sheepish. 'Forgive my bark, my dear. Your Shakespeare is something of a bee in my bonnet. I am – how do you say it – a fan. If only the rest of you had his understanding!'

'I'm sorry! I was hopeless at school.'

'What has that to do with the price of eggs? School is of no consequence here, I assure you.' It was clear that the doctor was possessed of strong opinions.

'So if we are not made of dreams, what are they for?'

'They have news for us. They tell us what we need to know – the thing we cannot face, the thing we try to hide. A dream is like a special kind of photograph – it is a picture of what happens in the depths where we cannot always see ourselves.'

'I sort of know that – I had therapy before.'

'My therapy is different.' The doctor showed the teeth, which were much in need of a dental hygienist. 'It is about leaving behind all the nonsense so that you see not only the thing you truly are but also the thing you may become. "We know what we are but we know not what we may be", as Shakespeare has that poor child say. Ophelia could have done with my therapy. You are lucky you do not end up mad and upside down in your petticoats in a river in Denmark.' He spat another olive stone and laughed rather too heartily, she thought, at his own joke.

She had somehow not liked to ask Dr Asklepios about her name. Angela, the girl, never used any, referring to her as 'ma'am' – which seemed out of place here on a hillside with the goats and the hooded crows.

'Dr Asklepios?'

The doctor did not answer at first. He had eaten all the little black olives and was now apparently preoccupied picking wax out of his ear. 'Ludicrous that we should still be saddled with these evolutionary precautions. Do you know what this is for? I tell you. It is in case I lie down on the ground and a beetle walks into my ear.'

'Who am I now? I mean, what should Angela call me? It feels silly to be a ma'am.' She hadn't liked it even in the old days.

'Do you not think I might have been permitted to evolve, in my corporeal form, beyond the beetle-stopping wax? Why do you want to know?' His tone was peremptory.

'Well, I feel I don't have an identity any more, I suppose.'

'Yes?' He sounded uninterested.

'You were saying about dreams telling us things. I had this dream last night – I can't get it out of my mind.'

This did catch the doctor's attention. 'The things which stick in the mind are always worth investigation.' His own investigations over, he seemed willing to listen.

'It was about a play,' she explained. 'Edwin, my son, told me about a play he went to with my . . . with his father. I mean, in real life he told me. It seemed to be about that.' She tried to recover the dream.

'So, you had better spit it out.'

Wherever did he pick up his funny English? It sounded as if he had learnt it from some old school textbook. 'Well, I think there was an actress, a leading actress, she wasn't able to perform . . . there had been an accident, or something, I'm not sure. I was asked to take over the part. In the dream I thought, "I can't do this, I don't know how – I don't know the plot, the story, or anything." And, you see, I wasn't sure who I was because people seemed to be treating me as if I was this actress who had had the accident. My husband was at the theatre already, in the audience with the children – with Eds and Hugh – and I thought, "It's OK because Eds will help me, he knows the story – he told me the story before." You know how it is, in dreams? Time gets sort of squashed up, so what has happened in the past is part of what is happening now. In the dream, I remembered that Eds had told me all about it.' She stopped to collect herself. 'It was the last time I saw him.'

He was watching her carefully now. 'And the story your son told you. Do you remember it?'

She tried to think back across all that had happened and a faint line of pain set in across her forehead. She had not been paying attention when her son had tried to tell her. Eds with his dear, grave eyes. It had been important to him, but she had not wanted to know then, in that other life, because he had seen the play with his father and she had minded still – about their father. But now, suddenly, it was desperately important that she recovered the tale her son had told her that evening, which seemed both like yesterday and, oh, such a long time ago. It was like a precious ring which she had lost, but knew she could find if only she could go back into the past and look for it with better

93

sight. She frowned, struggling to pull back her elder son's words.

'I think so. It was about Helen of Troy – no, it was about a sacrifice that the Greeks made in order to get to Troy. That was it. They needed a strong wind, the Greek army. And a goddess, the goddess of the hunt, Eds said she was ... Artemis – that's right, she was called Artemis – told their leader that if he wished to get to Troy, to get Helen back, he must sacrifice his most precious possession.'

It was coming back now – the dream or the memory, she was not sure which. Now, of course, she remembered. She remembered it all perfectly.

'There was this girl, a young woman, Iphigenia, his daughter and she thought she was being taken to be married ...

... they dressed her in white and put garlands in her hair, her maids too, all in white and the garlands. And perfume, she remembered the perfume of ambergris. Her mother said, 'He is the most peerless fighter in the Greek army,' and she was happy, her mother, that her daughter was going to marry such a man. Her mother gave her, for a wedding gift, her favourite brooch, the running deer made in bronze, and set her off, on her journey, laughing. The crowds roared as she left. It was a holy day for them – a holiday.

And when she got there, to the seaside where the army were camping, her father took her in his arms and seemed to weep – she thought it was for joy. He led her out and there were more crowds – lines and lines of soldiers waiting to go and fight at Troy to get back Helen who had been stolen. She thought they had come to join in the celebrations, her celebrations, and she smiled at them to show how happy she was and how proud to be marrying the most fearless soldier of them all. And they had applauded and cheered and cried out, 'Well done, Iphigenia!' and 'Good old Iphigenia!' for of course they knew what was going to happen. She was going to give them the wind they needed. They believed she was doing it for them. Her father led her up the aisle of soldiers with their swords held out like branches, until they came to a great rock, and even then she hadn't guessed but had turned and smiled at him, believing it to be some sacred place he had chosen for her marriage rite. Which it was – an altar to Artemis, the virgin huntress.

They bound her then with rope and laid her on the rock, and she could not cry out for her father stuffed a cloth in her mouth. Her father was crying. Then he looked up and she saw the tears falling down into his beard and dripping on to the hand which held the knife. Her own father's hand. And then he called out, so that everyone could hear, 'Now then, Artemis, listen to me! Take my daughter as you willed. Take the most precious thing in life as you commanded me to give. But hear me, Artemis. After this, no more. This is the final sacrifice!'

. . . she was crying and Dr Asklepios had got out of his chair and was holding her and rocking her in safe, strong arms as her nanny had rocked her when she was a baby; as she had rocked the children in the nursery school, and then Eds and Hugh.

When she grew calmer, he said, 'There. That is sacrifice. Now you know what it is like.'

He put a glass of red wine into the two hands of the woman who had once been Princess Helena, the future queen of England, and had lately had no name, saying,

'Drink this, Iphigenia, and then, when you are ready, Angela has cooked us fish. It smells good with the herbs and the wild garlic.'

II

FLUX

16

George had not intended to go to the rave which Fresh Start had organized. He was too done in in his head about the Princess. But Tina, his girlfriend, was on at him to go and had promised to bring her friend, Sam. George fancied Sam and thought there might be a chance to get off with her provided Tina was busy dancing with his friend Steve. Steve was an ace dancer and Tina loved to dance. Which would give George a chance to have a go at Sam.

Princess Helena had been the patroness of Fresh Start, the housing trust for young homeless Londoners. The rave had been her own idea, to have something a bit cooler than the usual kind of dance; she had wanted to come to it herself and maybe dance with a few of the guys. The guys had all been in training, hoping they might get to dance with the Princess.

George had gone to Fresh Start when he was living under the M4 bridge with Old George who'd died. Old George had taken him in, if you could take someone 'in' to a house made out of crates and supermarket boxes, though Old George's cardboard house was a lot more like home than anything he'd known before.

'Who give you that name, George?' Old George had said. 'That's my name too! Us Georges should stick together.' Before that he'd been in the Young Offenders' place on account of his adopted mother, which he didn't like to think of much.

It was Old George had made him go along to the club where the Princess had visited. They'd got up a football side and the Princess had come to a match where he'd played on the wing and scored a brilliant goal – everybody talked about it – against a big public school side. The Princess had arranged that, too, with the posh school her sons were at, lucky bastards – if you could call anyone who still went to school lucky. George never did school any more.

After the match the Princess had asked to meet him. She was ever so nice – even though he'd been the reason her son's school got thrashed. She seemed quite cool about it. There was a photo taken, with her smiling, her arm round him. He had the photo still, in the waterproof army folder which Old George had kept his medal in.

Old George had shown him the medal when he first went to live under the M4. It looked quite the biz – and it turned out that Old George was a war hero or something. He knew a lot, did Old George: how to make a saucepan out of a can of beans; how to sew on buttons; how to tell which bins to look into for food. When Old George had died of pneumonia, George had taken the supermarket trolley and had wheeled it, with Old George's collection of tins and his war medal, all the way to Wandsworth – where Tina and Tina's kid lived.

Tina lived in a basement where her Gran had lived. It was pretty damp and it had no curtains, which was a pain when you wanted to have a piss or something, but the landlord couldn't get Tina out because he had agreed to have her on the rent book before her Grandma had died. So now George lived there too. With Tina and the baby and the rats.

'You still on about her then?'

Tina was asking about Princess Helena again. George went rigid. He didn't want to discuss the Princess with Tina. He'd been one of the guys invited to walk in the funeral procession as part of the Fresh Start contingent. There had been one ticket for the actual service in the Abbey, which was going to be given to Mick who had cancer. But Mick hadn't been able to go. When he heard about the Princess he'd kind of turned his face to the wall and wouldn't eat or anything. So George had been offered the place instead 'cos of him having met the Princess at the football match.

'What you on about? I've got a cold.' He wasn't going to tell Tina what had happened at the funeral. She thought he was bonkers anyway.

'Liar! I seen you crying every time she comes on the telly.'

Living with Tina was not half as nice, if you wanted to know, as living with Old George. The only advantage was you could shag Tina, where's you'd have to be two stops past Dagenham to shag Old George. Still, Tina's place'd do for the time being.

The decision to proceed with the Fresh Start rave had been furthered by a discreet announcement from the Palace that Prince Edwin had suggested his mother would wish the event to continue. Edwin, where he was allowed to have a say, had been adamant that none of the events with which his mother had been associated should be postponed or interfered with in any way. He knew, better than anyone, what her wishes would have been. What nobody other than Edwin himself knew was that he was planning to attend the rave himself.

Edwin had spent some time working out how to fix it so's he could get away. On balance, he thought, it would be easier to escape school than any of the places he might have got permission to stay at over an exeat weekend. He'd considered Aunt Mary's place, because there he would be chaperoned the least, but even she would have the regulation detectives about if he was staying there. Also, he disliked the idea of deceiving Aunt Mary. She was dead straight and he kind of wanted to keep his behaviour straight towards her. Anyway, it was easier to evade his own detectives at school. He was practised at that.

It was useful having been reasonably docile in the past. Also, with the business over Mum, everyone was careful not to upset him. So if he said he wanted to lie down in his room, school let him without any questions. He'd mostly used these opportunities to write up his journal, which he needed to do to keep in touch with Mum.

They gave you part of the Nobel Peace Prize today, Mum. They're saying they'd never have got the land-mine thing going if it weren't for you. All the guys here think it's great. Well done, Mum! I'm proud of you.

That was his entry today – and now he could prepare himself. For the moment he wasn't going to mention his plan – not even in the journal. If it all worked out, he'd tell Mum then.

Most probably Mum would have felt fine about what he was planning – which, roughly, was to try and get some experience of the kind of things which she had thought important: seeing how ordinary people lived – unemployed people, the homeless and so on. This rave seemed a good place to start. Mum had discussed it with him. She'd been proud that it wasn't one of those stuffy events she used to have to turn out for – more real, more what real kids like – and they had worked out together the scheme of her going to dance there. She was going to wear a really brilliant dress: a shining metallic blue number with a halter top edged in silver.

'That's such a great idea, Mum,' he'd said. 'They'll just love dancing with you! You're such a fantastic dancer!'

What he had decided to do was to climb out on to the roof and get down the fire-escape by one of the master's rooms. This particular master, who was not part of the regular staff but was on supply, was having an affair. Edwin knew this because his detective had told him – one of the things about being Mum's son was that people told you things – so Edwin was ninety per cent sure Timmy Tiptoes (which is what he was called on account of his funny walk) would be safely burrowed down in some blonde's bed.

Edwin had some army fatigues from a visit he and Hugh had been on with Dad. He'd brought the gear to school last year, for a play his year were doing about Northern Ireland, which they'd not let him take part in 'for reasons of security'. Edwin was still furious about that. The gear was now in the acting cupboard and he knew how to pick the lock. (Sometimes it was useful having your own detective.)

At 9.30 p.m. on an October night the future heir to the throne climbed across the roof and slipped on to the fire-escape wearing army fatigues and a black balaclava (also courtesy of the acting cupboard). He had £100 in his back pocket which he had won in the school sweepstake when Man. United beat Feyenoord. Being a Man. U. supporter he had been over the moon anyway, and it seemed a brilliant way to use the winnings now. He found a local taxi firm's number in a call-box and ordered a minicab to take him to Brentford (who seemed to be heading down fast this season) from where, sweating with the novelty, he took a train to Vauxhall Bridge. It was the first time in his life he had ever travelled alone.

*　　*　　*

George wasn't really angry with Tina. She had been dancing cheek to cheek with Steve, and George had seen her rubbing herself against him, suggestively. Which was useful, wasn't it, when you wanted to pretend.

'You go on like that and I'm off. Coming?'

Tina was enjoying herself too much to abandon Steve.

'You can piss off! I'll come home when I feel like!'

'Yeh, great – I will.'

A chance to see if Sam was available. George almost crashed into a guy in army gear who was coming through the door.

'Watchit, mate!'

The army guy jumped and looked a bit upset and George, who was small for his age and knew what it felt like to be battered, touched him on the sleeve. 'Hey, no worries!'

The guy was looking around, a bit lost.

'Looking for someone?'

'Ah, yup. A friend of mine . . . said he might be here.'

'Yeah? Cig?' George held out a box of Marlborough. It was the Princess's 'do', wasn't it, so you had to try and be friendly. That's what was wrong with Tina – she'd no feelings.

'No thanks. But I wouldn't mind a drink. Any idea where I could get one?'

Some accent! George stopped and looked. He was a tall, white dude, quite handsome. Tina'd probably go for him.

'Yeh, sure. Over there. Fancy a pint?'

The other seemed a bit lost and George, who had not managed to locate Samantha, set off with him to the bar.

'You from the trust? One of the Princess's lot?'

'Ah, yes, sort of.'

He seemed a basic enough bloke.

'You in the army, then?'

'Er, kind of.'

George snorted, 'Shit, mate, you sound like you should be!'

The tall guy was fumbling in his pocket and pulling out a twenty-pound note. 'Look, would you get us both a drink.'

'Cheers, mate.' This was all right then. Who cared where the guy came from if he was flush and handing it about. George ordered a pint of Fosters. 'What you having, mate?' It was cool, anyway, to have a talk with a guy for a change. He was sick of Tina and her endless moans and the baby.

'Same as you?' George wasn't getting this. The guy seemed like an army guy, all right. He was big enough. But he didn't seem to know his way round. Maybe it was a cover – like he was SAS or something.

'You rate her then?'

'Sorry? Rate who?'

'The Princess, git! Why we're here. D'you like her?'

Edwin wasn't sure how to answer this. He took what he hoped was a practised pull on his pint. 'Yes. Yes, I do . . . um, did.'

'Well, don't go over the top then! I thought she was brilliant. Just brilliant. Listen, don't tell my girlfriend, but I cried like I was never going to stop when it happened. I still cry when I see pictures of her or she comes on the telly.'

At 4.30 a.m. the following morning, Prince Edwin climbed back up the fire-escape, across the roof and though his unbolted window. He checked the note he had left on the door: SLEEPING – PLEASE DO NOT DISTURB.

All quiet. Next door DC Swift was snoring.

I had a great evening, Mum. I went to a rave – the one we talked about. Your idea, remember? It was brilliant, I went in a mini-cab, then on a train, then back in another minicab – driven by a Sikh. He was nice. He told me his wife has a shrine for you with flowers she puts there every day. And your photo. (He didn't know who I was, of course.) I met someone, too, called George. He says he met you before when you got our school to play his club at football. It was George who scored the winning goal. He loves you! He told me he cried and cried – but he was proud of it. He lives in a flat in Wandsworth and me and him's going clubbing next week – if I can get out again.

He'd undressed and was in bed before he remembered and opened the journal again.

'Goodnight, Mum, sweet dreams wherever you are.'

17

It was late afternoon and they were sitting in the dry suspended heat under the translucent green-fingered leaves of a walnut tree. The doctor was eating freshly fallen walnuts which he picked from the earth at his feet. The fact that he cracked the shells in his mouth did much to explain the colour of his teeth.

He had become a regular visitor. Usually they would sit, as they were today. He would ask her about her dreams and she would talk about the memories and feelings they prompted, often telling him about the life she had left behind her. That afternoon she was describing to him a dream she had had, about her husband, when she noticed a movement at the doctor's feet. Looking down she saw a large tortoise with a distinctive patterned shell.

Dr Asklepios bent down. 'Good afternoon, Hestia.' He spoke as if he were addressing someone of importance. 'I'm pleased you have joined us.'

'What is it? A pet?' The boys had always wanted a tortoise. She wished they could see this one.

The tortoise looked at her with two very bright black eyes.

Dr Asklepios, again, addressed the tortoise. 'You must forgive her, my dear. She is a recent arrival.' He turned reproachfully to his companion. 'It is provoking to be referred to as "it".' He lent down and fed the tortoise a piece of cracked walnut which it took with one scaly claw. 'Would you like one?' – proffering the other wrinkled half to the young woman. 'I am told they are excellent for the skin. Aphrodite eats them for that purpose alone. For myself, I eat them because I am greedy.'

'You talk to her?'

The tortoise, who was rapidly consuming the walnut, raised its head. Dr Asklepios spoke hurriedly. 'Hestia is the oldest among us. When you have been informed of a body's name it is polite to use it.' He stroked the tortoise under the chin with a fat finger and the creature opened her mouth and yawned, revealing a very pink tongue. 'She's new, Hestia, still learning.' He sat back. 'We regard her visits as a privilege.'

'I'm sorry – I didn't mean to be rude.'

The tortoise stared a moment longer and then resumed her walnut consumption. Dr Asklepios cracked another nut and left one of the wrinkled halves beside the reptile's horned foot. 'There you are, my dear, an offering.' He turned back to the young woman sitting beside him. 'And the dream about your husband? You were saying . . .'

She frowned, trying to remember. Here, in the sunshine, beneath the walnut tree with Dr Asklepios and a venerable tortoise, her old life seemed absurd.

From what she could remember of the dream she and James had been walking down a long corridor. She had gone behind him, knowing that James was leading her to a room where an ancestor of his had gone mad. In the dream he was intending to lock her in the room and leave her there. She described this to Dr Asklepios who nodded his head.

'So, tell me, how does it make you feel when this husband of yours wishes to do such a thing?'

It was an uncomfortable feeling. 'He's not my husband any longer, actually.'

'Ah, you side-step.'

He extracted a recalcitrant walnut from his mouth and examined the shell which was glistening with saliva.

'OK, then. I was upset!'

'But not angry?' Dr Asklepios settled the weight on his buttocks. 'The man you marry leads you into a room where he proposes to lock you up and where, according to the logic of your dream, you will go mad. Or maybe, as part of the same logic, he insults you by assuming you are *already* mad. It seems to me that the dream describes, with some accuracy, the way you feel your husband treated you, and yet you tell me you are only "upset"? What is this "upset"? Were you not turned upside down with grief and rage?'

'Of course I was angry!' Stung, she spoke louder than she intended.

'Because he had jilted you for the other woman, yes?' Dr Asklepios looked quite maliciously at her. She noticed he had a piece of walnut stuck between his two front teeth. It was quite revolting. 'But you see, you do not say so! From this we must assume there is a violence you do not acknowledge.'

'Oh, really!' Why should she put up with this? She half started to her feet but he put out a restraining hand.

'Good. So we establish that you are the wronged woman. And you enjoy this role?'

He certainly appeared to find it enjoyable anyway! 'Not at all, if you want to know!' How dared he? What did he know about the shames and humiliations she had borne – this fat stupid Greek doctor who was probably gay.

'Are you sure you did not take a certain, ah, relish in this being victimized? It would be not unnatural, after all. Your husband offends you – you gain the public sympathy. You are wrong, by the way: I am not homosexual, although I am told by Aphrodite that I have a strong feminine side.'

'I thought you were supposed to be helping me!' Her voice rang out so that Angela, many metres away, heard it where she was fishing for crabs in the deep rock pools by the cliffs, and wondered whether she should come to help.

The doctor laughed an infuriating laugh and she rose again, half wanting to hit him, half wanting to run away. With lightning speed he flung out a hairy hand and gripped her soft upper arm.

'No. Do not be upping and offing. You are not any more the English princess: hoity-toity – do what you like. Here it is different. You stay where you are told!'

He lifted his big hand and, just for a second, she saw something flash in his eyes. Gold, like an eagle. Rubbing her arm she sat down, her insides churning. He dropped the hand and resumed the hunt for walnuts.

The tortoise was looking at her with little black eyes. Suddenly, she hated being here, wherever in the name of heaven it was. It had been balm at first, he had been so kind – worming his way into her confidences with his bottles of wine and comfortable conversations – but now he seemed only to want to persecute her. Angrily she muttered, 'What the hell do you know, anyway? You know fuck all about my life!'

The tortoise continued the unblinking black gaze and she felt suddenly scared at the obscenity. Surprisingly, Dr Asklepios looked pleased. 'That is so. Let me tell you a little joke of which I am fond. There is a man, he is a man of small education but he is clever. This fellow is put down by those he works with. They believe because his education is not so good that this man is not so bright – they try to pull the wool over his eyes. They try to diddle him. One day he becomes tired of this; he loses his temper. He says, "Listen! You think I know fuck nothing! Well, let me tell you, I know fuck all!" In this same way I am pleased to admit that I know "fuck all".'

'It isn't funny.' She never thought she would have missed the life she had before. But there at least she was admired. Here, with Dr Asklepios and his beady-eyed tortoise there were no compliments or signs of adoration.

'But you see, it is funny – if only you look at it the right way.' His voice was kind again. All at once she began to giggle. 'What is it? You laugh. Good. Now, tell me.'

'I was thinking . . .' giggles overcame her '. . . I was thinking that I should have pinched his bottom.'

'The bottom of . . . ?'

'My husband, James. In the dream. He wouldn't have known what to do.'

Dr Asklepios beamed.

'Excellent! You get the picture. A humorous nip to the royal bum, correctly judged, is worth forty of the screaming fits.'

'Do you really think I am violent?'

The question was not so awful now she was asking it herself.

Dr Asklepios threw a couple of walnuts into the air. 'I think I may learn to juggle – the great advantage of immortality is that one has time. Violent? Of course you are violent. Why do you think you are here?'

Above them a large bird, spread-winged, was circling, looking for prey.

'Well, I hadn't exactly known.'

Dr Asklepios shaded his eyes. 'A golden eagle.' The tortoise stopped eating and withdrew her head hastily. Dr Asklepios picked the creature up, stroking the humped shell with his plump hands. 'Their only natural enemy, you know.' He nodded at the tortoise. 'Watch, he's seen her.'

The eagle had spiralled earthwards and was circling purpose-
fully over their heads. What must their sight be like to be able
to spot such a well-camouflaged creature from that distance?

'So why am I here? You still haven't explained.'

Dr Asklepios looked at his patient. She was very pretty –
almost as pretty as the other Helen, the one they had all the
trouble over that time ago. But this one was nicer.

'There are several reasons.' He watched as the eagle began to
move away in search of less protected prey. 'You asked me, my
dear, if I thought you were violent and I answered that, yes, I
thought you were. Do not, if you please, take offence. It is a
violence, for the most part, not directed against others. The
violence is against yourself.'

'But if I have never hurt anyone else?' She felt tears were
collecting in the edges of her eyes. She did not want to cry.

He looked at her. It was hard work being a mortal.

'You make a mistake, you Christians – I suppose you call
yourself a Christian, though I find most Christians are pretty
much indifferent to their faith these days – when you imagine
that if it is against the self then it is not violence. The self is
precious. At bottom it is all you have. If there is to be violence,
better it is aimed at the outer world than towards the self.'

'But surely hurting other people is wrong?' She had a disagree-
able feeling that she was hearing something which was not to
her credit.

'Oh, sure!' His odd English was peppered with Americanisms.
'Although we here do not always share that view. Sometimes you
mortals only learn through hurting each other. All I am saying,
my dear, is that hurting another human being is not as wrong as
hurting oneself. Hurting oneself attracts violence in others.'

The eagle had returned from a successful kill and was rising
again, resuming its predatory flight. Dr Asklepios gestured.

'Take the eagle there. We do not blame him that he seeks to

destroy. He is a natural part of a dialogue of life and death.' He pointed at the tortoise on his lap. 'I do not spell it out – it is not tactful – but the eagle's prey must also take steps to protect itself . . .'

'But you wouldn't blame a tortoise if an eagle ate it?'

Dr Asklepios flapped his hands. 'Hush! be careful now. She is very old but her hearing is still quick. Of course not. But also if the protection does not work we do not blame the eagle. It is its nature.'

She looked at the tortoise on the doctor's lap. It was well battened down: no extremity was visible, only the prettily patterned shell. She lowered her voice. 'How do they do it – the eagles?'

Dr Asklepios cupped his hands around the tortoise's shell. 'Let us say the, er, dinner, is dropped from a great height. With the shell smashed . . .'

'Poor tortoise!'

Dr Asklepios bent towards her to speak softly. 'In a sense. But that is to look at things only from one position. You see, the tortoise, should the, er, protection prove ineffective, also gives itself up to another level of being.' Here the doctor pointed upwards, stabbing the air with his fat forefinger towards the disappearing eagle. 'It is not a thing we do here, but you Christians eat your god, don't you? Being eaten is a kind of sacrifice.'

'I'm not sure I understand that. I used to eat things when I was unhappy.'

The eagle had disappeared. Dr Asklepios set the tortoise down and she moved off with surprising speed, into the surrounding scrub.

'Well, since we've got on to that subject, that is what I meant about your violence.' It was said casually but she flushed and Dr Asklepios kept his gaze towards the purple horizon. 'It is what your unhappy twentieth-century jargon would call "a complex".'

Those hunted times – days of constant rigid vigilance – the desperate fight not to eat and then the wretched fight to get rid of whatever she had eaten: dreadful days. 'It was my marriage.'

'So, what was it about your marriage that made you hurt yourself?'

She shrugged. 'My husband made me feel I was plump – you know, fat. He teased me, before we were married.' She blushed again, remembering her naiveté: she hadn't known then about Jessica. 'I didn't like it when he teased me. I wanted to be beautiful.'

'And so you are, my dear. Very beautiful.'

'I didn't think I was beautiful.' She looked more than usually so in the tawny autumn light.

Dr Asklepios blinked. 'But it is not about beauty, anyway – this eating, not eating.' *The violet-eyed princess*, the blind poet would have called her. He hurried on. 'It is about controlling a monster within. Your husband, perhaps rather tactlessly, awakens the monster with his charmless British humour. But be sure that your husband's opinion is only part of it – distressing as I daresay it was. It is inside you that the monster lives.'

She pulled a face. 'So I'm a monster now?'

'Silly girl. You are not a monster. This is something you have acquired – one of the numerous accretions which life has attached to you. It is not what you are in your essential being.'

What was in the locked room in her dream? It was true she had feared it – not wanting to be taken there by her husband.

Dr Asklepios plucked the thought from her mind. 'Let us take, for example, your dream of the locked room to which your husband was leading you. In life, if your husband did such a thing, that would be an act of gross immorality. But your husband did no such thing. He was, from what you have told me, a decent enough man – perhaps a bit uptight, the public-school boy, yes? But this dream is yours. What does it tell us about you? It tells us that inside you, somewhere, there is a locked room where there is something about yourself which you believe is dangerous.'

An image of standing, swaying with exhaustion in the Food Hall at Harrods assailed her. A particular strawberry cheesecake – red and glistening. She had bought the whole cheesecake and hurried home and eaten it in the bathroom, before she had even unwrapped her other purchases. How disgusting it seemed now.

'When I was, you know, ill, I thought maybe I was going mad. I felt out of control – I couldn't stop myself.'

The old doctor looked at his patient. She was watching him, her pupils wide in the extraordinary irises.

'Good. So the fear is spoken. And it is not so terrible after all. Every being has a locked room and there is always something to fear in it. Let us say, then, that for you there is this kind of monster hidden, which tries to eat you up. Sometimes you feed it things, sometimes you starve it. Or you buy it pretty clothes because it feels ugly to you, and that makes you feel ugly also.'

'How does one get rid of a it?'

A small spider spinning a web had attached one end of the thread to the doctor's beard. It swayed now, on its invisible line, as he spoke.

'You cannot. There is nothing in life that can be got rid of. My old friend Parmenides, who was something of what you nowadays would call a physicist, knew this and I notice your modern scientists have seen the wisdom of what he had to say. Nothing really changes – only the shape alters. And what is true of matter is also far more true of the human psyche. Better we find the thread, as Theseus did with his Minotaur, which leads us to the monster's lair and then, who knows, it may prove useful. A monster can be handy – useful for getting rid of unwelcome elements. Those ungentlemanly press who pursued you, for example, might have been more respectful if they had had to deal with a Minotaur, perhaps?'

The thought was liberating. 'What is the thread, Dr Asklepios?'

The spider had spun its way from Dr Asklepios's beard across the gap between them and settled on her dress. She watched its delicate walk, not wishing to brush it away.

'It is consciousness, my dear, the hardest thing of all to follow. It is the finest of threads.'

'And if I find the monster and tame it, as you say, where will the thread lead to next, Dr Asklepios?'

But the tide was on the turn and soon he needed to be off.

'Find out!' was all he would offer, over his shoulder, as he set off with his quick, bandy-legged walk, down the path towards the sea and the boat with the green sails.

18

Henri had no difficulty in finding Christina. He got her number from Directory Enquiries and when he rang she recognized his voice immediately.

'Henri Astaffort! Well, good God! It *is* you, isn't it? Where ever are you? My dear man, come round here immediately. I want to see what you look like.'

Christina, on sighting nearer sixty than fifty (which meant she must have lied about her age all those years ago when she posed, nude, for him in the Rue Serpente), was refreshingly blunt.

'My goodness you've changed! Quite grey – though it makes you look like Harvey Keitel. But still got those ravishing biceps, I bet! Do you remember how you cracked my ribs and the hospital thought you had beaten me up? Laugh! We thought they were going to get the gendarmes! *Do* you remember? I often think of it!'

Henri, as it happened, had forgotten the episode but the mention of hospital made him uncomfortable. Christina, it seemed, was stuck in a time-lock.

'Now tell me, do you still have that adorable studio – God it was cold! You could have hung a tea towel on my nipples.'

Henri learned that the Marquis had gone the way of all flesh and that Christina now shared her Knightsbridge apartment with Alan, a young man of thirty-two.

'Such a poppet – he does something awfully clever with computers. They're a complete mystery to me, darling, but so lovely to have a young man like him warm my bed.'

Fuller in the figure, Christina had lost none of her youthful vigour. She enquired little about Henri's life but was enthusiastic about his work.

'Truly, darling, I love it anyway but when I hear or read the comments I positively *swell*. I want to say, "Oh, yes, I slept with him, in Paris, you know." But imagine the Marquis! He'd have a heart attack – wherever he is, poor sweetheart.'

'But he is, er, deceased?' For a moment it wasn't clear.

Christina's lively relationship with her past was misleading. 'Goodness, yes. Ages since. No, I mean what would the poor sweetheart feel if he were to know I was boasting in public about, you know, a past liaison? Disloyal, don't you think? So I keep mum. But, of course, I've followed your career with a *special* interest, darling.' She inclined towards him along the silk couch.

'Christina, so delightful.' Now how long should he hold off before trying the Fenton-Kirks on her? 'And Alan?'

She moved back a little along the expensive silk upholstery. 'Dear Alan. Such a pet and devoted to me, darling.'

Good for Alan. She was too decent a woman to do much more than offer provocative suggestion while she was actually involved with another man. And you had to hand it to her – sixty or whatever, she still had sex appeal. Pity he was feeling so preoccupied. He decided on a half-truth; she was a woman who once had a talent for kindness.

'Christina, it is a true pleasure to see you again and I have never forgotten our days of working together, but the reason . . .'

Bright as ever, she interrupted. 'You've got another mission in coming to London than looking up poor old me?'

'Christina, truly, to see you is also reason . . .'

But she was too fly for that, he reflected later, as he left her apartment to return to his hotel. She listened intelligently to his tale of the missing Alice and had been instantly engaged by the story of the locket. 'Poor mite – so she had a love child. Well, the English upper classes can be beasts about that sort of thing. Or were. I think they're losing the class war now. The death of the Princess, of course, has had a fantastic impact. Everyone was thunderstruck.'

'Yes, what about that? What did you think?' And really he wanted to know.

Christina was crisp. 'I thought it was a rap on the knuckles for the establishment. Blair, of course is cashing in on it all. He twigged there was some kudos to be had out of the poor child's death and jumped on to the bandwagon, legs neatly together. He's running the Royals now, poor darlings. They must be in a pretty state to trust a man with two rows of teeth. I'm sorry for them.'

'And her? The Princess?' He had forgotten how invigorating Christina's opinions were.

'Oh, her – she was a one-off. The Royals woefully under-estimated her. It doesn't matter that she could be a goose – it was being goose that made her loveable. After all, we're all geese at times, aren't we? She had what we used to call "it". I met her once – ravishing, and not at all stuffy. She danced a tarantella in a dress I would have killed for. She was a star, darling.'

He thought about it. 'I did not like her much but it is strange, you know . . . I have come almost to, to love her since the disaster.'

'Of course, darling.' Christina was emphatic. 'Who could resist that conjunction of love and death – least of all an artist? And whatever we may think of young Milu, they were in love. The death of a lover is always a shocking thing. Think of Keats. Think of Juliet. When life takes a lover we are all of us left staring into the hole they leave behind. I wonder what she thinks of it all now?'

She took to heart the story of the missing child and promised to see what she could do about turning up the Fenton-Kirks. Meantime he proposed to enjoy London. And why not, since he was here, take a stroll. Go and see where Helena had lived. Where they had kept vigil with candles and song for over seven nights; where those legendary flowers had been laid. He'd take a turn past the other palace too, when he was near St James's. Might as well be slaughtered for a mutton as for a lamb – if that was not too inappropriate an image in the circumstances!

19

The holiday was a mistake, James thought. For once his mother had been right.

'By all means, in a month or so,' she had said, 'but not yet, James. It is inappropriate.'

He had defied her, choosing the wrong moment to be defiant. It hadn't worked.

'You've gone off me,' Jessica remarked matter-of-factly one morning as they crossed a muddy, ploughed field. Lapwings were somersaulting in the blue sky.

'Oh, Jess.'

'No, really, it's true.' Her laughter was distressing. 'You don't find me attractive any more, do you?'

He knew what she was referring to. 'It's not that.' He had always found her the most desirable woman he had ever had contact with. His wife was an acknowledged beauty, but she had never moved him as Jessica did. There was a receptive quality about Jess which, for him, was extraordinarily attractive. 'It's just that it feels wrong.'

'It's OK.' It was her brightness he couldn't stand.

They'd had a row about it – they who never quarrelled.

'Don't treat me like an invalid whom you have to jolly along.'

'And don't you patronize me! I don't like playing gooseberry.'

'Gooseberry!'

'Yes. Don't you know that *she* is here with us all the time these days!'

'Well, then, you'll know how she used to feel!'

He'd never said such a thing to her before.

'How dare you! This was never my idea. I was perfectly happy with Michael.'

'Michael! You must be joking. Everyone knows he was never at home.'

'So, what's new!'

It was terrible, terrible, he ruminated to himself two days later after he had dropped her home. The breach between them shocked him. They had, on the surface, made up, of course. There was too much genuine affection between them, and too much breeding, for the rift to remain exposed. Both came from a long and practised tradition of rift-covering. And he loved her – even if he could not express it in the old way.

Feeling bereft of confidantes, for Jess had been his main prop and stay in that department, he rang Mary.

'Feeling mis, bro?'

Mary and he had quarrelled as children. She had been their father's favourite, where he, quieter, less self-assured, had had stronger affinities with their mother. Whereas the two youngest shared the parents' affection pretty equally, between him and Mary there had always been the difficulty of the other parent. But now he got on so much less well with Ma, and Mary had transferred her adoration to her extraordinarily nice husband, they had gradually been finding each other.

'How's Eddie?'

Mary was the only one Edwin allowed to use that abbreviation. And she had been superb with him, James reflected. He was sitting in her farmhouse kitchen with a large gin and tonic which his sister had served up herself from the capacious American fridge. Mary hated servants and preferred to do the housework herself. James noticed that she was still wearing her riding breeches on which traces of mud were visible.

'Not great. Hugh's still awfully cut up – but you'd expect that. The school say Eds is very pale and lethargic. Evidently he looks tired all the time.'

'Not sleeping?'

If you didn't know her you'd think from her clipped tone that she did not much care about her nephew.

James said, 'I guess not. I'm hopeless at communicating with him. He just sort of squeezes my hand when we meet and tells me he's "fine". I don't know how to react.'

'Just as you are, I should say. The kid usually knows what he wants.'

'Like his mother!' James allowed himself a grin.

His sister returned him an amused look. 'He looks astonishingly like her. Zoe keeps bringing girls back home in the hope that he will visit. They're all nuts about him, the twelve- to fourteen-year-olds, which gives her great cachet.'

'Lord, I hope he's not starting girlfriends yet.'

This was where he was going to miss the boys' mother. Whatever the private circumstances between the two of them, she would have known exactly how to handle all the complex implications of Edwin's future romantic involvements.

Mary, as ever, was practical. 'He'll have to someday. In which case he'd better start sooner than us. You don't want another family fiasco over his love life – Ma'd go ballistic!'

Which was putting it mildly, in James's view. They'd never

discussed their different marital errors, he and Mary. But now, missing Jessica, or rather missing an intimacy in which anything could be said, he felt tempted to pursue the subject with Mary. 'Where do you think they went wrong, the parents?'

Mary paused. She was folding linen and putting it to air on the Aga. He watched her small hands folding a pair of Tom's rugby shorts. Mary's family were lucky.

'I don't know that it's fair to say they went wrong,' she began, unusually cautious. 'I'd say it was us that were "wrong" in listening to them.'

'But could we do anything else?' He genuinely didn't know.

'Yes and no, I guess. It seems to me they had to tell us what to do – that was their job and they didn't know otherwise. But did we *really* have to listen? I don't know about you, but I knew they were talking rubbish – and I still went along with it. It's that which maddens me now.' She shook out a pillow case. James noticed again how like their mother's hands they were. Light hands with the rein.

'I don't think I did – I think I thought they were right to suggest I marry Helena.'

'Well, I was always more of a rebel than you. But, then, it was easier for me. I didn't have your responsibilities. Another?' She gestured at the gin bottle.

'I'd better not or I'll be caught drink-driving and then, can't you imagine, it'd be all over the press: "James Rat-Arsed!!" They'd love that!'

'Oh, Jams! Are you on your own then?'

And he was. Lately he had taken to jettisoning his minders, slipping out at night from his country home. The stars and the owls comforted him. Once he had heard a fox barking, 'clear and cold'. It reminded him of the poetry he used to read late at night.

All that had disappeared when he had married Helena. He had blamed her because she knew so little of culture. She was a creature of instinct, as he had written to her when there was still the possibility of a passion between them. But the pop records, the dancing, the endless following of fashion got on his nerves and made him irritable. Bit by bit, he didn't quite understand how, Bach and Elgar, Shakespeare and Dylan Thomas had lost their place in his regular life. He had never, anyway, felt confident that these were suitable pursuits for a king. But in these times, when even his sister was acting out of character, he could maybe return to his old loves – specially if it wasn't working with Jess.

'In more ways than one, Mary.'

'Things not OK with Jess?'

Mary had managed his relationship with Jessica well. It was interesting that the press line on Mary was that she was tactless, because when you thought about it she had handled the whole family situation with a tact that was positively Eastern. But then, you hardly went to the press for accuracy.

Sighing slightly, he said, 'Not great.'

'I'm sorry. It must be tough on her.'

He agreed. 'I'm not exactly brilliant company and she never saw that much of me even before.'

It was as if Helena was a presence even in his sister's kitchen. In his mind, James could hear his wife's infectious laugh.

'James, this may be a silly question . . .' Mary was looking at him with the kind of expression she wore when taking a very nervous horse to a difficult jump. 'Have you, well, *seen* anyone?'

'How do you mean?' he was tempted to make a joke about mediums, but even to Mary that would seem in bad taste.

'One of your psycho cronies – a shrink or anyone?'

'Do you think I need to?'

She looked at him. He was still the big brother she had been proud of and wanted to protect. He'd had a far worse time of it, being who he was and who he had to be, than she had had.

Intellectual and reserved, he should have been a scholar or a monk. 'Well, don't you think you need to *talk*?'

'"It's good to talk",' he impersonated the BT ad. People forgot that, like his mother, he was a good mimic. 'But I'm talking to you, aren't I?'

'Me!' An exclamation of laughter. 'I'm a non-starter at shrinky stuff. I'd probably whack the kids if it weren't for Tom.' Tom, Mary's husband, personable, modest and extremely sane was devoted to her. It said a lot for Mary, James thought, that the devotion was reciprocated.

Later that night, after driving himself with unusual care back to his own house, James got out the volume of Dylan Thomas that he'd had at university.

'Now as I was young and easy, under the apple boughs/ About the lilting house and happy as the grass was green . . .'

What did it mean to be 'happy as the grass was green'? The grass outside his wife's home had been green once. Had he ever been happy as the grass was green? His thoughts turned to his elder son, so dignified, so modest. Was Eds happy? How could he be at the moment with his mother gone, but had he ever been? That was the sort of question Helena would know the answer to. 'Lord, yes,' she would have said. 'Our Eds? Happy as a sandboy!' And despite his reservations about her judgement, her words would have soothed him. It was only now that he was becoming aware how much Helena had, in fact, contributed to his security, especially his security in being a parent. Whatever her faults, his late wife had been an excellent choice of mother for his boys. The best.

If only he could tell her so now.

20

9 NOVEMBER 1997

*Saw George again yesterday, Mum. You'd really like him. He's got
a stud in his nose and an ear-ring – left ear, so he's not gay – not
that you'd mind! I haven't been to where he lives. I think he's
embarrassed about his girlfriend. She's got a baby – not his! – and
it sounds as if they don't get on that well. I told him I knew all
about that from home – you taught me that: how to use what
happened to you to talk to other people, so I hope you don't mind!
I had to tell him something about me so I told him I was an army
cadet. Didn't say where – he doesn't seem to know much about
that sort of thing so I've been vague. Mostly I ask him things – he
doesn't ask any questions.*

*George is adopted. He doesn't know anything about his father.
His adopted mother told him that his mother wasn't fit to keep him.
She sounds pretty grim. I thought of how you'd have felt if you'd
not been allowed to keep me or Hugh (Hugh's better, by the way
– though he does miss you. I do try to look after him, Mum,
promise). George looked kind of sad when he told me about his*

mother. Can't people find their natural parents these days? You'd know about that. I wish George could meet you. He was in a Young Offenders' place because he stole some things from his adopted mother. Sounds as if he'd been treated pretty badly and he started to steal as a sort of revenge. You told me once that it was a good sign when people stole because it meant that they hadn't given up hope – so I told George. Don't know what he made of that! When he got parole he went to live under the M4 in a cardboard house with another George, an old chap who'd been a soldier and sounds as if he'd got shell-shock (another one for you, Mum!). When the old George died, my George went to live with Tina – that's his girlfriend. I think he really misses Old George. He says he preferred being under the M4, even though it wasn't a real home. I guess it was because Old George sort of cared about him. You'd understand that.

He took me dancing and we met a friend of his, Steve, who is a really cool dancer and was going to dance with you, if you'd been able to get to the dance where I met them all. I'm sorry you missed it but I'm glad I got to go instead. Steve offered me some dope – they call it 'puff' – but I didn't take any. I said, 'It's up to you what you do, it's your business, but that stuff makes you paranoid.' I told them what you told me about the Vietnam veterans being given dope in the war to make them paranoid and make them hate the Viet Cong. I was a bit worried they'd think I was a prat. Peer pressure! But they were cool. Seemed interested. George agreed about the paranoia. He said they were all on it at Heston and after he came out he was paranoid all the time. I don't know if he does drugs much now, but don't panic! I know what you would say about that. I'm not daft and I've taken in everything you told me about them.

I miss you Mum. I hope you're OK.

21

'Hallo, Hallo.'

'Darling, you sound like that French character, what's his name, in *The Pursuit of Love*.'

Henri was irritated. The old persona of flamboyant lothario had begun to irk him. His telephone manner was born of anxiety rather than the desire to seduce this flickering flame. But he had asked Christina's help and it was necessary to be polite.

He tried for the old vein. 'Christina, cherie, if only we were young and in Paris again . . .'

'Listen, you old sham, I've got some information for you about the Fenton-Kirks, but I shan't give it to you unless you buy me lunch.'

'Christina, you are an angel.'

'Yes, but a hungry one, darling!'

They met at a small Knightsbridge place, Christina's recommendation. Henri, in whom years of poverty had inculcated habits of meanness, looked askance at the prices. A memory came back to him of Christina tucking in to a meal at Maxim's which had cost him a month's rent. She had, it appeared, in her better-heeled old age lost none of her delight in expensive dining haunts.

'I love this place; the waiters are so sexy.'

A young man with an exquisite bottom passed and exchanged an insincere smile with Christina, who settled her own behind pleasurably into the wire chair. Henri, who preferred a veal chop and a *pichet* of wine for his lunch, read the outlandish menu making rapid inner accounts. London prices were an abomination.

'So, you are in luck, sweet: there seems to be only one Fenton-Kirk family in the South of England.' Christina was enjoying herself. 'This mango and crab is divine, by the way. A pal of mine knows them slightly – but it would take a bit of social engineering to organize a meeting, and Molly is nosy and would want to know the whys and wherefores, et cetera and I'm assuming all this is sub rosa? But what she did tell me, en passant, is that the Fenton-Kirks are selling their family home, and Mrs F-K is very cut up about it. So, if you wanted to, you could nip down to Wiltshire and plonk the old shoe in the door by looking round the property. I'm told it's quite a pile.' She was triumphant with her news.

This was worth any amount of expensive pap. 'Christina, when I get to heaven I will make sure there is a very special throne for you.'

'With a nicely laden table, darling.'

Christina had even managed to find the name of the agents who were selling Halt House – 'You see what a veritable mine I am? I expect a dinner at least when you return! – a firm called Stoke and Stone, whose branch at Market Twinning was more than happy to arrange a visit to Halt House for the impressive-sounding Frenchman. A man young enough to be Henri's grandson rang through to ask if Mrs Fenton-Kirk would prefer that he accompany M. Astaffort or, if they were home themselves, perhaps . . . ? In that case, M. Astaffort would be along there this very afternoon.

So far the gods had been on his side, Henri decided, which boded well for the Fenton-Kirk encounter. He studied the glossy brochure which the agent had given him. A lovely eighteenth-century house with a bricked wall garden. If this was, indeed, Alice's family, she had left behind a visible paradise which posed some interesting questions about what lay behind that charming façade.

The gods had also arranged for Fenton-Kirk Masculine to be 'in town' that day, leaving a wife with a baleful and bloodshot eye to Henri's skilled charm. After only one tour of the house and garden he was sipping a gin and tonic in the large light drawing room which looked down across a bosky valley.

'Of course we hate to be going.'

Mrs Fenton-Kirk was a lush. She had finished her first drink and her eye had slid already towards the drinks tray. It was not quite noon.

'Philip won't have anything to do with it. He's up at his club now. So poor little me is left to manage all the vile viewers – present company excepted, of course.' She smiled archly.

Henri thought, 'May the good Lord spare me from having to go to bed with this woman.' Aloud he said, 'Your family, Madame, they are all grown, flown the nest . . . ?'

There were photographs on the grand piano. He strolled across, using a foreigner's licence to pick up and inspect them. A silver-framed group of three girls wearing Laura Ashley-style frocks were seated under a tree. His heart contracted. The unmistakable eyes of a young Alice looked out at him. Beside her, a slimmer but recognizable version of the woman beside him.

'This must be you with the wonderful bones. And these? Your belles – your lovely daughters, Madame?' His accent was taking on an extra emphasis.

'Linda, do call me Linda. That was the summer of 1980. Me and the daughters, yes. A monstrous regiment of women, Philip calls us.' She sighed.

Henri's ear was quick on sighs. 'Daughters, they grow, cause problems. Ah, Linda, if you heard what some of mine get up to!' And why not invent a few daughters while he was at it?

'Do you have daughters, too? Another gin? Thanks. Not too much tonic for me. Then you'll know how it is. Yes, Emma has two of her own now. They're very busy, Piers is in a merchant bank and you know what that means – he's out all the hours God sends. And we all feel Julia has gone slightly potty – she's making hats. Though, rather to our surprise, they seem to be quite successful. There was an article in *Harper's*.'

'And the other?' Outside he heard some animal make a sound like a sharp cough. It distracted him for a moment from her face. When he looked again her skin had mottled.

'Alicia is dead. We tend not to . . . And you, tell me about you. You are a sculptor. What an extraordinary thing. You know someone once told me I should sculpt. Apparently I have an eye . . .'

Five gin and tonics later she said, 'Alicia isn't really dead . . .' and burst into tears.

22

It was a fine afternoon – though all days on the island seemed fine, as if a pane of smeared glass had been permanently removed so that colours had a peculiar vivid brightness. Dr Asklepios, though she had been expecting him, had not arrived in the boat with the green sails. Angela had gone off on her own and her mistress found herself at a loose end.

She walked down the scrubby path towards the beach. The sea round the island was still warm and she felt like some exercise. She was making her way towards the bay where she half-hoped she might see a green shape tacking across the water when she saw another, smaller path she had not noticed before leading towards a group of olive trees. A little way off, along the path, she thought she saw something hanging from one of the trees. There was plenty of time to swim, so she followed the path to investigate.

Closer up she saw it was a sack with what seemed to be leaves stuffed inside it. She was inspecting the sack when a clear voice made her turn round.

'It's a target. Want to try?'

For a second she thought it was a man. Then she saw it was a woman who spoke. She was half-leaning, half-lying, propped against the whorled grey trunk of one of the more substantial olive trees.

'At shooting, you mean?' A bow was lying on the ground beside the androgynous-looking woman.

'What else?' The woman uncoiled herself from her semi-supine position. When she stood up it was apparent that she was unusually tall. 'Here you are.'

The bow she was handed was made of what looked like the peeled bough of a tree. It was big – taller than her own height.

'Golly, it's huge – it must be over six foot.' Which made the stranger six foot plus.

She stood there – feeling rather daft – uncertain what she should do next.

'Hold it in the middle.' The tall woman spoke abruptly. 'That's the job. Now pull the bowstring back with your other hand; wrap your fingers round, that's the ticket. Now, between the thumb and the first finger.'

'I can't – it hurts my fingers!' And apart from that she was nowhere near strong enough to pull back the tight gut which was stretched across the bow.

The other took the weapon from her. 'Watch.' Pulling an arrow from a quiver at her back the tall woman held the stem of the arrow behind the flight feathers between her thumb and fingers, as though holding a cigar. 'We don't use gloves.' The implication was that gloves were for weaklings. 'We release the arrow, not the string.'

The woman pulled back the arrow, notched in the bowstring, until the gut formed a vertical line between the bow's extremities. Then, squaring her shoulders, she pulled deeply. The bowstring strained a moment then suddenly gave a tremendous thrum and the arrow leapt forward and out into the heart of the sacking target with a dim thwack which reverberated through the grove.

The whole action was thrilling. Involuntarily, her onlooker applauded.

'Wow, that's brilliant. How did you learn to do that?'

'It's my job.' The archer turned unblinking grey eyes upon her. 'The trick is in the breathing. Here, have another go. When you feel the strain, breathe out and pull through. Then keep yourself from breathing as you release. That way your body stays still. It's about control.'

After twenty or so efforts, she was beginning to get the hang of it: you had to overcome a resistance. At the moment when her instructor said, 'Square shoulders – breathe – now out!' you had to pull. It was like running up a steep hill and coming down the other side.

'Try and form a diamond. The power lies in the space between the bowshaft and the string.' They went on, with her pulling, exhaling, pulling again, until she was exhausted.

'I'm shattered,' she said, collapsing under the olive tree. 'My ribs! I feel as if I've been in an accident.'

The other put down the bow and sat cross-legged beside her. 'For that too it is a possible cure.' A lizard on a nearby rock ran across the ground and settled on the long shin.

'I was in an accident.'

'Yes,' said the tall woman in the still afternoon. 'I heard.' There was no other sound but the faint perpetual background hum of dry heat. 'Smoke?' She offered a packet of cigarettes.

Another smoker! Maybe it was because they were Greek? They seemed dangerously oblivious to health risks here. 'No, thank you. I don't. It's terribly bad for you, you know, especially the ones without tips.'

Her companion spat out a shred of tobacco. 'Doesn't affect us, of course. We can do as we choose. Although my father dislikes it. Says it's unwomanly.' She had a laugh rather like James's sister: a kind of gracious seal's bark.

'Who is your father? Does he own here?'

For reply there was another bark before the woman with the bow said, 'Oh, him – *he* owns everything.'

It was hard to tell how old she was. She had a smooth brown face and eyes which gazed at you very straight. It was as if one had met those eyes somewhere before. Slender and striking as she was, the tall woman had an unusual, faraway feel, as if she were not as young as she appeared.

'Sorry about the accident. You'll find this helps.' The tall woman waved a long brown hand towards the target.

'Do you mean learning how to shoot? I'm afraid I don't like the idea of hunting. I liked learning to pull the bow and so on, but . . .' The struggle to overcome the bow's resistance was exhilarating but she didn't want to kill anything with it.

'Hunting isn't just blood lust, you know.' The tall woman had lain down on her back and was smoking her cigarette at the sky.

'What is it then?' Her husband's girlfriend had hunted – with hounds. Horrific.

'That's a big question. Not sure I can answer it.' The woman blew a smoke-ring.

She had tried to stop her husband hunting because she had thought it merely an excuse to see his girlfriend. Maybe he hunted now?

A noise some metres away in the scrub made the tall woman start. Evidently she had quick hearing. 'Not really my department, those sort of questions. The doctor might be able to help you. So long then – see you around.'

The tall woman had sprung lithely to her feet and vanished between the trees before Dr Asklepios arrived sweating.

'I see you've met the Aunt.'

'Is she your aunt? Goodness, she doesn't look old enough.'

Dr Asklepios leaned his shoulders against the olive tree.

'Appearances are deceptive. Your mortal life should have taught you that. This is her island, as a matter of fact.'

'She said it belonged to her father?'

'Ah yes, the "universal landlord".'

'What? Dr Asklepios, who are you all?'

Dr Asklepios thought for a moment. She had been there nearly three months – a quarter of a mortal year. There seemed no harm in her learning more. After all, she had now met the chief mover in the plan.

'It was Herself, in point of fact,' – he nodded towards the vanished figure – 'took you up.' He spoke confidentially. It was not unlike conversations she had had in her past, with members of James's family. 'My father is her brother. He has an island entirely to himself – Delos, they call it. No one lives there, but in the old times worshippers went there to sacrifice. It's only the tourists who go now.'

She had heard of Delos. Wasn't it the sun god who was supposed to have been born there? James had gone on about it – wanted to go there in one of his Cambridge friends' yachts. She hadn't liked the suggestion – too highbrow for her, she'd thought then, afraid she would have been excluded. But now she was almost sorry James wasn't with her, hearing about it too.

Aloud she said, 'Was that where the sun god, Apollo, lived?'

Dr Asklepios carried on as if she hadn't spoken. 'Anyway, the boss, the big feta, who is also my grandfather – we are all a bit inter-related here – gave Auntie this island for herself, to balance out any sibling rivalry, you know. Grandpops was fond of our mother. They had' – here Dr Asklepios lowered his voice suggestively – 'an *understanding*. We brought you here because it is so private. It is on no mortal map, so there are no visitors – which suits the Aunt. She's not a great socializer.'

Hearing about Dr Asklepios's family was rather like chatting to James's grandmother, which she had done often before she was married. James's grandmother had tales of what she called 'Family goings-on'. She used to take nips, during the tellings, from a little silver flask she kept in her knitting bag. 'For medicinal purposes, my dear,' she had said. 'Keeps me in the pink, don't you know. Don't mention it, will you, to my daughter?' Families were the same everywhere, she supposed, though clearly the daunting long-limbed woman with the bow, Dr Asklepios's aunt, was not an object of awe to him.

'Why did you bring me here, Dr Asklepios?'

They had begun, by unspoken agreement, to walk back along the path. Looking down she could see Angela on the beach.

The doctor cleared his throat. 'Oh, you mustn't give the credit to me – it is not I who brought you here. My – how shall I call it? – my remit is strictly confined. In our world we have our particular jobs. Mine happens to be healing. Aphrodite looks after lovers – or doesn't,' he laughed loudly. 'For Ares it is fighting. If Saddam Hussein gets stroppy then that is Ares' department.'

He flapped his hand as if to dismiss Saddam Hussein.

'Strictly speaking, you were brought here by *Moira*, what you would call Destiny, most powerful of all in our domain. The Aunt won't tell you herself because she's shy, but she developed a fondness for you when she saw you being hunted in your mortal life, so she put in a special request. Destiny – who, by the way, works on unfathomable lines: even we cannot second-guess her – decreed that if you continued to make the kind of mess of your life that, let's face it, most of you generally make, then the Aunt would have to relinquish any rights over you. In that case the usual procedures would have applied.' Here the doctor moved his hands suggestively. 'But if you continued down a certain path, then, it was decided, you would be given over to Auntie's care.'

Some white gulls were sitting on the water like paper boats. 'What "path"?'

She had made paper boats for the boys when they were little. They floated them down the stream together at her father's house.

The doctor had shaded his eyes to watch the gulls. 'Let me put it like this: in life you attracted a certain quality of existence. It is true there were, let us say, perturbations, but with those perturbations you learnt to make efforts. We do not trouble to bring across those who have made no efforts. They just get melted down – put in the pot on the back boiler to be served up again and again.' He flicked his wrist as if to indicate a passing triviality. 'My task, for what it is worth, is to help you to see what you are – in your essential self. Together we sift the wheat from the chaff – an image, by the way, which your Christian gospel writers pinched from us.'

'I tried to kill myself once.' The words were out before she knew what she was going to say.

The flotilla of paper-boat gulls took off suddenly and passed above them, a shaky arrow in the high vault of the sky. Dr Asklepios contemplated the birds' formation.

'But of course you did. When a beloved is lost – and the loss of the beloved's affection is as great a loss as death for some – then usually a human chooses either to create or destroy. It is all one, if you see it from our point of view.' He seemed unsurprised by her revelation.

'But why did I do it? Is that what you were telling me before? I don't understand.'

'In a sense. It was the part of your being that you fear, that works against your self. But a part which also, I have been trying to show you, has its own place. In your world you have spring and summer, but you also have autumn and winter. There is birth but there is also death. The urge to destroy is only the other pole of the urge to create. Both are part of a whole. This is why we brought you here.' They were walking past a bramble bush and he stopped to pick some blackberries. 'Like one?

Aphrodite has an excellent recipe for making jam with these. I must bring you some. What was I saying?'

'Something about creation and destruction being much of a muchness, I think?'

'Ah, yes.' He resumed their walk. 'What, after all, is the distinction between the hunter and the hunted? They are different sides of the same coin. Remember the eagle and the tortoise?'

An image of broad, wheeling wings in the blue sky. 'Yes – but I'm afraid I don't quite see. What have they got to do with me?'

The doctor glanced a trifle nervously along the path. 'Have you seen, Hestia?'

'No.' She hadn't met the tortoise since their first encounter.

'Good. I do not wish to offend her, but she makes an example. Let us say you begin your existence by being the tortoise – here, you learn the other side. It is like this: in the eagle's belly, which is eagle and which is tortoise? In the end they are the same.'

'Oh, Dr Asklepios,' she was almost laughing. 'So have I been eaten then? What has eaten me up and why?'

The sun, turned to a red ball, had begun its rapid descent into the sea. Dr Asklepios was observing it. 'One day you might get a chance to ask that question of my father.'

More riddles. She tried again. 'Dr Asklepios, are there only the two choices then – hunting or being hunted?'

'Of course there is always the hunting and the being hunted, the endless cycle of this and then of that, until, if one is lucky, one gets beyond both,' he replied and if it were not Dr Asklepios one might have almost imagined he was sad.

'So,' she plucked at his sleeve, 'how does one do that? How does one get beyond both?'

The red ball had dropped finally beneath the sea, leaving only a scatter of red-gold on the horizon.

'You will know,' he said. 'Your past life, even the end Destiny chose for you, taught you a great deal about faith and courage.

And now,' briskly, 'I have things I must attend to: Aphrodite's husband is acting up, throwing his tools about and generally causing commotion and I have promised my help in calming him down. You would like him, by the way: he limps.'

She looked as if she were about to interject and he patted her, familiarly.

'No, no, I tease you. When you practise tomorrow with the Aunt, you can relieve your anger by pretending you are shooting your arrows at my ugly mug. It is good that you learn archery: besides what we have spoken of today it teaches you aim. In the life to which Destiny has brought you, aim is important, Iphigenia.'

23

The remnants of Alicia Fenton-Kirk's life looked pathetic. Mrs Fenton-Kirk, overcome by gin and sympathy, had drawn Henri two flights up the oak stairs to a room at the top of the house where he was shown a rabbit with a torn ear, some childish paintings and a photograph album.

The photograph album showed Alice from chubby babyhood to youthful sylph. In the last two pictures he saw that her face had resumed her childhood roundness. Linda Fenton-Kirk looked at the photograph of her daughter.

'You can see she's getting fat, there. She was an attractive girl once.'

She spoke angrily. Henri had grown disturbed looking at the pictures of the young Alice. An image of her huddled form in his bed flashed across his mind and he found himself wishing he were back in the Rue Serpente. What was he doing here with this unpleasantly drunk woman? Why ever had he started this bizarre search?

'When did you see her last?' He tried to speak gently, but something in his tone must have alerted her.

'It wasn't me, it was her father,' she spoke defensively. 'He started it all. Of course, I'd had my suspicions. You do, don't you?'

Henri, well versed in the variety of distasteful issues which can arise between parents and children, was reluctant to get into the details. Even had she wished to, he doubted this woman was capable of speaking the truth any more. His guess was that the gin was an attempted antidote to a life of justifying and untruthfulness. He shrugged, grateful for the protection of the Gallic gesture.

'Children, parents . . . this is the way of life. Your daughter was pregnant?'

'Little tart!' The viciousness was startling. 'We had to send her away. Cost a fortune. Obviously, it had to be adopted. She wanted to keep it – I mean, can you imagine!'

'There was a problem? I am not sure . . .'

'Of course there was a problem!'

This was a very violent woman. Henri began to wonder if it was wise to be alone with her. He felt his armpits dampen.

'It was a little bastard, wasn't it? And anyway . . .' She paused, looking uncomfortable. Was she going to let slip that 'it' was her husband's child? But muttering, 'Excuse me a moment,' she stumbled off towards the door.

Henri waited until he heard her clattering down the stairs and another door bang in the distance. Opening the photo album, he flicked through to the end. On the last page but one he found something. Another picture, this time of a young woman holding a baby. The face was not smiling but frowning slightly at the camera. No doubt though, it was Alice. And the small bundle she held in her arm must be her baby – 'Baby Fenton-Kirk' whose plastic wrist-band he had here in his wallet. But whoever the father had been it was not Alice's own father – whatever her mother's insinuations about that relationship. Baby Fenton-Kirk, whatever else he wasn't, was, most assuredly, black.

Henri listened. No sound from below. He turned to the end of the album. Inside the back cover were some folded papers. Pulling them out he read, 'Dear Mummy and Daddy . . .' The address at the top spelled 'St Margaret's, Sere Westonbury, Wilts.'

A noise on the stairs warned him and, shoving the papers into his pocket, he turned the pages back to a picture of Alice on a bay horse.

'Do forgive me . . . the ravages of age, waterworks not what they were.'

'Your daughter rode?'

'Oh, yes. She was a champion eventer. She could have made a career at it if only . . .'

'The child? Surely it is not such a crime these days . . . ?' Henri had hoped to draw her out further, but the effects of the gin were subsiding. Now she would be worrying at what she might have revealed. As if in confirmation she repeated her earlier remark,

'We never speak of her.'

But at this he couldn't resist: 'A pity, if I may say so, Madame. She is charming on her horse here. Do you know where she is living? Time is the great healer, is he not?'

'Not in this case.' She closed her mouth. 'One of her sisters heard something, but I really couldn't be bothered to find out more. Now, if you'll excuse me . . . Philip . . . the six-thirty train will be in soon.'

'But of course.' He almost bowed in his imitation of a Frenchman. 'Forgive me, Madame, would that be the sister who makes the wonderful hats? I am looking for a hat for my niece . . . And meantime I shall consider your beautiful house.'

You always get such people with greed, he reflected as he drove away again with the card for Mad Hatters in his pocket. Linda Fenton-Kirk could not pass up the possibility of encouraging a potential purchaser and had thus given him the next small clue in the distressing discovery of Alice's past.

Over soup and a double scotch at the Woodpecker, Market Twinning's most comfortable-looking pub, Henri took out the papers he had removed from the photo album. Two letters. Both were written in fountain pen on blue paper. He found the looped inky writing strangely touching.

Dear Mummy and Daddy, the first letter began, *Things are not too bad here. There are quite a few girls my age and the nuns are kind. They let me have a vegetarian dinner.*

(Henri made a face at this – if Alice was a vegetarian she had concealed it from him.)

We don't have very much to do, so most days I walk. I miss riding and can't wait to get back to Turquoise. I miss her. I know it will be difficult for you to come and visit me so please don't worry about it. I am fine.

The letter was signed. *Your loving daughter, Alicia.* There were three kisses.

'Turquoise' must have been her horse. Maybe that had some bearing on the turquoise locket? He had it still in his breast pocket and he took out the blue heart now. It was certainly a lovely piece. He smoothed out the next letter which looked as if it had had something spilt on it.

Dearest Mummy and Da,

   I know this is very difficult for you but I think if I can't keep Hector I will die. I love him so much. He is so sweet and if you could just come and see his little face and his tubby knees and little squidgey feet – and his toes and fingers. His fingernails are completely perfect and his mouth is like a

kitten's, Mummy – like the marmalade one you and I both
loved in Betsy's last litter.

I know you will say I am mad but I'm going to bring
Hector to see you because if I don't I think you won't forgive
yourselves. Your first grandson.

Please believe that I love you very much and I'm sorry if I
make things difficult for you.

Your loving daughter, Lissy XXX

P.S. Hector sends you a kiss each.

There followed two more crosses.

Henri realized that what he had imagined was something spilt
on the page was probably tears. His own looked like adding to
the letter's illegibility. For a moment he sat, not eating his soup,
until the waitress called over,

'Everything all right, love?'

Unable to find any language he merely nodded. Poor Alice.
His own behaviour towards her returned to mind, appearing,
with what he now knew of her life, unspeakably brutal. He spread
out the first letter. Where was it written from? The waitress was
passing again.

'Forgive me, I am in a reverie. This soup is magnificent!' She
smiled, suitably flattered. 'Forgive me, do you know a town, no
it will be a village, Sere Westonbury?'

The waitress, new to the area, called over to the bar,

'Des, d'you know a place called, what's it? Sere Westonbury?'

A young man with a ponytail came out from behind the
bar. 'Yeh, s'about ten, twelve mile from here. Near Lower
Westonbury.'

'The name, Sere – it is unusual. It means decay?' But on that
matter the ponytail was ignorant. He did, however, direct Henri
to a pleasant hotel ten miles on in the next village, where Henri
found he was savagely exhausted. A manic hunger gripped him

and he tore into a second meal, this time of duck and red cabbage.

After the scotch, two bottles of claret, and a good but over-priced armagnac he lay in the soft hotel bed. Thoughts of his past life filtered through his mind with the light of the moon through the curtains. In that life there had been many, many women – few had been more than passingly important. The relationship with Alice had been no more than a pleasant distraction from his work. It had been his work he had loved – all true erotic expression he had made through his sculptures. Yet now the thought of Alice's child, and the sad little cameo he had stumbled upon of her own childhood, aroused in him a feeling more powerful than any passing lust. As powerful, in its way, as his feeling for his work.

That night Henri dreamed. He and Alice were galloping on two black steeds over marshlands, she far ahead of him. 'Where are we going?' he called out to her and she cried back, across the grey salt-marshes, 'To find my son, my son, my son.'

24

'So what happened?'

Edwin and George were walking to the station. It was the third night he'd been out to meet George and he'd got the drill down to a fine art. Minicab, train, minicab back to near school, then through the fence and up the fire-escape. It was expensive though and he'd had to borrow from Hugh. Lucky that Man. U. were doing so well because he'd got them for the whole draw.

People didn't recognize you out of context. George certainly didn't. They were talking about George's adopted family and how he had landed up in the Young Offenders' place.

'Reckon they never wanted me, really.'

George was surprised to find that he didn't mind talking to Ed about his past. Mostly it was a subject he shied away from, but Ed was different. He made you feel OK about the things you'd done. 'Guess I treated them pretty bad.'

'Depends how they treated you.' Edwin remembered his mother. She had yelled at Dad quite a bit and once Dad was very angry with her because she'd gone to a party where Dad's girlfriend had been a guest and said some things to her. But then could you blame her for it? Probably it was the same with George.

'I don't think you should judge people if you haven't been in the situation they have been in.' It was the longest pronouncement he had ever made to George and he instantly began to blush. He must have sounded a prat. But George seemed pleased.

'Yeh! They treated me pretty shit.'

'What did they do?' No one at school knew anything about this sort of life – the kind George had had.

'Oh, hit me about and that.'

'And you let them?'

'Didn't have no choice, did I? Anyhow, I stole their stupid things. Still got some of them. Paid them back.'

'What did you steal?' Edwin, fascinated, was careful not to sound too interested. 'Where d'you keep them?'

'I hid them before I got nicked. Then when I was nicked I gave some of them back. But not all. I reckon some of it's mine. Or my real mum's, I should say. I remember when I was a kid my adopted dad, before he went back to Jamaica, saying she left the things with me when I was a baby. Course, when I told them that at the court, my adopted mum said it was a lie'

Edwin said, 'George, if the things were yours, you can't be sent to prison for stealing them. That's a miscarriage of justice.'

'Yeah, well jail weren't as bad as living with my adopted mum. Anyhow, who's going to believe me? – so what's the difference?'

'It's a matter of justice. That's very important.' Edwin was confident about this. As a matter of fact, both his parents were hot on all that stuff: people getting sent to prison for the wrong reasons.

'Look, if you wouldn't mind me seeing the things, we might be able to trace them. See if they were yours really.'

'How we going to do that?'

George was more eager then he appeared. The silver and some

of the other stuff he had taken had been returned to his adopted mother. But he had kept the small silver horse. He loved that horse. When he was a little boy his adopted dad had let him play with it.

'Well, we might find your real mother. What d'you think?'

'Dunno, never thought about it.'

Which was probably untrue, Edwin decided, as he drove away in the minicab.

What would Mum say? She would say, 'Go for it!' – wouldn't she? It must be right to know your own mother. After all, what would he be without his? Suddenly her absence struck him full on. He hoped she was safe. She was fragile, Mum was. But she was strong too. He was ninety-nine per cent certain she was all right somewhere. Which was more than George had to hang on to. Funny they were both without mothers. Next weekend he was due to stay with Aunt Mary. Maybe the cousins would help. They knew about things. Edwin settled down for the journey back up the motorway.

'They say he's tired all the time.' James was talking to his sister by the Aga where she was scraping mud from her riding-boots.

'Bloody things. Sorry, Jams – why shouldn't he be tired, poor sausage? He's had a helluva shock.'

'But d'you think we should do anything?'

'If it comes to that, his father doesn't look too special.' She had been observing her brother, whose face had grown more crumpled and anxious over the weeks. 'Are you sleeping, Jams?'

Of course, he wasn't. The effort of dealing with it all: his mother, Jess, the boys and, most of all, this terrible grief which he could share with no one – for whom could you tell about the grief which comes when you lose someone you've learnt to love too late? 'And death shall have no dominion.' But it did. Death

150

took the brightness from your mistress's smile and the colour out of the autumn leaves. Death, Helena's death, kept him sleepless at night with nothing but his books of poetry to give him comfort. 'She's good being gone.' The words Shakespeare gave another bungler who mourned his dead wife too late.

The line had come to him that day in Paris. What a day. Thinking now of the scene where he had taken leave of the boys' mother made him indescribably sad. What might he have said to her, when he and she were alone? He had been absurdly inhibited. She would have teased him about it! He had been trying to recall when they had last been alone together and it was an irritant to him that he could not remember. In all his memories of her they seemed to have had other people around them. Maybe that had been the trouble? Mary and Tom guarded their privacy jealously.

'Jams?' Mary was looking at him, concerned.

'Sorry, I was in a brown study.'

'That seems to be pretty much par for the course, these days. Look, Eddie is coming here next weekend. I'll have a chat with him. We get on pretty well together, Eddie and I.'

By the time Edwin had returned to the school all hell had broken loose. His house-master had roused the Head and both had woken DC Swift whose face was looking like a piece of uncooked lard when Edwin pulled himself up and through the window.

'Christ, mate, give us a break,' were the detective's words which greeted Edwin before the wave broke over him.

It seemed that the house-master, following up a comment from the art master who had opined that Edwin was 'peaky', had disregarded the notice on the boy's door and had entered the room, allegedly to see if he was sleeping.

'How bloody daft. If I had been asleep he would have woken me up! Anyhow, he had no right to do that,' was Edwin's comment when he was questioned by an anxious father who had driven over from his sister's house.

'Nonsense! He had every right to check up on you if you behave like a bally idiot!'

James was unintentionally sharp. The news that his beloved elder son was not in his room had terrified him. He thanked his stars that he had happened to be at Mary's and near by. 'For God's sake, Edwin, think about it! The whole country was about to be put on red alert. Can you imagine what would have been thought? All manner of ghastly possibles! If you hadn't turned up when you did, I shudder to think what would have happened next. Wars are started for less.'

'Oh yeah! And what a nuisance I would have been to you then, wouldn't I just?'

Edwin had never spoken like that before. James was shocked. 'Well, yes, since you ask, you would have been. And you pretty damn near got yourself shot, by the way. What in the name of all that's serious were you doing in that army gear?'

But his son wouldn't answer. Already he was turning over in his mind the problem of George and Hugh. He had promised to meet George at the club in four days' time and if he didn't turn up there was no way of getting in contact with him. Now getting away to meet George was going to be impossible. And he had given a promise to his mother that he would watch over Hugh. How could he do that if they were grounding him?

In the short conversation he had had with the Head, after the army fatigues and balaclava had been removed, he had been told that he was to stay for the time being with his aunt. Evidently they were fearful of taking too tough a line with him, so a 'rest' was being advised. His father had even spoken of him 'seeing a doctor', which made Edwin very angry indeed.

'I don't need a bloody doctor – I'm not crazy! I want to stay here. I've told you I'm *fine!*'

But it was hopeless. No one listens much to a boy of fifteen, even less when that boy is in line for the throne. Not for the first time, Edwin cursed his family and his destiny. George didn't have these problems! No one told George what to do. And how was he, anyway, going to solve the problem of how to tell George?

25

She woke with a worry about Eds in her mind. Lying there, patterns of light filtering through the shutters, and thinking of her two sons, the day started badly. Who would be there for the boys? And where was Dr Asklepios when she needed him? He had not called to see her for days. In his high-handed way, he hadn't even bothered to let her know that he wasn't coming. More than once she had waited for him by the walnut tree. Probably he was sorting something out in his troublesome extended family. Obviously he had no time for her!

Thinking to go and look for him, she took the path towards the cove. The stones were still warm under her feet. Back home it would be freezing – she hoped someone was seeing to it that the boys were keeping warm. Walking so much barefoot her toes had turned brown and her soles had grown hard, like leather. To think once she'd had three hundred pairs of shoes!

By an outcrop of rocks, a little way before she reached the place where the path turned off towards the olive grove, something scratched her foot. She snatched it back, fearing snakes, then, looking down, saw it was the tortoise, Hestia.

'*Festina lente* – which, translated, means, hurry slowly or, to make one of your country's proverbs of it, more haste less speed.' A squeaky dry voice made her start and look about, but there was no one to be seen. 'I don't suppose you speak any of the ancient tongues?' It was the tortoise.

Hastily, recalling Dr Asklepios's stricture about respect, she replied, 'I'm afraid not. I was never much good at school.' How lucky that her old life had brought her all kinds of unusual encounters. If nothing else, it had taught her to be diplomatic!

Hestia made a noise as if she was blowing air through her nose. 'Don't give me that. You remind me of Aphrodite, beautiful as the day is long, so she pretends to be a ninny. The fact is that madam can beat the others into a cocked hat any day for brains.'

'She's the goddess of love, isn't she?'

The tortoise blinked approval. 'That's right. Be grateful you haven't fallen under her care. The things she puts 'em through!'

For a moment she remembered Milu. 'But it's wonderful, being in love.' Funny how little she thought about him here. She could barely remember what he looked like.

The tortoise made the sound through her nose again. 'Hmm! You're young. Wait 'til you get to my age and you'll think different. Anyway, hurry along, you're late.'

'Late?'

'It's a joke. Think about it! Not a very good one, I grant you. The doctor likes it – he stole it from a programme he used to listen to on your wireless.'

'It's called the radio nowadays. What programme?' But the tortoise was steaming ahead of her now at a tremendous pace and she had to hurry to catch up.

By a rock Hestia turned away from the path. 'Along you go.' She inclined a wrinkled head.

'But where?'

'You'll find out,' the tortoise enigmatically declared. 'I'm taking eighty winks.' And she withdrew into her shell.

Hestia had led her to the outer edge of a circle of rocks set high above the cove where Dr Asklepios beached his boat. Looking down she realized she was searching for him and experienced a flash of anger. What right had he to appear day after day, making her depend on him, and then just not show up?

The rocks formed a kind of protected basin and entering the warm shelter she saw a naked woman stretched out upon one of the flatter rocks. She was apparently sunbathing.

'Oh, I'm so sorry.'

'Please.' The woman had a lazy voice which sounded as if she were half-asleep. She made no effort to cover up her nakedness; indeed, she rolled over so that it was possible to see that she had a perfect figure. 'Don't go – I was about to be bored.'

The naked woman had long, copper-coloured hair which wreathed and tendrilled round a heart-shaped face. Looking at her it was difficult not to feel inferior. Did Dr Asklepios know this woman, she wondered?

'I was looking for Dr Asklepios, actually.' She was conscious that she sounded rather stiff.

'He's an old sweetie-pie, isn't he? Bless him!'

'You know him?' She felt her heart churn a little – as it had, too often, in the old days.

'Course. Everyone knows old Asklepy!'

What a cheek the creature had – talking about her doctor like that. Who was this harpy?

As if reading her mind the naked woman gave a gurgling laugh. 'No need to be jealous – he's my great-nephew – I played the drums on his bottom' – she gently slapped her own belly – 'when he was knee-high to a cicada.' The belly was golden-brown and quite rounded.

Another relative. And what beauty treatments they must have here! The woman was stretching her body now and clambering down from the hot-spot on the rock. She pulled a long white dress over her head, belting it with a leaf-green cord. Closer up she did seem older, with something of the faraway look of Dr Asklepios's aunt. But this woman was definitely not shy. Indeed, she acted as if they were, not exactly old friends – but as if they already knew each other – pen-pals, almost.

'Pleased to meet you at last,' said the woman extending a hand with pearly-pink nails. She was ever so slightly vulgar-looking. 'I was expecting you would turn up. Drink?'

A bottle of wine, some glasses and a bowl of nuts and luscious-looking fruits were visible on the rock on which the woman had been sunbathing.

'No thanks, I don't drink in the day. Especially not with all the sun. It's not good for the complexion.'

'You'll be all right here. I use walnut oil – eat 'em too. Good for the skin. Like some?'

An image came to her of Dr Asklepios feeding Hestia walnuts under the walnut tree. 'You're Aphrodite!'

The other woman grinned delightedly. 'You've heard of me, then?' she said.

'Dr Asklepios has mentioned your name – he seems fond of you.' Perhaps that was rather a presumptuous thing to say in the circumstances? After all, she was his great-aunt, improbable as that seemed. 'And Hestia, too,' she added.

'Ah! Our oldest inhabitant.'

'I met her on the way here. She, er, spoke of you . . .' She trailed off because Hestia, she remembered, had been rather tart on the subject of the goddess.

'Nothing good, I fancy!' Aphrodite seemed quite unabashed.

'She's past all that herself – I expect she told you. But even before, when she wasn't a wrinkly . . .' She gave a chortle. Like Dr Asklepios she seemed fond of her own jokes. 'She wasn't in favour of "*It*", you know. Looked after hearth and home whereas I – I break 'em up!' she concluded cheerfully.

You could hardly get more direct than that. 'Don't you worry about doing that?' Her own home-life had been broken into a thousand desperate pieces.

'It's not my nature to worry, I'm afraid.' Aphrodite was certainly candid. 'Anyway, you people like falling in and out of love.'

'Not out of love, I assure you!' Painful memories half-scuttered back. 'Do you never worry?' Such brazen disregard seemed hardly possible – and more than somewhat immoral.

'Never! What good does it do? My husband worries.' She laughed the chortling laugh. And really, one had to admit it was attractive – like a calling blackbird.

'What about?' This must be the husband with the limp Dr Asklepios had referred to.

'Me, I should think. I have a lover, you know.'

'Oh, dear – doesn't he mind – your husband?'

'Of course he minds – but it's his own fault – he shouldn't have married me.'

'I know how he feels!' And that was heartfelt. Whatever he was like, Aphrodite's husband had her immediate sympathy.

The goddess had seated herself on one of the lower planes of the rocks and was examining her face in an exquisite silver hand-glass. 'I expect you do,' she said. 'Perhaps that sounds callous but – no offence intended – I doubt if you understand love. Though I daresay you think you do.'

'I certainly never got it right – at least . . .'

'Oh, don't say that! You got much of it right – more than many mortals, I would say. They tell me you were an excellent mother and a loyal friend, though, of course, all that isn't my forte.'

She was becoming used to this. 'Not your department?'

'That's right. I'm strictly Desire.' And the goddess pursed her lips and made kissing motions.

'It's true, I wasn't good on that.' All thoughts of Milu had vanished from her mind.

Aphrodite sprang up. 'Doesn't matter,' she said comfortingly. 'It's not important, you know. The other kind, the one you're good at, kids and things, that's what sees a body through. I'm really for stirring folk up. Then, if they've got any nous, they learn.'

'What do they learn?' Conversation with Aphrodite was certainly stimulating.

'They learn what matters,' the goddess replied. 'Now, I must fly.'

There was a gentle whirring noise and a flock of doves appeared over the headland and descended from the cloudless sky. They clustered around the goddess, then, in unison, rose together back up into the brilliant air and she found herself alone once more.

Coming back along the path she met Dr Asklepios standing at the point of the cliff-top where the path turned inland towards the stone house. Seeing him there, her heart lurched.

'I thought you weren't coming.' Somehow the words came out more angrily than she intended.

In reply the doctor shrugged. 'I had business.'

She had been right. 'More important than me?'

The doctor looked at her but said nothing. For the first time she noticed he had green eyes.

'I've missed you. Where have you been?' The moment the words were out she wanted to take them back. She knew she sounded petulant. She tried to correct herself but the tone came out wrong. 'I needed you this morning. Why didn't you come? I found your great-aunt but it was you I was looking for.'

How could this be happening to her again? And why wouldn't the bloody man say anything? He was standing there, like a block of wood, just looking at her. She tried to stop the words but they came tumbling out. 'Do you love me, Dr Asklepios?'

Dr Asklepios still said nothing. Instead he took her arm, threading it through the crook of his own, and walked on, so that she was forced to almost run to keep up with him.

She hurried beside him trying to hold them off but she couldn't stop the tears. Something dropped on to the large hand. As a rule, tears got short shrift with Dr Asklepios, but now he stopped on the cliff path and spoke very gently.

'You have been wounded, my dear, in your heart. There is another meaning to the arrow you learn to shoot. It is also Eros's arrow. You have lost more than one beloved in your, we must say, short life. Now the wound in you seeks to turn me into another occasion for its pain.'

'You don't love me?'

'I am humbled by your words.'

'Can't you . . . ever? No one else has understood.'

Dr Asklepios was staring into the sun so she could not see his eyes. He seemed to be looking to the crimson, glowing disc for words. 'I am older than the hills, my dove, and immortal. There are many compensations for immortality – the "long perspective", as one of your poets called it – but love such as visits the human heart is not one of them. Lovely as you are, and you are very lovely, I cannot return the feelings you believe you have for me. It is not in my nature.'

She turned away from the light glancing off the sea so that he shouldn't see her face. 'Why is it always like that?'

'Do you mean why do you always choose impossible people to love?' He spoke to a drooping shoulder. 'One of my imitators your age is so proud of, Dr Freud, would say it is because you have the streak of masochism in you – that secretly you like to be tormented. And about this the good doctor is not entirely wrong. There is in you humans a strange attraction for the painful. You all have a crazy love for what makes you unhappy. But for all that, I do not share Dr Freud's opinion. He was a sincere man but he liked the idea of misery too much. It is a one-sided view.'

'It hurts so much.'

There was a cry in her voice and the doctor, for all his claims, might have flinched.

'It is the arrow of Eros which wounds you and you suffer. But Eros is also a great teacher. The suffering of love disciplines. It teaches those who are prepared to make the effort to look deeply.'

'I should have thought I'd had enough of suffering.'

His instinct was to soften the words but it was a moment where another way was necessary.

'Now you are feeling sorry for yourself. That is understandable. And I seem not to be so sympathetic again. Like your husband, perhaps? This is a picture you have of yourself. The picture says, "Poor me, how I suffer: the cruel husband, the stupid doctor, they do not understand me. I am a victim." But this is not a true image of how you are.'

'Why are you so unkind?'

'Because I take your wound so lightly, you mean? But I do not. I speak so because, on the contrary, I take you seriously. You have chosen a very difficult path – one which few have chosen. But if you take this path it is important to distinguish between the wound of love and the wound of self-pity, Iphigenia.'

He watched her as she ran away from him towards the stone cottage. The light was already at the window and smoke was coming from the chimney. The girl would be there to comfort her. It was kinder not to stay.

161

All the same, the doctor stood for some time before he made his way back to the seashore.

'O cruel immortality . . .' He spoke the words aloud to himself, unfurling the green sails to cross the darkening sea.

26

Mad Hatters was a lemon-painted boutique in an alley off the Fulham Road. Henri had a pleasant time finding it. The skirts were very mini this year and he enjoyed himself assessing the legs of the passing women. The English had good thighs but he missed the French ankle. It was a pity designers didn't appreciate a well-turned ankle these days.

But hats, it seemed, were back. Reaching the boutique at last, Henri observed a pretty one, trimmed with a coquettish black feather, in the window. It would have suited Alice. For a moment his eyes blurred. Foolish to have these thoughts which were not much use to either of them now. For he was as sure as he could be that the black horses of his dream were the horses of death.

Wise after the event one could never be quite sure, of course, but he was fairly certain that he would have recognized the woman who smiled at him, as he entered the shop, as Alice's sister — even without the information on the card her mother had found for him.

Like her sister, Julie Kirk had abbreviated both her names.

Her fine-boned face was so reminiscent that Henri almost turned on his heel and left. She was shorter, though, than Alice – and although she looked in better health she was inherently less good-looking.

Looking at her sister, Henri could see how handsome Alice must once have been – before the booze and the drugs worked their ruin.

'May I help you or do you just want to be left alone to browse?' Again the voice was reminiscent but had held more of its refined origins. But the sweetness of manner was the same. Usually, it would have been a pleasure to be allowed to browse. But that was not his present purpose.

'Thank you, but I need some help, if you would be so kind. Hats are not quite my . . .'

'Of course. Is it for your wife, or . . . ?'

Again, a tact which was so like Alice. Alice had never asked him where he had been when he failed to return at night. Not once had they had a scene – except when she was drunk or crazily needing drugs.

'Alas, I have been careless! At present I have no wife. But I have a niece whom I thought to give one of your charming hats.'

'Lucky her. My uncle always buys me book-tokens. I think he knows I don't read much.'

'Ah, you will in time. Reading is not for girls.'

Mistake. She clammed up at the compliment. 'Hardly a "girl" – I'm thirty-eight. Was there any hat in particular?'

By the time she had tried on several hats for Henri, he had recovered her desire to please.

'I think the one with the black feather – but what do you think? You are about the same build and colouring as my niece – in fact, I have been pondering – have we perhaps met before? I seem to know your face.' Which was, after all, true.

'I don't think so. I like the one with the feather, too. I never

164

wear my best hats, but if I had to choose for myself it would be that one.' Julie put it on again and a version of Alice's face stared out at him from the mirror. 'I'm afraid I don't remember meeting you, sorry.' She sounded apologetic.

Henri, who had planned to leave without making a purchase said, 'Then let it be the black with the feather. I have a credit card if you accept those?' He took out his wallet with its secret cache. 'But you are so familiar. Could I have met a sister? Do you have sisters?'

She flushed and said, 'Thank you – Visa is fine. My eldest sister doesn't look like me at all and I doubt if you'd know my youngest sister except . . .' she paused '. . . you don't live in Paris do you?'

His stomach contracted. 'In fact, yes.' He was going to hear something.

'My sister . . . Look, let me get this card through or I'll get into a muddle.'

They both waited while the machine interrogated Henri's account. For a moment he panicked, fearing that perhaps it was in a state of disarray – he had left so importunately – then it hiccuped and spat out the docket to sign.

'I always think it's like coitus interruptus,' she giggled and looked shy at her own boldness. It was not a very good joke but he laughed, also nervous. It was as if they both knew something important was going to transpire.

'My sister was living in Paris when I last heard from her. I don't often hear – from time to time she sends me a card. I'd love to know how she is.' Alice's eyes looked pitifully out at Henri from her sister's face.

'And you don't have her address?'

Julie Kirk fiddled with the feather on the hat. 'No. She was treated very badly by our parents. They slung her out and she went to Paris to get away from them, I guess. I went and saw her there once, but she was on drugs and I sort of couldn't bear it. We lost touch and I didn't hear for ages. Then there was an article about my hats which gave the shop's address. She must have read it because she started to send me these cards. Look, I've got one here.' She pulled open her handbag. 'D'you think you've met her?'

She held out a sepia card with a view of the old Paris flower market. Henri realized that he had never consciously seen Alice's handwriting. He turned the card over. 'May I?'

She nodded. 'Of course.'

Overleaf Alice had written:

Darling Jules, Keep hoping we'll bump into each other here one day. Wouldn't it be a laugh? If you see Emma, and you think she'd want it, give her my love. Lots to you, Lissy. XXX

It was dated 15 August 1997. A few weeks after he'd chucked her out.

'Emma?'

'Our sister. She didn't, by the way, want Lissy's "love".'

'And your parents?' As if he didn't already know.

'Oh, them! Look, do want this?' She had wrapped tissue paper round the feathers of the hat to protect it. Now he nodded, speechless. 'Are you sure? In which case, would you also like a box? They're another ten pounds, I'm afraid, but they do protect the hats better and they give a nice finishing touch.'

Henri found his voice. 'By all means the box. Your parents do not care about Alice?'

It took a moment for each of them to work it out. He got to it first and blushed dark red: the signature had been from 'Lissy'. Only someone who already knew the name would construct 'Alice' from the abbreviation. She was there a second after him.

'Who the hell are you? A private dick?'

'Mademoiselle, please . . .'

'How dare you! Tricking me like that – I think I'd better call the police!'

She was at the phone already when he placed a hand on her arm. 'Please, no, please understand. I am a friend – I know, knew, Alice, Alicia. Look, I can prove it.'

She struggled away from him but waited while he fished the tissue-wrapped parcel from his breast pocket. At first he couldn't find it and a wild fear that he had dropped it somewhere – at the Fenton-Kirk house, in the tube, along the Fulham Road – set his heart beating arrhythmically. He was breathing painfully by the time he found it.

'Look!' He unwrapped the turquoise heart.

'That's Lissy's. How do I know you haven't stolen it?'

She was white too. Her hair had worked its way loose from the velvet scrunchie which pulled it back from her face.

'Intuition. Do I look like a thief or a detective? I am, in fact, a fairly well-recognized sculptor. Look, my card.'

She examined the card carefully and then, anticipating another customer, moved towards the shop door, turning the sign to register that the premises were closed. The woman outside swore audibly but neither of the two inside turned to look. Although barely three o'clock it was already dark.

'So you know about Alicia.'

She had sat down. Henri noticed she had good ankles.

'A little. The little she told me – and then some I learned from your mother.'

'You've spoken to Mummy?' She looked alarmed.

'I fear that I also practised some deceit on her. I feel ashamed, but somehow I did not think I would be given information if, out of the blue air, I arrive and say, "I am the French lover of little Alice!" What do you think?'

It worked. Laughter. She rocked the chair on to its back legs

167

– a habit from which he had never succeeded in curing Alice.

'No, not much chance of getting Mummy to talk with that for introduction. But if you are my sister's lover why don't you know where she is?'

She had gone to the heart of the matter. There seemed little point in prevarication.

'I think she may be dead. I am so sorry. We had a quarrel – more than a quarrel, a row. I do not apologize too much because she set fire to my bed. My bed I do not mind so much but, unfortunately, it is in my studio and in my studio is my work. So, I threw her out. I have to hope that this was not the reason she died. Maybe I am too fond of my work . . .'

'No, no – a fire, that's bad – you couldn't be expected . . . But why? Lissy wasn't violent.'

'Absolutely not. It was . . . she got . . . she became not herself, you see and . . .'

'Was it the drugs?'

'I am afraid yes. But always worse in the summer. Then, you see, I found her locket and *tiens* – there is the explanation.'

He looked at her. Her eyes, less striking than Alice's were more candid.

'What is the explanation? Hector, is it Hector you mean?'

'Hector?' Just for a moment he was puzzled.

'Her baby, she called him Hector. He was the sweetest babe you ever saw.' She looked as if she was going to cry and he'd had enough of tears.

'Of course – I forget. One does not think of a baby called Hector. But, yes, it is so that there were mementoes of a baby inside the locket.'

Both looked at the turquoise heart as if it might speak in Alice's voice and tell them where she had gone.

'How did you come by it?'

But he chose not to tell her. 'She left it behind with a note.

I thought to keep it, unless . . .' Desperately now he did not wish to surrender the jewel.

'Oh, no. You keep it. It's yours. Daddy gave it to her when she won a big horse event. Her horse was called Turquoise, you see. Lissy would have wanted you to have it. Are you sure she's dead?'

'I think so, though I have not been successful in finding the body. But the heroin – it was always a matter of time.'

They talked until past the time the shop would normally close. Unsure how to proceed next, he stood up.

'May I buy you a drink?'

'I think I should buy you one. But my flat is just round the corner. Would you like to . . . ?'

They walked to the nearby mansion block not quite arm in arm, occasionally knocking into each other. Henri felt uneasy in her presence. His mind did not stray to thoughts of bed with her. Yet she was an attractive woman – solider than Alice, – more his usual type. They had got on immediately too. She told him about her family – hinting at bedroom secrets with papa – her eldest sister's establishment life – her mother's alcoholism, 'Though I think that's because of Lissy.'

There was a nasty little sequel to the letters he had read. It seemed that Alice had arrived home one day in a taxi, from the nursing home, Baby Hector in her arms. Her father had refused to see them and her mother had finally shut the door in Alice's face after calling a taxi to take her back to the nursing home – a taxi from Salisbury, rather than a local firm, so that the matter might not get around in the immediate neighbourhood.

'And they never saw her again?'

There was no cruelty like familial cruelty.

'Not so far as I know. None of us did – except me that once. I'm the only one she even wrote to.'

'And the baby?'

It was late. Henri felt he was getting old. He could not take too much more.

'He was adopted.'

Henri flexed the calf of his left leg which had slight cramp. It was impossible, this foolish quest he had commenced. Who did he imagine he was? St Nicholas? 'And so he too has disappeared into anonymity, like his poor dear *maman*.'

It was a statement, but she answered as if it were a question. 'No. I know where he went. I know who the adopted parents were. I saw the file, you see.'

27

It was common knowledge that Ted Mallins didn't care about anyone in the world except Aunt Mary. Ted had used to work in Granny's stables where Mary had learned to ride as a little girl. She would get Ted to put her on a horse too high for her, and make him walk beside her until she fell off into his arms.

When Aunt Mary married first, Ted had handed in his notice – which was not a thing people did with Granny. But when Granny saw it she refused to let him go.

'No, Mr Mallins,' she had said (Granny didn't hold with using people's first names). 'I see you have resigned but I do not accept your resignation. You will do me a favour if you go and work with my daughter. No one else appears to have any influence over her!'

Ted had also helped teach Edwin to ride. He was no respecter of persons and used to swear at Edwin horribly when he turned his heels down wrong. Which is one reason Edwin liked Ted. It's awful being with people who feel they must smarm over you all the time.

Even on this occasion, Ted wasn't doing much smarming, which was a relief when everyone seemed to have decided that Edwin had gone slightly mad and were consequently treating him with a horrid kind of carefulness. Even Aunt Mary had offered to bring him breakfast in bed – which would have been nice if you didn't know that she hadn't even allowed Uncle Tom breakfast in bed when he slipped a disc in his back playing rugger.

'Exercise is good for backs,' she had said firmly, and poor Uncle Tom had had to hobble downstairs bent nearly double.

Ted had merely said, 'Guess who it isn't!' when he had seen Edwin and had laughed, showing his bare gums. 'Buckin' school? Don't blame yer. Don't learn anything in school these days.'

Ted was the only person who never made any reference to Mum, either – not even by his silences. He just acted as if nothing had happened to disrupt your life – an attitude which was very calming.

It was said that Ted had had a wife once who had removed her presence for good from his taciturn life, taking with her their only son.

The day after his arrival from school, helping comb down a mare, Edwin said, 'Got any work for a likely lad, Ted?'

'How d'yer mean?'

The answer came slowly enough. Edwin took a gamble.

'Friend of mine. Been in trouble.'

The departure of Mrs Mallins was alleged to have occurred after she had discovered that Ted had once spent a short stretch at Her Majesty's Pleasure for breaking a man's jaw. Granny, who had known all about Ted's past before she employed him, was rumoured to have been rather witty on the subject of Her Majesty's Pleasure and Mrs Mallins's displeasure.

'Oh yeah.' A little later Ted said, 'What kind of trouble?' and Edwin knew that he was at least in with a chance.

It needed another piece of organization, though, to make the plan work.

'Look, Matt, can I ask you to do something for me and tell absolutely no one?'

Edwin's older cousin looked bothered. Usually he would have agreed without a protest, but you had to remember who Eds was and, seemingly, he hadn't been great since the business of his mother.

'Hey, Eds, not sure that it's too cool to do things behind the scenes right now.'

'No, listen,' Edwin felt slightly desperate. It was Saturday and George would be expecting him. If he didn't turn up he would probably never see George again. 'It's something I have to do for Mum – but you know how it is – they probably won't let me in case I get upset.'

'OK. So give.'

'There's a boy Mum was photographed with once. She was going to see him at a dance for one of her homeless do's, then for obvious reasons she couldn't. Anyway, I heard he was very upset he hadn't got to see her.'

'Hey, all kinds of people are upset about your mum, Eds.'

'But this one's different. Mum talked to me about him.'

Matt thought a moment. He knew that Auntie Helena had often discussed her particular plans with her elder son. Matt also privately thought that this business of Eds being sick was exaggerated. Obviously he was missing his mother – just about everyone did. But there seemed nothing dramatically different about his cousin. If anything, Eds seemed more sane than usual.

'OK. Where do I find this guy?'

Later that night a navy Porsche drove up the Vauxhall Bridge Road. Edwin had promised to meet George by the club entrance. It was tricky explaining this part of the arrangement to Matt.

'So how can you be so sure he'll be outside? I don't get that!'

The area was off Matt's usual beat. He was fond of his younger cousin, but he didn't fancy getting beaten up by local roughs.

What to say? How could he be sure? 'Er, I sent a message on Mum's writing paper to say that he should wait outside the club to receive something from her. I didn't think they'd let me meet him, so I was going to get my driver to go.' Necessity was the mother of invention.

Matt still looked doubtful. 'OK. So, how was your driver going to recognize this chap? Does he have any distinguishing features at all?'

Edwin thought. He had not, truth to tell, taken that much notice of the way George looked. He tried to assemble George in his mind's eye.

'He has an ear-ring,'

'Yeah?'

'And a nose stud.'

'Cool! Anything else?'

'Well, he's quite small.'

'So, I'm looking for a little guy with rings in his ears and his nose. Anything else?'

'Yes,' said Edwin, 'there is one more thing. He's not exactly white.'

Which he suspected was going to be a problem with Ted. Matt and he went to school with boys of all nationalities. But Ted was not known for his political correctness. Any more than Grandpa was.

Imagine what Grandpa would think, Mum, if he knew about George! I'm trying to get him a job here, with the horses (George – not Grandpa!) I'm hoping Ted'll take him on – which would be brilliant, don't you think? Just your kind of idea. They've got me off school staying here for a while. I'm absolutely OK, but it means I can't see Hugh – sorry, Mum.

*   *   *

Edwin had not worked out how he was going to explain himself to George. Explaining things to Matt was a push-over by comparison. How did you explain that you were not an army cadet at some military school but someone rather more particular? There would have to come a time when he explained who he really was. Meanwhile, the note would have to be written with care so as not to alarm George and therefore alert Matt, in case Matt was there when George read it. Edwin thought for a while then, tearing a page from a his journal, wrote:

Dear George,

I've been kept in so I can't meet you. There's a chance that you might get work at my aunt's place. She has quite a few eventing horses (that's horses which are shown in events) and the guy who runs the stables (he taught me to ride) might give you work if you want it. If you do want it you should ring the number below and ask for Ted. It's important you tell Ted you're Ed's friend. He's expecting you to ring. Hope to see you soon. Cheers,

Ed.

P.S. In case you need money to get to see Ted here's £40. You can pay me back later if you want. No worries.

P.P.S. My cousin is delivering this for me. He's OK.

Edwin wrote the stables' number on the bottom of the note. That should do it. Time enough to explain himself further if George ever got here. Which, in itself, must be doubtful. He felt suddenly very tired. When he had given the note to Matt he went upstairs, lay down on the floor of the bedroom and fell asleep.

He knew it was his mother by her smile.

'Edkins!' she said, and opened her arms. It was good to feel their strength round him again.

'Are you all right, Mum?' he asked and she had smiled again. She smelt of flowers.

'How is Hugh?' she asked, and he explained that he had not been able to look after him lately.

'It's all right, my duck,' she said, 'as long as he knows you are there.'

She took him up a hillside to a place which looked out over the sea. Then they had walked, holding hands, down the hill towards the beach 'til they came to the sea and there was a boat with green sails.

'Shall I get in, Mum?' he had asked.

She had kissed him and smiled and kissed him again and when he woke it was morning and his face was buried in the black sheepskin rug that Dad had given Aunt Mary when she won a bet, racing him in Scotland, when they were still children.

28

They had left the walnut tree and were strolling along the sea-shore. Dr Asklepios was, rather ineptly, playing ducks and drakes. 'Hades! I can never get the knack. Aphrodite can make a stone skip across the water at least six times.' He looked put out.

'It's how you flick your wrist.'

He raised his eyebrows and she picked up a flat flint to show him. She let the flint fly.

'Look, you're holding it wrong. You need to keep your wrist at this angle then use it like a gate swinging.' She let the stone fly and it jumped in ever-decreasing lengths over the sea's surface.

'One, two, three, four, five, six, seven.' Dr Asklepios looked admiringly at his patient. 'Better than Aphrodite. I might get you two together for a competition.'

He looked at his pupil. She had grown stronger over the months. Under the Aunt's tutelage her arms and hands, now adept at stringing and pulling a bow, had grown firmer and browner, and her teeth looked whiter than ever in her tanned face. Her beauty was the equal of Aphrodite's.

'So you are reconciled to being a huntress?'

'Isn't it funny – I like it now! It's a marvellous moment when you pull, and you think you can't do it, and then, somehow, you get through that resistance and then the arrow flies like a bird.' She understood why Dr Asklepios's aunt had said it might help.

'And you see better, how only those who fully understand both sides of the coin really know how not to do harm?'

She nodded, eyes serious. 'I guess I had one of those pictures of myself you talk about. I never knew what you meant. I'm slow.'

'You are Hermes himself compared to some!' And it was true she had grasped the point as few could have done. 'Tell me, what was the picture of yourself?'

A pause. 'I think I saw myself as part heroine, part victim. Plucky, you know? Battling to keep going against all odds – against my husband's family, really. I suppose I didn't admit my own power.'

No doubt about it, the Aunt had done well in bringing her here. He was going to miss her. 'Ah! But they see it now, your husband's family. They feel the lack of you, believe me.'

'I'm not hearing right! Dr Asklepios, you're paying me a compliment.'

'A little bird tells me it is the case,' he said, pretending not to hear. 'And you know, you are not alone by any means. What is rare is to recognize it. All mortals have pictures of themselves which put them in a good light – enough to fill the Alexandrian library – that is,' – seeing her uncomprehending look – 'or was, before it burnt to the ground, a great building, something like your British Museum.'

'Why do we do it, Dr Asklepios? Why do we make up pictures of ourselves?'

'That is one of your tendencies we find hard to understand here. Compared to us, you are complicated creatures.'

178

She remembered Aphrodite's unabashed admissions; the Aunt's straightforward manner. 'The truth is . . .' she hunted for the word, '. . . simpler, isn't it?'

He watched her. She had pulled up her long saffron-coloured skirt and was paddling in the sea. 'Ah yes, "The truth shall set ye free."'

'I s'pose it does. I forget, who was it said that?'

'A man who was once called by his followers, "The Wounded Snake" . . . What is it?' She had made a sudden exclamation. 'You have been bitten by a crab?'

'No, but I dreamt about a snake last night. I suppose you guessed that!' She had become used to his intuition for such things.

'Indeed? That is good sign.'

'Is it? I thought they were supposed to be phallic symbols.' She laughed, slightly flirtatious, remembering how she had believed herself in love with him.

'This phallic nonsense is a foolish twentieth-century fixation.' He was a touch annoyed. Her recovery from infatuation had been rapid. 'The snake is an ancient and sacred symbol. My father's place, at Delphi you know, was the home of the snake Python, an old beast, even older than us Olympians. My father set up his own oracle there – perhaps you've heard of it?'

She half-nodded. 'I've heard of the oracle – I've never visited, though.' James had wanted to. Poor James. She hoped he was enjoying his hunting now.

'You should. We must arrange something. It's full of tourists these days. But there are ways. We might persuade Pan to start a riot – he enjoys that kind of thing – spread word there's a landslide brewing, get the place shut down for a day. But if it comes to a visit, I would prefer to take you to my own sanctuary. It is more modest than my father's place, but it was famous in its day. I'm fond of it.'

'Did you have snakes, too? Look, there's Angela!'

Together they watched her companion at the far end of the beach. She was walking towards them accompanied by a dog she had found one day, straying on the hillside, and brought down to the cottage. The black-and-grey spaniel bitch, whom Angela had named Persephone, was never far from her rescuer's side.

'She is a good little bitch, that one.' Dr Asklepios spoke with approval. It was unclear whether he referred to the hound or to the girl. 'To answer your question, there are no sacred snakes now at Epidaurus. Once they came, the pilgrims, seeking a cure for their ailments, or, in the case of a few, enlightenment for their souls. They lay all night in the labyrinth, inside the Tholos, the dwelling in the sacred area. My snakes slept inside the Tholos too, in the hidden heart of the labyrinth. It was part of the cure to be bitten by a sacred snake – a sign of great favour. This is why I am happy with your dream.'

'But the snake didn't bite me.' She was seeing how far she could hop now, as Hugh had liked to do.

He gave a mock shiver. 'You English with your hardy constitutions! Are you not afraid you will catch cold? It is true that you have not been bitten by the snake yet. It is only very few they bite – and their bite is said to be lethal. But in that lethal bite lies the cure. Forgive the paradox but, as my philosopher friend Zeno will tell you, paradox is at the crux of life.'

She knocked a pair of stones together as if they were castanets. Once she had danced with castanets at a President's dinner. 'Sounds like homeopathic medicine.' Her husband had been keen on all that.

Dr Asklepios, who was picking up another pebble from the shoreline, beamed. 'Clever girl. Exactly. The poison, in a measured dose, is the cure. Like a gate, you say?' He flapped his wrist and the stone fell dead into the water. 'Dis! I think you and Aphrodite must cheat. All women cheat.'

'Nonsense, Dr Asklepios, Aphrodite and I have no need to cheat. You wouldn't let us get away with such a feeble justification. You aren't doing it right. Look!' She skimmed another stone across the water's surface. 'Now then, you were saying. The poison and the cure. Explain how it works.'

'It is the wound that heals,' he resumed rather grumpily. 'You, for example. You were much hurt in life. This we know. Your heart was hurt by a husband who, in your eyes, betrayed you with another woman. You were hounded by the newspapers, excited by your not unpleasing face and figure and this none too seemly story of betrayal. You were driven, hunted, a tormented creature, like a young deer, until, bang! – you are hunted so hard you are driven to a seeming end upon the hard surface of life. Hey, I think I acquire the knack –' Here Dr Asklepios threw another stone which skipped twice before it fell beneath the surface. 'Ah, it comes! I see it is how you say, all in the action of the wrist.'

She jumped over a more than usually steep wave.

Dr Asklepios was watching. 'You will be good in our Olympics. I must mention it to Herakles. Like yourself he passed across – although I hear he's got wind of some film they've done of him and I gather he has become impossible lately. Aphrodite tells me is wearing Levi jeans, very tight.'

'Oh, yes! I wonder if Hugh has seen it yet?' She would have made sure Hugh saw the cartoon. Maybe the boys' aunt would take him to it? 'You were saying, about me coming to an end . . . ?'

'On the contrary, I was saying, you have not come to an end. Something constellated in you elected to survive. You had begun already, before the gross event which brought you here, the hard lesson – which is that suffering, taken rightly, is a means not an end. You had already begun the work – I . . .' And what had he done after all? 'I have merely helped you to complete it.'

He watched while she jumped more waves. She hardly looked old enough to have borne children.

'Here you learn to take the hurt. And, I fear, your old doctor sometimes adds to it. Sometimes I am rough with you. This is how you learn to accept the bite of the snake. To see more clearly what your own part in all this tragedy has been. And then, my dear,' – he looked at her, really she was a child still herself – 'we see the start of something new. The tragedy begins to end and we have something greater than tragedy commence.'

He flipped another stone which skipped four times over the bay. 'Aha! I get the trick. So, the teacher learns something from the pupil. That is also a sign of progress.'

Angela and Persephone were approaching and she spoke hurriedly. 'Dr Asklepios, the dangerous bit in me – you know, the monster in the locked room – do you think the snake I dreamt about was that?'

But he was absorbed in trying out his new skill and Angela and the dog were soon abreast of them.

Later, when Angela had gone to bed, Dr Asklepios sat before the fire smoking his pipe.

'The smell of wood dried on the beach beats all the sacrificial smoke on Olympus. Sometimes I thank Gaia for my immortality because I shall have the chance of such a smell for eternity. Speaking of which, it was your carpenter god' – he cupped his hand over the pipe's bowl to encourage a draw – 'the one who got himself killed in order to defeat eternity, who was called the "Wounded Snake".'

'You mean Jesus Christ?'

'If that is what you wish to call him.'

'Why do you call him a snake? I don't think the Church of England would approve.'

The doctor made one of his impatient noises. 'I have no time for this Church which knows precious little about snakes, which

182

it thinks are the devil, and even less about the Carpenter. We here see a snake change its skin, so for us a snake is a symbol of transformation. The Carpenter's suffering was transformative. The dark night of the soul, the dear boy called it.'

She said nothing for a while, raking the fire.

'I wonder what he had to give up.'

'The usual things – marriage, a family, his life.'

A piece of driftwood had burnt right through leaving its shape intact. She prodded it and the shape disintegrated – falling to gold-vermilion embers.

'Dr Asklepios, do my boys know I am all right?'

The pipe was over and he spent some time knocking it out and scraping it with a piece of sweet chestnut rind.

'By and large they do.'

'But will I see them again?'

She didn't plead and it was the measure of her growth that she did not. He looked at the young woman who was kneeling on her heels and looking levelly at him. The light from the embers danced in her remarkable eyes. She would not be a patient for much longer.

'Yes, you will see them again. That I promise. Now, I do not know about you, but my immortal bones are tired. Go and get yourself some sleep. Some day soon, I think, I take you to Epidaurus.'

29

'I was visiting Lissy when the social worker came to the nursing home.' Julie Kirk poured another glass.

Henri nodded, blinking. He felt quite drunk. He had visited the nursing home at Sere Westonbury the night after he dreamed of Alice and the black horses. The nun in the old brick house with the big garden had shaken her head. 'They have taken the nursing home from us, monsieur,' she had said. Her accent was impeccable. 'For many years we have cared for the young mothers on behalf of Our Lady. We are no longer considered experts. For us it is sad that the Mother of God has no longer an influence.' Henri thought it was sad too, that the modern world no longer trusted the good sisters.

Julie took another slug. 'It turned out I knew the social worker slightly. She'd been at school with a guy I was going out with at the time.' Henri nodded again. He seemed to think they had downed almost a whole bottle of whisky between them.

'Afterwards I went to see her, the social worker, at her office in Salisbury. Lissy's file was on her desk. She excused herself and went out of the room. She meant me to read it, obviously. It made pretty grim reading.'

'Because . . . ?' He wanted to lie down, go to bed. Not with Alice's sister, much as he liked her. His head hurt and his skin was sore under his clothes.

'Because the notes suggested she knew how Lissy felt about the baby. The social worker was shocked, you could tell, at Mummy and Daddy's reaction. I think the social worker tried to get Lissy to change her mind and keep the baby after all but there was this stubborn bit in Lissy. Once she had decided something, even if it wasn't to her own advantage, you couldn't shift her. Do you know what I mean?'

Indeed he did. Images rushed in: Alice in the street in her petticoat; Alice with a kitchen knife running it down her forearm; Alice blocking his way as he tried to put out the fire she had started. He knew about the stubborn streak, all right.

'But it, the adoption, the procedures all went through?'

'Oh yes. I think Lissy gave up the ghost. They took the baby away after six weeks and she just sort of disappeared, as if there was no one inside her any more. I remember because it was the day Lady Helena Grey got married. Funny really, because it was Lady Helena who got Lissy's job at the nursery after they sacked her because she was pregnant. Not that Lissy blamed Lady Helena. She rather liked her, actually.'

Another connection. 'It is strange – since I heard of the death of the Princess, I have been so sure that your sister too . . .'

'They never met, but people used to say they looked alike. Perhaps they share a fate?'

The black horses dream had made Henri allergic to anything of that nature. Anyway, mediums, astrology, tarot card readings, things like that made him nervous. He reverted to more terrestrial ground.

'And the adoptive parents? To whom did the baby Hector go?'

'That's almost the worst part. He was half-black, you see. Lissy told me she never knew if the father was a pal of Emma's, a Ghanaian polo player from Winchester and Oxford, or Tom Thumb the Black Poet – I don't know what his real name was, but he was called Tom Thumb because he was so small. I liked him, actually. He had bare feet and dreadlocks and used to do rap by Stonehenge. But he was kind to her. I always hoped it was Tom – the other guy sounded like the worst type of upper-class jerk.'

'And how did this affect the adoption?'

'It's policy. Hector had to have a white and a black parent – poor little twiglet. It wasn't so easy. In the end he went to a couple where it sounds as if it all went wrong.'

'You know?'

'I made a few enquiries – neighbours and things. I had seen the file, remember? The mother was still living in Acton when I last asked. Evidently the husband had pushed off back to Jamaica. But no one seemed to know anything about Hector. He'd just vanished.'

'And your parents?' He was exhausted with that pain in his chest. Really he must go to bed soon.

'Oh, predictable. Didn't want to know. Mummy gets sloshed and occasionally cries a lot and then she might refer to Lissy. Daddy just clammed up. Mostly they act as if she's dead.' Suddenly she began to weep. 'Which I suppose she is now. Poor Lissy, poor, poor Lissy.'

It was 2 a.m. before Henri managed to detach himself from Alice's drunk and grieving sister. There were no cabs in sight and he walked back to his hotel through the clammy fog of the late November night.

It was suddenly cold. A vagrant huddled in a doorway, begged a cigarette, and, thinking of Alice, Henri gave the bundled figure a twenty-pound note. He was too self-aware a man not to recognize that superstitious impulse to avert disaster from his own life through acts of generosity to others.

Desolate thoughts of Alice plagued him through the night during which he slept restlessly on the too-hard mattress. Before he left the Fulham flat, he had given the hat with the black feather to Julie. 'You say you never wear your own best creations. Please, I should like you to wear this for your sister,' he had said. 'For the grief we both share.'

But that night images of Alice visited him in his semi-somnolent state. 'How dare you!' she had said. 'It's my hat. You never gave me anything. Why are you giving it to my sister?' And when he awoke, protesting, it was nearly 8 a.m. and the maid was knocking at the door with early-morning tea.

Later that day Henri, increasingly tired, made his way with the help of an A–Z, from the tube station at Acton Central to Harbour Road.

Harbour Road was difficult to find. It was a long depressing run of shops with boarded-up windows and dirty maisonettes above. He rang the bell on the magenta-painted door at number 345.

A woman of indistinguishable age answered the door. Henri, who had learned to assess whether a woman would go to bed with him within ten minutes of meeting her, thought he would have been exercised by this one.

'Yes?'

'Mrs Botswana?'

'Who wants to know?'

'Excuse me,' Henri removed his hat. 'I should have introduced myself. I am Henri Astaffort.' Deliberately, he gabbled the name.

'So?'

'And you are Mrs Botswana?' Henri tried smiling.

'What d'you want?'

'I would like, if you would be so kind, to speak with Mrs Botswana. You are she?'

'She's my sister.' The voice was terminally angry. He too, Henri thought, might be angry if he had to live in such surroundings.

'So you are . . . ?'

'That's my business. Who are you?'

Henri, who had a passion for the cinema, had once seen a film in which a husband had got access to a house by pretending that he was a solicitor.

'Forgive me, Madame, I represent the estate of Miss Fenton-Kirk.'

'You're French aren't you?'

'Most certainly. I am also a solicitor. May I . . . ?' he moved towards the door and she stood back. Privately, Henri thanked the screenwriter of the forgotten film.

The interior of 345 Harbour Road was even less appealing than the outside. Henri sat down carefully on a tall stool which appeared to have only three fully functional legs. A TV in the corner showed a highly made-up young woman in a yellow suit talking brightly to a green puppet.

'My sister's in hospital. I live here with her. What was the name?'

'The name of my client?' He did not particularly want to repeat his own to become the property of this woman. 'Fenton-Kirk. I act on behalf of her family.'

Which was true in a way, he reflected later as he hurried back down the road to the tube.

Iris Fisher had explained that her sister, once Mrs Botswana now Jackie Fisher, was in hospital with a collapsed womb. She seemed not to recognize the name Fenton-Kirk, but she did speak pretty freely about the boy her sister had adopted.

'He's in a home for young offenders, as far as I know. My sister never sees him. Nasty little thing. Black, you know. They're all the same. 'Course, she adopted the kid to please her husband. I couldn't think why she'd married him, because they all sleep around, don't they?. Thank your lucky stars you didn't get Aids, I told her. He told her he was a teacher! I could teach him a thing or two.' A sharp laugh. Henri involuntarily felt for his scrotum. 'Still, she's best off out of it. And the boy too. Little criminal.'

'It was the boy I had hoped to find.'

Iris Fisher's pupils dilated at this.

'Why? He's no good. He took drugs. Stole from her – after all she'd done for him, bringing him up by hand.' Judging by her sister's face, Henri thought, no doubt there was plenty of 'hand'.

'Naturally, I must be discreet for professional reasons, you understand, madame,' – as with Linda Fenton-Kirk, Henri brought his accent to bear – 'but I think it can do no harm if I mention that my late client had a few *objets* – nothing of great value. The boy was adopted. I must ask for the greatest discretion here but, I believe, a blood tie. A nephew perhaps?'

It had worked. Long ago Henri had decided that the most sensitive part of a human being is his or her wallet. Iris Fisher, scenting wealth, had subtly altered her script.

'Mind you, it was difficult for the lad,' she had said, back-pedalling fast in case there was a profit to be found in this unexpected visitation. 'His so-called father hit him when he drank. You can see how he might have acted up.'

Henri had passed on one of his bogus cards on which he had written the hotel number in case Jackie Fisher chose to call him on her return from hospital. But he had the important information anyway. Baby Fenton-Kirk, Hector, Alice's baby, was in some sort of delinquents' home on the outer stretch of West London.

The import of this didn't strike him fully until he was dining with Christina later that day in Wheeler's. Her choice again.

'Poor scrap,' she said, squeezing a lemon and delicately forking out an oyster. 'I've always been against it. The Marquis and I

189

couldn't, you know, have children, but we were both agreed about adoption. He was against it, poor sweet, because he had this thing about his blood, being so terribly blue, you know, and I was against it because I couldn't bear the idea of messing up someone else's kid. It would have been fine with one's own, don't you see?' She ate a slice of buttered brown bread thoughtfully.

Henri said, 'Alice would have been in despair.'

'At the adoption?'

'At him being in the delinquents' home.'

'What will you do about it?'

She was a nice woman, he thought. Greedy and egocentric, but she was not unusual in that.

'I am going to find him, quite simply.'

'And if he is a little "tough" – which, my dear, he surely will be?'

It had been a long day. But he had reached a conclusion. He had not been sure what had set him on this quest to find Alice's adopted child. Perhaps it was his age – perhaps it was that odd conjunction of Alice's disappearance with the English princess's death. Whatever, he was not now going to give up, go home, resume his life of easy bachelorhood. Quite when the decision had been taken he was unsure. Somewhere, perhaps on the Circle Line – which was surely auditioning for a set location as one of the circles of hell.

'I, too, have been, what you call "a little tough", Christina. It is, at least, a condition I know about. If I find him I will judge what must be done. He has no one, it appears. And I owe his *maman*. I was not so good to Alice in life. I would like to try to be at least a little good to her in death.'

30

Edwin looked out for George's arrival every day for a week. Then he asked Ted, 'Heard from the chap I was telling you about?'

But all Ted said was, 'Nope!' After another week, Edwin stopped asking.

It was strange being at Aunt Mary's. Dad seemed to have more or less moved in, which was comforting in its way. He sat upstairs in the spare room reading poetry. Once Edwin had gone in and Dad had asked him if he was 'happy' – which wasn't the sort of question you could answer easily. It was quite boring, too, with none of his friends and he missed Hugh. Dad made him do school work every morning but thanks to Aunt Mary he was allowed to go and work with the horses in the afternoons.

'No point in him staying here if he moons about indoors, Jams,' she had said to Dad. 'He's much better out getting the roses back in his cheeks.'

And Dad had not objected. He seemed different somehow, since Mum had gone away. More gentle.

One afternoon Edwin was on his way to see Dad's horse,

Artemis, whom Dad had brought over to have Ted keep an eye on, when Ted stopped him. 'Your friend's here,' he said. 'He's down the meadow.'

Edwin's heart jolted. He had pressed his cousin for all the details of the note's delivery – 'Sure thing,' Matt had said. 'I met him – little guy, with an ear-ring. He got the note, Eds. I can't do more.'

So when he heard nothing Edwin had given up on the plan.

Now, with it seeming to have come to something after all, he was going to have to explain himself to George. Which wasn't too easy. Ted, who had an almost telepathic understanding of horses, showed the same gift with certain people. He suddenly said, 'I didn't tell him. He don't know who you are, do he?' and showed his gums.

'May I go and see him?'

You might be going to be the king one day but you didn't presume with Ted. When it came to stables business, Ted was in charge.

'Nothing stopping yer as I can see.' Edwin was about to go when Ted stopped him by saying, 'Yer didn't tell me he was black.'

'So?' Edwin stared at Ted pointedly.

'Nothing – just wondered where you met a darkie?'

Edwin was about to challenge him when he saw that Ted was laughing at him. 'I'd rather you didn't call him that, Ted.'

'If he wants to work here, he'll get called worse'n that!'

Which at least seemed to mean Ted had accepted George, Edwin thought, as he walked down to the big meadow. It was common knowledge that he called the lads (which included the girl stablehands, of course) the most appalling names. It was rumoured that he'd once called Aunt Mary 'a stupid cow'. No one spoke to Aunt Mary like that, but Ted Mallins was an exception.

Tomorrow was the shortest day of the year and the old man's beard and the strings of scarlet berries along the hedge reminded him of walks with Mum and Dad when he and Hugh were still kids. Mum would have liked the berries: she had a dress that colour.

George, looking smaller than Edwin had remembered, was standing in the meadow holding a long rein. Lightfoot, one of the older mares, was walking round him. Edwin approached slowly so as not to frighten either the horse or the boy.

'Hi,' he spoke quietly and for a moment George didn't hear. Then he turned round and saw Edwin.

'Hey! This is brilliant!'

George was grinning and Edwin realized that he had half expected George to be angry with him. Relief surged now through his belly. 'She's a beaut, isn't she?'

Edwin watched Lightfoot. She seemed quite calm. Horses always knew whom they could trust. She was a placid mare but even so the fact that Ted had given her to George showed he was taking George seriously.

'You betcha!' George was in his seventh heaven. He had been suspicious when the guy in the flash blue Porsche had driven up to the club and given him the note from Ed. First he thought it was some kind of trick Ed was playing. He'd shown the note to Steve, who'd just said, 'You don't wanna move outa the city, man. You got contacts here!' He hadn't shown the note to Tina. One night he'd come home to find Tina and Steve out of it, on a trip together in the flat. The kid was yelling her head off and George, worried, had taken her to the hospital where he had had to fend too many questions.

'What you wanna do a stupid fing like that for?' Tina had yelled at him.

And he had said, 'Look, she's not my kid – but I can't stand the way you treat her. So I'm off, OK?'

'Suit yourself,' Tina had yelled after him. 'You'll be back, Mister God Almighty!'

But he hadn't gone back. He'd kept the forty quid Ed'd sent him hidden in his bus pass, and he'd gone to the coach station that very night and taken a ticket to Gloucester. Arriving late at night, he'd slept in the coach station and the next morning he'd rung the number on Ed's note. An old guy had answered the phone and told him to come over. The old geezer had said very little on the phone and said even less when George met him, but there was an atmosphere that any friend of Ed's was all right by him. He'd reminded George of the only decent screw in the nick, Jim, who'd played snooker with him and some of the others on A-wing.

'Know anything about horses?' the old guy had asked, and George had had to admit he didn't.

'Don't matter — either it's in yer blood or it ain't,' the old guy had said and had given him this really cool horse to take out.

Later, after the two boys had stabled Lightfoot, Ted said, 'Guess we'll get yer up on Mandy tomorrow. Yer've the build for it.' Then, turning to Edwin: 'Aren't yer gonna show yer friend to his quarters?'

Edwin showed George the barn which Aunt Mary had converted. There was a dormitory for the boys and a separate one for the girls — and a kitchenette with a hob, a microwave oven, a washing machine and a tumble dryer, and a sitting room with a snooker table and a TV.

George didn't like to say what he really thought, which was that it looked liked bloody heaven to him so he just said, 'Great.'

'Is it all right?' Edwin was anxious. 'It's a bit rough, I know, but it's clean. And the other lads are good fun — that's girls too.'

'No, honest, it's great. Fantastic.'

George hoped Ed would go away because he was afraid he was going to cry.

'I'll leave you to settle in then. Oh,' – Edwin turned back – 'did you bring a bag?'

'I forgot it.'

Edwin thought for a minute. 'I can let you have a toothbrush, razor and so on, and some pyjamas, though mine'll be big on you.'

'This your aunt's place, then?'

Edwin flushed. He knew this was a conversation he had to have, but he couldn't bring himself to have it yet. Being a future king had never felt more embarrassing.

'Yeah. She's OK. You'll meet her, I expect. Look, I'll fetch some stuff for you. If you need anything else we can buy it in Gloucester.'

George felt suddenly paranoid. There was something fishy about all this. It was too nice. There must be a catch. Ed was acting funny. Maybe he was trying something on. 'So, why you doing this for me?'

Edwin paused. Outside, the December sun was hanging low in the afternoon sky. Above the blue-grey line of hills in the distance were streaks of pink light, heralding fine weather tomorrow. Words that his mother had spoken to him the day he started school came back to him. 'Be brave, darling,' she had whispered, 'and remember who you are.' Even then, Edwin had known she was not referring to his title. She meant something harder which had to do with courage. He took a breath.

'George,' he said, 'remember how we met, at the Princess Helena rave? Remember how you told me you had met her – how you had your photo taken with her? D'you remember how you wondered why I was there?'

George stared at Edwin. Now it's coming, George thought. It's what I thought. He's some kind of special agent or something. One of those undercover jobs you hear about. He knows about me doing drugs. He's going to do me to the police.

Edwin looked at the sun again, a red-gold plate in the sky. He hoped his mother, wherever she was, could see the sun, too. He took another breath. Despite the cold he was sweating slightly and he felt dizzy.

'You see, George, Princess Helena . . . she is . . . she was my mother.'

31

'It is no good,' Henri said to Christina beneath the sky-blue ceiling of the dining room of the Ritz on Christmas Eve. 'I have failed. There is no trace of the boy.'

Christina, who was drinking Kir Royale, took a swig. 'I do love the Ritz. So sweet of you, darling. It reminds me of the Marquis.'

The experience of looking for the boy called Hector had so affected Henri that he did not even wince at the choice of venue. In his mind this meal, in one of England's most celebrated hotels, was a kind of wake – a fitting lament for Alice and her lost son and the wealthy life she had left behind.

Christina, remembering her manners, said, 'Tell me about it, my dear. Last I heard, you were going to that perfectly *foul*-sounding place – in Ruislip, wasn't it? – with the introduction I got you from Toby?'

'Heston.' Henri spoke grimly. Christina's contacts had turned out to include an Inspector of Prisons who had engineered a meeting with the Governor of the Young Offenders' Institute in

Heston where Iris Fisher had said her sister's adopted son had been committed.

'Toby always fancied me.' Christina was ruminative, swilling the raspberry-tinted bubbles round the glass. Alan had been made redundant from his computer firm and had taken to hanging around the flat asking her where she was going. A man with his work cut out, inspecting England's malfunctioning prison system, might be a jollier bet. So she had been pleased to instigate the contact with Toby Marcheson.

Henri, his eye half on the brunette at the next table while Christina visited the Powder Room ('So sweet, here – they let one change from top to toe – I once had to change even my stockings, darling!') recalled his visit to the unlovely building in West Middlesex which constituted the last leg of his search for Alice's boy. Quite what he would have done with the child if he found him he had never determined. It was all academic, anyway: of the whereabouts of the lost boy-child of Alicia Fenton-Kirk there was no clear record.

The governor, whose institution had been inspected by Christina's Toby Marcheson, was on his toes. 'I've dug out the lists – as you see, we have several Botswanas and three or four Fishers.'

How appalling, Henri thought, that so many of England's youth should be confined in this unremedial atmosphere.

Scrutiny of the records revealed a George Botswana, with a date of birth which matched little 'Baby Fenton-Kirk', whose relics Henri now carried in his pocket everywhere. George Botswana's address was given in the dismissal records, as 345 Harbour Road W6. Of course, Henri had thought, the Christian name too would have been changed at the adoption. He had never thought to ask the name of Iris Fisher.

The record showed that George Botswana been out since last April on parole. The parole was up in June; it seemed there was no way of tracing him beyond that time. Henri knew he had not returned to the Harbour Road. Iris Fisher's greed would have told him.

'Is there, perhaps, an address besides . . . ? The parole officer maybe?'

The Governor did not remember the boy himself but he was keen to be obliging. Toby Marcheson's last report on the institute had criticized it on forty-nine points. There had been questions asked in the Commons. The Governor's job might well rest on his capacity to oblige this Frenchman whose connection with the late inmate of Heston remained mysterious. Christina had done her work well: clearly her prison-inspecting friend had put the fear of God into Heston's Governor.

The Governor telephoned a local probation service while Henri inspected the print of Van Gogh's bridge on the facing wall. 'Do you think my pictures will ever sell?' the destitute artist had asked his brother. Poor Vincent! Incarcerated for so long himself his sympathy would have all gone to these young spirits who were also incarcerated. But how his passionate individuality would have deplored the bleak surrounds.

'They'll call me back. Tea?'

'Thank you, no. I drink only coffee?'

'Oh, I think we can rise to that, y'know!'

It was interesting how cordiality, in the wrong environment, could be experienced as assault. Henri found himself, more than ever, empathizing with Alice's son. 'Thank you, I take only coffee made with beans.'

The Governor, his hospitality worsted by French fastidiousness, settled into a restless silence. Henri could feel patches of sweat collecting under his armpits.

It was apparent that the Governor was not a man who liked waiting. It was interesting to reflect that his job was the supervision of an organized wait for many thousands of young lives.

'I think we'll try one of the officers. They're known as "screws" here – even by us, I'm afraid. The inmates have other names for them!' The man behind the vast desk had smiled conspiratorially and Henri, to deflect the impulse to punch him, asked the question.

'What names?'

'Oh, "kangers" – from kangaroo, you know, it's all rhyming slang. I had a female from one of those new universities on at me the other day. Wanted to do a thesis on it. Extraordinary, don't you think? It changes, of course, all the time. I heard "XR2" recently. Kind of car. Do you have them?'

They were both relieved when the officer, who had been summoned, knocked at the door.

The officer, Jim, knew the name immediately. 'George, sir? Yes, I knew George. He was on A-wing, sir. Bright lad, could've made something of his self, sir.'

'A-wing is our therapeutic wing. We're rather keen on it,' the Governor explained. 'They do group therapy – that sort of thing.' Henri speculated that a few good modern paintings or pieces of sculpture about the place would have been likely to be more beneficial to the inmates.

'All the wings are named after birds here. A is for Albatross.'

Dear Lord, Henri thought, what great mind in the arena of penal planning came up with that idea?

Of the prisoner officer he asked, 'Do you have any notion where the boy might have gone, if he did not go home, that is?'

Jim was apologetic. ''Fraid not, sir. Some of them exchange names and addresses and that when they're let out, but George didn't mix much. He was always a bit of a loner, know what I mean?'

And he did, of course, know what Jim meant. Henri's feet clattered coldly on the steps as he walked down from the Governor's office. The probation service had rung through with a hostel address for George Botswana. The Governor had insisted on ringing it himself.

'It's not much, I'm afraid, but it's the best I can do. They're not the most inviting of places. But maybe if you ask . . .' he trailed off, reluctant to admit his inability to help further the visitor's enquiry.

Henri walked back through the overwhelming noise of the visiting hall. A fight had broken out between two gangs of visitors and Henri saw the prison officers gag and haul two of the inmates away to cries of 'XR2, XR2 – dirty kangaroo, dirty kangaroo, you went behind the dustbins and did a dirty poo.' An image of Alice, sitting naked on the copper *Madonna* singing – flashed into his mind. What was it she had sung?

The thought obsessed him as he made his way back toward the tube station. He was becoming quite an aficionado of the London underground. No wonder there was a collapse of values here if people were required to travel like this – like convicts going for hard labour. The visit to Heston Young Offenders' Institute had depressed him profoundly. If this didn't work he would give up, abandon the search and return to Paris. Anyway, there was an official unveiling of *Madonna* planned for the New Year and he should be there.

So now, a week later, he was sitting, in this very different ambience, taking leave of England. From the depths of Heston to the sublime Ritz – the extremes of England. The hostel had thrown up no clues. Only a man dressed in leathers, about Henri's own age, had remembered a George Botswana.

'Yeah, I remember George, like,' he had said, taking off dark glasses to reveal dilated pupils. He was plainly smashed on something. Life, probably. The hostel looked as dire as the prison. 'He weren't here much. Truth to tell, he was living under the M4 most of his time here, right? They don't check once you're here. They say they do, but they don't. Near Chiswick way, right? He was cool, Georgie. Tell him "Cheers" from Dave, yeah?'

Recalling that visit, as he hailed a cab to take Christina home, Henri thought, how can they expect England's youth to find any level of decency in such an environment? He remembered his own wild young days and praised the Lord for the brothels of Paris. Only the kindness of experienced older women had saved him from actions which would have surely led to prison. Instead of which he had found a way of stamping his spirit on the world by means of copper rather than, so to speak, lead piping.

Suddenly the song that Alice had sung him as she had sat that day in his studio, swinging her legs on the copper sculpture, came back to him. 'The darkest hour is just before dawn.' But for her there had been no dawn. He had failed her and now he had failed in his search for her child, Baby Fenton-Kirk – Hector – otherwise known as George Botswana.

32

There came a day when Dr Asklepios arrived and asked her to join him on the boat. They set out to sea with a wind behind them. It became apparent he was an accomplished sailor.

'It is a good lesson, you see,' – he was paying out a rope to let out the sail – 'tacking. It is a lesson for life. You make an aim and you steer towards it but the progress is not straight.' Here she had to duck as the boom swung across by her head. 'No, it is from side to side one must go.'

'What is our aim now, then? Where are we going?'

And really she did not mind where. It felt free on the water.

'Across to the mainland. I have my own route. We go past the cave of Proteus, the Old Man of the Sea. If you are lucky we will see some of my Great Uncle's dolphins.'

The boys and she had swum with dolphins.

'Look at the sea! "Wine-dark" the blind poet called it. What a temper he had, but his poetry' – Dr Asklepios gave an admiring whistle – 'I swear we've never heard sweeter since.'

The water didn't look much like wine to her. 'It's not red. Why did he call it "wine-dark"?'

He was tacking along the far end of the island. 'Porpoises, see?'

Ahead and to the right she saw them leap like curved silver arrows – a whole school of them. Hugh would love them. Eds too. How were her boys? Dear boys. Dr Asklepios had said she would see them again.

'It is because the Ancients used to add the wine to the water.' Dr Asklepios steered neatly through the porpoises. 'It made the water dark with wine – opaque. Would you like some, by the way? My immortal throat is parched. There should be a bottle in the basket down below. Angela packed us a picnic.'

Some hours later they dropped anchor in a bay surrounded by rocky cliffs. A colony of dark, long-throated birds were calling harshly from the craggy ledges.

'Ithaka,' said Dr Asklepios briefly. 'Odysseus's island.'

It appeared they were spending the night. She usually changed into a white night-gown to sleep in; it transpired that Angela had packed that too.

'Dr Asklepios, you are a mystery monger. Where are you taking me?' But he was busy coiling rope and didn't answer.

They ate the picnic – bread, cheese and tomatoes with glasses of wine and a couple of crabs she caught for them on a line over the side. Afterwards Dr Asklepios pointed out the planets in the night sky.

'There's Aphrodite – you call her Venus – Zeus knows why you have taken over those vulgar Roman names – and there's her lover Ares, Mars to you.'

'Yes she told me about the lover.'

He looked at her questioningly across his pipe. The moon was almost full and its near-circular reflection in the water below illuminated her face as if from a lighted looking-glass. Her expression was quite serene. 'Ah, Dr Asklepios. I am past all that, thanks to you.'

And to be sure she had stood the test well. Needling no longer brought on any jealous protestations.

'Aphrodite was not always so composed. Once she too lost a love.'

'And what happened?'

'There is a flower. She grieved so deeply, my father brings him back each year in the spring.'

So Aphrodite did have feelings! 'I'd like to see the flower.'

'I expect you will. Where I am taking you the anemone grows wild.'

The next day they set sail accompanied by two dolphins who made hoops above the sea beside her. Seeing the dolphins reminded her of something.

'Dr Asklepios, should I have said good-bye to Hestia?'

'That one has her own way of doing these things.'

'I only talked to her once, but it seems rude . . .'

'She *spoke* to you?'

'Yes, didn't I say?'

So Hestia had recognized the signs. There would be no further need of him soon. He sighed. Success, though gratifying, was not always welcome.

They anchored off a rocky cove and she rowed them ashore, the dolphins coming part of the way, in a small round coracle which took some handling. 'No, really,' she had said. 'I'd like to. I need the exercise.'

On the cliff-top was a familiar sight – the forest green van with the snake emblem on its side.

'What a long way I've come since you brought me in that!'

She did not lie down in the back this time. Instead she sat between the driver, a young man wearing a hat, and Dr Asklepios whose bulk created quite a squash. The young man lent her his hat which she wore, turned back to front like Eds's baseball cap, to shade her eyes from the wintry sun.

Driving along, Dr Asklepios sang an ancient Greek song all about the slaying of some centaurs, and she taught them both an early Beatles song, which was the oldest song she knew. Dr Asklepios got quite carried away singing the 'yeah, yeah, yeahs' and had to be calmed by the young man who, she noticed, had a snake tattooed on his arm.

'More snakes.' She nodded at the tattoo to Dr Asklepios but he had fallen asleep with his mouth open and was snoring.

'Are you one of his team?' she asked the dark young man. He had not said anything, only joining in with the 'yeah, yeah, yeahs' in a convivial sort of way.

'I am part of big team,' he replied. 'I move folk about.'

And, indeed, he moved the green van with a speed and efficiency that was almost like flying. Once they came to a crossroads where she would have sworn she saw an old-fashioned carriage pulled by mules. She had tensed up, waiting for the young man to brake but he sped by negotiating the obstruction smoothly.

The countryside was bare and hilly; light from the winter sun fell in pale gold tranches. The van must have had a special air-conditioning system because there was an aromatic smell, like pine – unless it was the smell of the trees which they passed. She filled her lungs with the energizing smell.

A subtle exhilaration was seeping through her – almost she felt it filling her physical tissues with excitement. Dr Asklepios was still snoring. She turned to the young man.

'Do you know where we are going? You must.'

For reply he merely nodded. Maybe he did not speak her language. He was not so much taciturn, she decided, as reserved. Keeping his own counsel. But friendly enough. After all, he'd lent her his hat.

She twisted the hat round on her head and felt something

soft, like a flower or a bird. Taking it off to inspect she saw two small dark feathered wings on either side of the brim. It was not at all cold in the van but she shivered. The young man smiled at her.

'It is useful,' he said, 'when you wear – people not see.'

'I could have done with it in the old days.'

'You look.' He reached across and pulled down the blind so that the mirror was in front of her face. 'Look,' he said again.

Nothing there. She could see half of Dr Asklepios's slouched belly and the van's green interior. But of her own face, which should have been staring back at her – nothing. It struck her then that she hadn't looked in a mirror since – well, before it all happened. There had been no mirrors on the island.

'Where have I gone?' It made her giggle. 'Is it a kind of trick?'

'Watch,' said the young man.

They had drawn into a filling station and he jumped down and started to open the cap for the petrol. A woman came out and spoke to him. After a moment he gesticulated towards the van and she reached inside, picking up for him an oily cloth wedged under the driver's seat. It was evident, from the garage hand's movements, that she could see only Dr Asklepios asleep on the far side of the van. The other passenger, the young woman in the yellow gown, wearing the hat with wings, was wholly invisible to her.

Some miles down the road she asked, as if about to solve a puzzle, 'Why are you here?'

'I am – what you say – escort? I take across – from one side to the other.'

'Of course he doesn't mix with the people much.' Dr Asklepios spoke conversationally. They were walking through a pine grove where the driver of the green van had dropped them after

207

negotiating the path with his usual skill. 'I see he has lent you his hat. Without it he will be seen, visible, and that he does not like. I've not known him lend it before. He must have taken a shine to you.'

They were coming towards a gate. She could see a notice. The words in English read EPIDAURUS: ANCIENT SITE.

'Your home?' she enquired.

He smiled, pleased, and she saw he had somehow acquired a rather crumpled blue denim suit and a pair of sun-glasses.

'You', he said, answering her surprised look, 'have no need of any change.' He gestured at the hat. 'No one can see you. But I must assume the invisibility of the commonplace. Therefore, behold, I am a doctor, a psychiatrist from Thessaloniki. You approve the transformation?'

A hassle broke out over the price of the entrance-ticket. Dr Asklepios wanted a senior citizen's special rate but could produce no proof of his birth date.

'This is a farce even Aristophanes could not write! Here I am, nearly as old as Time, and I do not get the half-price ticket even into my own home!' He disappeared and returned with a Magnum ice-cream.

'Like some?' he enquired, licking the chocolate vigorously.

'Absolutely not!' she replied. 'I gave those up long ago. Wherever did you get such tastes?'

'It is good for the blood sugar. This business of being human is stressful.

'Also, it is the great advantage of immortality,' he explained a little later, as he conducted her down a rough pathway, 'one has the opportunity to acquire an infinity of pleasures. And this, too, is such a pleasure – to show you my home.'

They had strolled, in a companionable way, until they came to an area which was roped off. It looked as if there was archaeological work taking place. Tools were lying about but no workers to be seen. Although December, it was still very mild and a late butterfly, deceived by the warmth, flittered past.

'Look,' she said, 'a Brimstone.'

Dr Asklepios looked at the delicate yellow butterfly which was opening and shutting its wings in the sunlight on a tumbled wall. 'Psyche,' he said. 'For us it is the symbol of psyche, or soul, if you prefer. The butterfly.'

'I dreamt about a butterfly,' she said, looking at the roped-off remains. It must have been once part of a circular building. 'Last night, in the boat. There was this bug sort of thing. Brown. Maggotty. It was revolting-looking – I didn't like it. There was a fire – I think like the bonfires we used to build with Daddy, at the bottom of the garden, at home – and I chucked the maggotty thing into the flames. And then I felt awful that I'd done it – you know, killed something living. But then as I watched the flames, sort of horrified, I saw a butterfly emerging from the heat and the smoke. It flew up and over the flames and I was so relieved and happy that I hadn't killed it. It was quite beautiful . . .'

. . . it was dark in the round house, the Tholos, they called it. I had to leave all my things, all my clothes behind. They gave me a white robe to wear – nothing on my feet. It was cold too – though the sun was shining outside.

Someone came and blindfolded me – even though it was so dark I could hardly see my hand before my face – and led me inside the labyrinth. They turned me round three times – like when I played as a child, with my brother, in our father's garden – then they let me go. I had been told before I entered that I might never come back.

I went on, feeling my way along the stone wall – curving inwards – whenever I came to a branch in the track I always chose to go inwards. At the beginning I had made a decision – if there is a choice, take the inward turn. It smelt worse as I went further in. I didn't know now if that had been the right choice but I made it anyway. In, in, into the dark.

After a while I came up against a wall and I stopped and drank from the flask they had given me. I thought it would be water from the sacred spring – but it wasn't water – it was wine. Sweet wine.

The wine warmed me and helped me decide what to do next, which was to feel my way along the wall until I found a ledge just wide enough to take a body stretched out. I stretched out my body and waited in the dark.

The dark was old. Older than the sun and the light which I knew from my life outside. And I knew that the god who lived here was older than the earth. As old as the cosmos itself. I had heard about the snake – it was why I had come – although I couldn't quite remember now why I had come at all. Everything from the old life seemed so far away.

I must have dropped off for a while, for suddenly I was wide awake and aware of a tremendous presence – no sound, just an immense silence going back, one might guess, to the beginnings of time.

And then, just as I was being lulled by the silence, there was the pain – a pain so sharp and so fierce that I knew I could not survive it – too terrible to cry out – no time to say good-bye to the old life – only a hiss as it slithered away and my mind slithering away too, following the creature into the heart of the labyrinth, before me only two faces from my past . . .

'. . . the boys,' she said. She was half-sitting, propped against Dr Asklepios's arm. The sun was shining through the pine trees. They were quite alone.

Dr Asklepios was no longer wearing the denim suit but was back in his familiar gown.

'Here, drink this.' He handed her a bottle. 'Just a few drops on the tongue, if you please.'

She tipped the bottle obediently. Small drops of fiery sweetness. 'It's like the wine in . . .'

'Just so. And we examine now the bite.' He extended his plump hand to her foot. 'Healing nicely. A touch of tincture of myrrh, I think. But you have excellent antibodies. There will hardly be a scar.'

Looking down at her left ankle, on to which he was shaking a dark brown liquid from a small phial, she saw a scarlet wound. It made a coil round the ankle bone. 'It's like a snake.'

'But of course.' He spoke matter-of-factly. 'Can you walk on it? I am afraid we do not have the luxury of Hermes for our journey back. They are very stingy with their resources at headquarters. It is like those department stores which have the escalators going up and then, after you have made the expensive purchases, the stairs down.'

It was no longer a matter of novelty to her that Dr Asklepios knew about department stores. If she had met him at Saks, Fifth Avenue, she would not have been surprised.

'Will we see him again?' She had liked Hermes. 'Oh! his hat. I forgot it. It must be in the . . .'

'They will send it on. They are accustomed to lost property there. And he can always pick it up himself.'

There was an off-hand tone in Dr Asklepios's voice. Was he jealous? She sensed he did not wish to pursue the topic of their dark young driver.

For a while they pressed on through the pines until they came to a natural clearing where they paused. Looking down, she could see the ancient site beneath them.

'That is the Tholos,' he said. Below you could make out remains of round marking in the herbiage. 'You see it well in winter.' She squinted down. A young man, clearly an archaeologist, was talking to a group of tourists. 'And that, over there, is the theatre. They still put plays on there today.'

He pointed towards a high semi-circle of tiered seats. 'It is the most famous thing about the place now. Very few, these days, know about the other.'

'The Tholos, you mean? Do you mind?'

He was having, she could tell, one of his occasional patches of melancholy. Suddenly she felt a rush of fondness for him. He had been hard on her, over the months, but she thought she understood now why. Realizing this, she knew she loved him very much, but not in the silly fixated way of before. On an impulse she hugged him.

'Hey, what is this? I am older than the hills, remember.' None the less she saw he was pleased. 'No, I don't mind, since you ask, that they come merely to gawp at the theatre. It is a fine specimen, even if the imbeciles have restored it rather badly, and it keeps the philistines away from the sanctuary. Only the true initiates come to the Tholos, where the healing is.'

'Am I a "true initiate", Dr Asklepios?'

He looked at her. Her gown was hitched up where she had belted it at the waist to give greater freedom to her long stride. Tall and graceful, her expression looked out at the world, tentative but unafraid. She looked quite at peace. The yellow gown, tucked over at her waist, gave the impression of folded wings.

'You, my dear,' he came towards her and placed the lightest of kisses on her brown forehead. 'Look at you. You have become a butterfly. A beautiful, rare butterfly.'

INTERVAL

If you take the coast road from Athens, driving south, you will come to the ancient temple to Poseidon at Sounion where the delinquent poet Byron famously carved his initials in the dazzling-seeming marble. But there is another route to Sounion, by an inland road, and if you take that less-travelled route perhaps you will pass, on your way to the great temple of the god of the sea, a signpost to the small hamlet of Vavrona, home of the ancient site of Brauron.

At ancient Brauron the sanctuary of Artemis Brauronia lies at the foot of a low hill just beyond the little Byzantine chapel of Ayios Yeoryios – St George, to you and me. There, if you go, you will find the remnants of the old cult of Artemis, for Artemis was a goddess known in these parts long before the Greeks of the Classical period found her and made her theirs. Here you can see the remains of the heyday of her worship: the stoa shaped like the Greek 'π' where the 'little bears', the young girls who served the goddess, lived in small chambers round a great court-yard; and the steps hewn out of rock, the 'holy-steps', as they were named, which led up to the Doric-columned temple.

In the small museum a visitor may see some of the most charming sculptures of the ancient world: a child carrying a dove, a small girl with a hare – emblems of the goddess's affinity with young children and animals – for, despite the fact that Artemis is the goddess of the hunt, she is also goddess of childbirth, of fertility and healing. And you may see, too, the ancient bridge, old as any bridge in the West, which the young girls would cross when they went to fetch water.

In the dried-up pool before the temple, where the sacred spring once bubbled, archaeologists have found votive offerings – at least they call them this, but I wonder. Have you noticed how often we take for true what we read? Imagine an archaeologist (and it is the case I am imagining a male archaeologist, for by and large men are less astute in their imaginings than women) imagine then, if you will, some male archaeologist in the year 7000 (for that is how far ahead you will need to travel in your mind if we are to keep the parallel exact) trawling through your possessions. The possessions he trawls will be randomly chosen, for chance and nature will have sifted off the bulk of your things and only a few will survive the evolutionary principle of time. These are the survivors of your life.

Let us suppose then, just as example, that it is the contents of your bathroom cabinet our imaginary archaeologist finds. If it is anything like mine it will contain something like the following: a box of sticking plasters; a bottle of gargle; a blunt razor; two mascaras, in colours which make your eyes sting; a spray cologne which you gave your husband or your boyfriend, or even your son last Christmas and which he is too polite to throw away; bath oil which he gave you – ditto; a blue eye-bath which no one ever uses; a small plastic toy which your younger son took from your elder son in the bath twenty years ago and which caused such a row between them that you confiscated it – both your children now have beards but you can't bear to throw 'Greedo' away because it reminds you of when their skin was soft and they cried when you left them at play-school; an ear-ring which might belong to one of the sons' girlfriends but you aren't quite sure which and since it may be the one that came just the once, when the regular one was in Hong Kong, you can't ask for fear of making some awful blunder; some throat lozenges; a device for getting blackheads out of your nose; a purple flower on elastic, for keeping your hair out of the bath; some oil of spike lavender; a heel cushion. 'Obviously,' – the male archaeologist of the year 6098 is going to pronounce, anxious to retain his credibility with the scholastic community – 'these are votive offerings.'

Well, yes, of a kind. You see, I think that those bronze mirrors and combs, the jewelled belts and rings and small ornaments, seem more like the pretty artefacts that women and girls the world over take pleasure in having about them. And maybe Artemis was not so different from the rest of us women. Maybe she had no need of the 'votive offerings' we read about on museum cards.

Let me tell you about the 'little bears'. They were so called because this is the site of Artemis Brauronia, Artemis of the Bear. It is said that long ago Agamemnon's daughter, Iphigenia, came here from Tauris bringing with her a great wooden effigy of the goddess and accidentally killed the sacred bear who had guarded the site for Artemis. The story of Iphigenia is interesting, because she is one of those men or women (there are more of them about than our Christian civilization would have us think) who, like our own God's son, have died and returned to life. Her father, Agamemnon, sacrificed Iphigenia for a wind – a mistake you may say, to sacrifice your favourite daughter, especially to a goddess like Artemis who was defensive of young women. Poor Agamemnon got his comeuppance though, because his wife murdered him a while later, and I can understand that – a daughter for a wind? The wrong priorities, you might say. (Though there is more to it than this, in the story of Agamemnon and his wife but that is for another day.) Right now I am telling you about Iphigenia because cunning Artemis watched how she went to her death, bravely and with her head held high. Artemis is a ballsy goddess. She likes courage. So, I suppose, she thought, 'That's too good to lose,' and she let Iphigenia appear to die, before whisking her away to one of her own fastnesses.

First she whisked her to Tauris, a savage-sounding place in the Crimea, but after a while she brought her here, to ancient Brauron, where the bear was. Somehow I doubt that Iphigenia killed that bear. She learned to be a huntress but she doesn't sound to me the bear-slaying type. More likely, I think, the bear

217

represented a side of Artemis – the fierce side that will swipe you with its great paw if you do not respect her. The young girls, who were chosen every four years to serve at the temple, were called 'little bears' as a kind of pretty compliment to this fierce side of the goddess whose life-giving side you can also find in Ephesus, were she is shown with many breasts.

By the humble little Byzantine chapel to St George, which I recommend you visit if you have the time, is a rocky cavern. It is said that when the priestess of the goddess Artemis finally died, she was buried here and that this is her tomb of Iphigenia. Through the centuries the shrine has always been visited by local people, sick in body or sick at heart, for the priestess of the ancient sanctuary of Artemis Brauronia was credited with powers of great healing. At dawn or dusk, over the years, a lone woman has occasionally been seen there, seeking a cure for barrenness, or a mother might bring her crippled son, or a wife a husband on whom the doctors have given up.

Early one evening, in late March, Spyros Nicolaides was walking with his wife Caroline in the sanctuary at Brauron. The spring solstice was approaching and the evenings had begun to lighten. Spyros, who was a poet and still believed in the ancient goddesses, was pondering a poem he was writing. His wife, who collected all kinds of animals but especially amphibians, had gone off with the net she carried in their car for such occasions. She was hoping to catch tadpoles in the nearby marshy swamps of Vavrona.

Suddenly their dog, Titus, began to bark. Spyros tried to calm Titus – the sound of the barking dog was disturbing his sense of metre – but the dog refused to be quieted and rushed off into the bushy growth which surrounds the Tomb of Iphigenia. An answering bark fuelled Spyros's suspicions. There was a bitch around somewhere. Caro always refused to have her dogs castrated, 'I wouldn't do it to a human male,' she said, 'and frankly

I prefer dogs to most men – so why should I do it to Titus?'

Spyros didn't necessarily agree with Caro on this matter but in their day-to-day arrangements she was in charge of the animals. 'Nature is your goddess,' he used to say to her. For his part he still believed in the old religions.

But now it looked as if Caro's indulgence was going to mean some bitch was going to be impregnated by the ebullient Titus. And not every dog-owner wants the trouble of disposing of mongrel pups of unprepossessing antecedents. Titus, though a handsome dog, had no pedigree at all – which was another reason Caro liked him.

What Spyros did not like was the idea of having to deal with some irate dog owner on the subject of Titus's dynastic urges. Wishing that his wife would hurry back from her tadpole hunt, he plunged into the undergrowth.

Andreas Hylades had also been to the shrine that day. He had been teased and chidden more than he could bear at the school which was run by the local priest. The priest was old and could no longer keep order. He preferred to sit in the sun and smoke and let the older boys keep order, which they did by bullying.

Andreas had been born 'not quite the full shilling', as the Irish say, which made him a ripe target for the school bullies. His mother had tried to abort him when she was four months pregnant. She had been unsuccessful in her attempt but the boy child had been born with a twist in his spine and slowness in his speech. His grandmother, who was devoted to her love-child grandson, called him 'child of Zeus' after the father of the gods who was known for his tendency to sow his seed widely and profusely. Andreas's grandmother, who had no time for priests, had taken him to the shrine when he was only four years old. 'See here,' she had said. 'You pray to the Lady Iphigenia. She will watch over you.'

Andreas's grandmother had died last year. When he missed her, he went up to the sanctuary. Few people went there outside the summer season, and if there were tourists he could dodge them and hide in the cave which was the tomb of the Lady Iphigenia. He knew the way through the top of the cave, where the rocks have lain fallen since before the birth of Jesus.

Andreas, too, heard a dog barking that day in late March. He liked dogs and, believing that one had maybe fallen into the cave, he climbed down himself to investigate.

Maria Massourides had lost her fourth baby in the summer. Each time she had gone the full term and each time she had prayed to the Holy Virgin that she may be delivered of a healthy child. But the fourth baby had been stillborn, like her brothers and sisters. Now Maria's husband was threatening to divorce her. 'You are not a proper woman,' he had jibed. 'Look, my comrades all laugh at me. I better find myself a proper woman.'

An old woman from her mother's village, Loutsa, had told her once that she should go to ask favour from the shrine of Iphigenia, priestess of Artemis, at Vavrona. 'She was the goddess of child-bearing since long ago,' the old woman had said. 'When I couldn't fall pregnant first, I went to her. She sent me seven children, heaven help me!'

Maria had taken the Fiat and driven out on the inland road from Athens. Her husband was watching football that evening down at the stadium.

All three visitors to the shrine of Iphigenia, if asked, would have said they had seen that afternoon or evening two young women but not a soul else. The smaller of the two women had a dog, a black-and-grey spaniel who had welcomed the advances of the Nicolaides' dog Titus with a playful zeal. The other woman was, all would have agreed, unusually tall. She was wearing a yellow gown and a kind of light emanated from her. To each she had appeared and spoken but what she said was kept by each secret. Each recalled to themselves that she had the most compelling eyes.

Spyros the poet, who was subject to melancholy, astonished his wife, when she returned with a jar brimming with tadpoles, by whirling her round in a kind of madcap impromptu dance. They drove back to their home in a leafy suburb of Athens singing old songs and the following day Spyros wrote an epic poem.

When Maria returned home she was surprised to find her husband there before her. 'Where have you been?' he asked angrily.

'Just out,' she replied.

'I don't want you wandering about with other men looking at you,' was his surprising response. 'You're too attractive to be safe. I want you to stay close to me from now on.' That night they made passionate love and it was not to the Virgin Mary that Maria prayed the following morning.

'O, Artemis,' she murmured, on her knees in the park, 'if I have conceived, please keep the baby safe.'

The boy Andreas had no one to speak to after the encounter. His mother had left to work in Athens. After his grandmother died, Andreas had lived a makeshift sort of existence between various aunts and uncles, belonging fully to no one household. He remained in the sanctuary after he had met the tall lady, holing up in one of the other rocky caves which people said were also tombs.

III

RESOLUTION

33

'There is nothing in life that is not better faced.'

James's godfather had said this to him once and, instinctively, James had known the truth of it. His godfather's words came back to him now. It was nerve-racking to be in Paris again. But it was also right. Shadows were better faced.

He had needed to return to the place where he had seen her last. To settle things inside himself. And the great cathedral, Notre Dame, nourished and calmed his mind. Looking up at the high dark-blue wheels of light, the rose windows that faced each other across the cathedral transepts, he thought of the thousands of anonymous artists who had died giving their life to the place of worship named for the Mother of God. They had never known the legacy of long delight they had left behind them. That was what true humility was, James speculated: when you offer what you have, your gift, he supposed it was, without thought of personal return. In her own way his mother knew about that.

The 'official' cause of the visit, the unveiling of a new statue by Henri Astaffort – a sculptor James had hardly heard of – was not, in itself, enticing. But the setting for the new work, the Jardin Shakespeare, was. James, himself, had half-thought of a Shakespeare Garden at home. Looking up at the light streaming through the vivid blue mandalas set on the arms of the cathedral's cross, it had seemed almost as if they were winking at him, as if sharing some vast celestial secret. If he had a gift at all it was for recognizing what was worthwhile in England's heritage. And working to save it because, slice it how you liked, all governments were the same. Whichever way you vote, the government gets in! Look how this one, with all their talk on education, were butchering the arts.

The Prince was surprised to find that the new sculpture was very much to his tastes. Astaffort's *Madonna* had just the blend of the traditional and the contemporary he enjoyed. And there was something about it too which touched him. Large and curvaceous as the image was, it somehow reminded him of his wife. He motioned to his secretary to ensure he had a chance to talk to the sculptor.

Henri felt a mixture of excitement and dismay when he descended from the Eurostar at Waterloo. It was late March, over three months since he had been in England. Irrevocably now the place was associated with the fruitless search for Alice's son, which he had abandoned last Christmas.

Since the disappearance of Alice, Henri had become curious about the Royal Family – for there had been set up in his mind that link between Alice and the English Princess. It had given him an interest in her husband, Prince James. And then there had been the splendid piece of fortune: the Prince, over in Paris, had been so taken by the copper *Madonna* that he wanted one of his own in the new garden he was planning, which was to be laid out with the flowers mentioned in Shakespeare's texts.

Republican as Henri was, he was nevertheless flattered to be working for a man whose taste in culture redeemed him from the usual charge against the English aristocracy of philistinism. James not only knew who Henry Moore was, he had likened his work to Henri's.

'I like the maternal quality,' James had said, patting one of the copper *Madonna*'s generous breasts. 'It is archetypal. When can you come over and do me something similar?' When he talked about a subject which touched him, the Prince had a most winning smile.

So, back in England, where the search for Alice's son had defeated him, Henri was on his way to the house in Gloucestershire to survey the new Shakespeare Garden which James was planting.

It had been tough for Edwin, leaving Dad and Aunt Mary and, especially, George and returning to school after Christmas. Just as he'd got things sorted with George too.

At first George was pretty knocked out by his confession and had gone all strange and different. He had called him 'sir' a few times, which Edwin had found really creepy.

It had got better though, gradually, over the Christmas holidays. Ted had helped enormously by treating Edwin with his usual sour humour. Once when George had fallen off Mandy and had looked as if he was upset by it, Ted had rescued the situation by gesturing at Edwin. 'Look at himself now,' Ted had said. 'He's bin arse over tit more times than I've had hot meals. Mind you, he's like his Dad, not got a bad seat these days.' Which was praise from Ted.

Christmas was something they had just sort of had to get through. The first one was bound to be the worst. There had been one good moment though. One day he had been hanging round the yard – George had been off on Mandy with Ted –

and Aunt Mary had gone off to Tesco's to get what she referred to as 'Christmas grub'. Matt and the cousins had gone with Hugh to give their presents to Great-Grandma. Somehow, he had not felt like going so he had been allowed to send his present – a foot-stool he'd been making – with Hugh. Hugh was giving Great-Grandma a sauce-boat.

They had all gone and he was wondering what to do, enjoying the chance to be alone, when a van had drawn up at the bottom of the lane. It had disappeared before he got to the gate. Lying beside the mail-box was a big wooden crate with a notice on it: LIVESTOCK – PLEASE HANDLE GENTLY. Stuck on the crate besides was a green envelope addressed to him.

Inside the envelope was an import licence, a set of instructions for hibernating tortoises, and a cryptic word: Hestia.

Dad had been very concerned and had telephoned the London zoo and all kinds of people. It seemed the tortoise was a true bill. All the import papers were in order and no one seemed to know anything about her. So Edwin was allowed to keep her – although he had so far only peeked through the straw in her box. She was asleep – the tortoise – in her high-domed yellowy patterned shell. And heavy! It had taken a wheelbarrow to get the crate up to the stables.

Edwin hadn't said so but he kind of guessed that the tortoise arriving like that had maybe to do with Mum not being with them at Christmas. And, he couldn't have quite said why, it helped. The unexpected arrival of the tortoise had also helped break the ice with George, and bit by bit they had become real friends. It was hard thinking of George at Aunt Mary's learning to be a 'lad' while he himself had to go back to school where they guarded him as if he was a prisoner or something. Not that he ought to joke about that because both George and Ted had really 'done time'.

Edwin had heard them one day. Ted had said to George,

'You done H.M.P. then?' and George had said,
'Y.O.I. – nine months.'
'I done ten,' Ted had said. 'You get parole?'
At which George had nodded and Edwin had felt quite out
of it when George had explained later that Y.O.I. meant Young
Offenders' Institute.

Another time Ted had said, 'There's no drugs allowed here,
see! Any drugs and yer out on yer arse – whoever yer has as yer
mate. See?'

Later, when the two of them were alone again, Edwin had
said, 'Do you do drugs, George?' and George had said aggressively,
'No but I used to. Puff, Pox, H, Tackle, Brown, Gear, Rocks,
Acid, E's – you name it, I've done it. All right?'

They hadn't spoken much for a few days until, one day in
the yard, George had muttered, 'Sorry mate, dodgy subject. No
offence?' and everything had been OK again.

It was a comfort to think of Ted keeping an eye on George.
He was keen to impress Ted. That would stop him going back
to drugs.

It was good to get back home again from school for the start of
the Easter holidays. He and Hugh were living with Dad now but
they all still spent a lot of time over at Aunt Mary's. She had been
really great in helping him and George move on this business of
finding George's real mother. And really they had done brilliantly,
Edwin thought to himself. George had been to all the social
workers, who had helped him get hold of his birth certificate. It
looked as if it mightn't be too hard to find George's mother
because her name was quite unusual. Aunt Mary had known the
procedures from her work with children – it was her had told
George exactly who he had to ring.

Edwin's aunt had never asked why her nephew had taken up
with the small new stable lad with the nose-stud and ear-rings.

'As long as he's happy, I don't mind,' she had said to her husband. 'Anyhow, Ted thinks the kid's a natural horseman.'

'Oh, well, if *Ted* thinks he's all right . . .' Tom had joshed her.

James was looking forward to the arrival of the French sculptor. The best part of the past three months had been the way he was able to enjoy art and poetry again. *Madonna*, the copper piece in the Paris garden, had moved him. There was something in the sculpture's free lines which reminded him of the boys' mother when she was nursing them as babies.

'I'm seeing this Parisian sculptor first thing tomorrow,' he had said to Mary, who had rung to invite him to Sunday lunch. 'But, yes, after that I'd love to come over. I'll send the boys on ahead, shall I?'

But Astaffort's views on art were too absorbing to cut short. They had been discussing an Indian miniature they had both seen in Delhi – the departure of a husband from his young bride – when Astaffort said, 'You know, I have always loved this work for its delicate line and colour, but recently I lost someone and suddenly I understand the painting better.'

'Yes?'

'Forgive me,' Astaffort had said, looking embarrassed. 'I know you too lost someone.'

If he wasn't expected at Mary's he would have asked Astaffort to stay for lunch. James picked up the phone.

'Mary?'

'Yup.'

'I say, would you mind if I brought this French chap over to your place? He's rather fascinating and I'd like the boys to meet him.'

'If he doesn't mind risking his health with our English beef he's welcome.'

*   *   *

230

'Aunt Mary?'

'Yup.'

'Would you mind having a word with George? He's got something he needs your help with.'

'Just as soon as I've finished making the gravy. Your father's bringing some French sculptor over for lunch and I bet he's fussy. The French are, particularly about anything to do with the trough.'

'Hugh'll do the gravy, won't you, Hugh? Only it's urgent.'

'Course,' said Hugh. He liked to cook when anyone would let him.

Sighing slightly, Mary went outside into the yard. Edwin's friend was standing there looking scared. Edwin spoke for him.

'George has run up against a prob.' His expression was serious. 'He's just rung the only number in the name of his mother's family and a very posh-sounding woman answered.'

'George?' Mary turned to the stable lad. She had seen him up on Mandy earlier that morning in the meadow. Ted was right. He had a wonderful seat.

'Reckon I panicked, didn't I?'

'So what can I do to assist?'

George was looking at the ground, so Edwin took charge again. 'It's like this, Aunt Mary – me and George want you to ring this woman – kind of sound her out. Then if it seems, you know, like she may have something to tell George, you can tell him and he'll take it from there.'

Secretly, Mary was impressed by her nephew's crusade. He had guts – the kind of guts the country needed. And this friendship was no bad thing either for a future king of a population that was now such a mix of people. 'You want me to suss her out, is that it?'

Edwin smiled his heart-stopping smile. 'Exactly. See, I knew she'd get it. Aunt Mary's brill.' He thumped his aunt on the back.

'Wow, watch it! You're strong enough to knock me flat. OK, then, flatterer, give me the number and I'll ring it after lunch. What do you want me to say?'

'Can't you do it now? People go out after lunch and there's Dad and his Frenchman coming here. You can say it's to do with your charity work, can't you, Aunt Mary?'

Which, in a way, it is, Mary thought smiling to herself as she went to telephone the number her nephew had pressed on her. What a will the boy had! No one had better try and stand in his way when he thought something was right. The Family wasn't going to know what had hit them when he reached his majority.

Mary rang the number – a Wiltshire exchange. An answerphone, with the 'posh-sounding voice' that had repulsed George, asked her to leave a number. Might as well. She didn't see it could do any harm. And if her own voice and number could help the boy, why not? He had good hands, too. Why not give them a jolt and tell them who was ringing? That would, at least, prepare the ground for George. They weren't likely to quarrel with having her as a connection!

Henri had accepted avidly the invitation to lunch at the house of Prince James's sister. He knew she was a famous horsewoman and even before his recent conversion to the Royal Family he had admired her. She was chic, too, in that careless, fair, English way. Fine hands. He would like to do a carving of them.

It was during pudding that the telephone rang. Henri was describing a day he had spent at the Chantilly races involving a complicated betting scam, which was making Mary's husband Tom laugh so much that tears were collecting on his cheeks.

'Damn!' Mary said. 'I forgot to put on the answerphone. It's probably that Fenton-Kirk woman.'

No one could have been sure whether it was Mary herself or M. Astaffort, their guest, who, at that moment, knocked over the wine which spread across the old white damask table cloth like a guilty stain. Everyone jumped and Edwin rushed over to the phone.

The caller had given up. Edwin dialled 1471.

'It was *that* number,' he said meaningfully to his aunt, accompanying her to the scullery from which she was fetching cloths. 'Will you ring her back?'

But M. Astaffort had followed them.

'I am so sorry – forgive me – I am clumsy . . .'

'Good heavens! It's only a table cloth. And there's stacks more wine.'

'I am mortified but, you see, I received a shock. The name of your caller was Fenton-Kirk?'

Mary looked at Edwin and it was he who replied. 'Yes – Aunt Mary was trying to get in touch with her for something I wanted.'

The Frenchman looked very white and his forehead had beaded with sweat. He clutched Edwin's sleeve.

'I think I know this family. A good friend of mine – she died . . .' Suddenly he remembered – this was the Princess Helena's beloved elder son. '. . . forgive me, I think she died about the time your mother . . .'

Edwin's aunt, usually protective of her nephew, especially with strangers, turned suddenly on her heel and left the scullery. For a moment Edwin could not speak. Then he said, 'I have a friend too. He was adopted. His mother was called Fenton-Kirk.'

Henri thought, 'It is the Prince's Shakespeare Garden brings me here and now this is like a play of Shakespeare's.'

'Where is your friend?' His voice was rough; he too was near tears.

'Please, will you wait here?'

Edwin left the scullery. It seemed a long time before he returned with a small dark boy with black curly hair.

233

Afterwards Henri thought it was as if his own genes had responded to the boy. 'Hector!' he said opening his arms.

'And the wonder of it was the boy knew who he meant,' Mary said later to her brother who was helping her dry up the wine glasses.

'Not really,' said the Prince. 'He had read his birth certificate. More wondrous is that he and his mother's friend should both happen up in your house. That's your hospitality, my dear.' He felt more than usually affectionate towards his sister.

'Your love of your old Shakespeare, rather.'

She was pleased for him. Edwin was over the moon at the discovery that Henri Astaffort had known his friend's mother. And Hugh, who had cooked them all tea, was almost as joyous.

'It's called synchronicity,' James had said to his sister and he explained it later that evening back home, to his elder son, after the younger had gone to bed.

'It's the idea of meaningful coincidence.' Edwin, who was on the sofa had left George with his excitable new 'uncle'. Dad had allowed him to bring Hestia into the sitting-room. She had woken up a few days earlier and now she was sitting on the hearth looking into the fire with little bright black eyes. It was nice being there, just the three of them.

'If you live your life in a random kind of way,' his father continued, 'the things that happen to you happen by accident. But if you start to live from inside yourself – doing what feels right to you, even if it contradicts what other people say or think you should do – then what happens to you becomes part of your fate. It becomes "meant", not in the silly way people often use that term but in a much more profound way. Synchronicity happens when a person is living his or her destiny.'

Edwin looked at the mantel-shelf where the housekeeper had placed a vase of coloured flowers. Anemones, like the flowers the nurse in the crowd had given him.

'Do you think what happened to Mum was accident or part of her destiny?'

His father looked out of the tall window down towards the Shakespeare Garden where Astaffort was to place his statue. It was with Helena in mind that he had commissioned it. She had done a marvellous job on their sons. Edwin and his friend, George, had both lost mothers – maybe on the same day – from what Astaffort had been able to determine. It was that, perhaps, which had made the boys friends. But it was Edwin's gift of warmth, his lack of stuffiness, his willingness to mix, even (one couldn't help smiling) if it involved duping his school and his detectives, which had forged the link which had ended in his friend beginning to be able to trace his real mother. There was no doubt – Edwin was his mother's son.

'I thought at first' – he spoke so as to communicate his mind as truthfully as he could – 'it was pure accident. I even thought, God forgive me, that she had, maybe, brought it on herself – by being careless, you know?' He looked anxiously at his son but Edwin simply sat looking at his father with his grave eyes and made no comment. 'Then, when there was all the public reaction, the extraordinary grief, I had that row with Granny. I began to see that I, that we, all of us, had under-estimated her – misjudged her.'

Outside, in the dusk-gathering garden, a male blackbird was calling to a female. James listened to the distinctive call, envying the bird its single-mindedness.

'We had our differences, your mother and I, and I am sorrier than I know how to tell you that you and Hugh got caught up in all of that. It must have hurt you both. I'm deeply sorry.'

He looked straight at his son as he said that and Edwin smiled back at him, flushing slightly. 'But we were so different in essence. I think the alchemy between us could never have worked. Except, of course, that it produced two pure nuggets of gold – you and Hugh.'

He leaned almost as if he was about to get out of his chair and reach across the wide room to his son. 'Maybe that was what we were for, Mummy and I, to bring the two of you into the world. But I'm sure, too, that she was made for something else. She had the capacity to reach into people's being and move them. To make them value life, however hopeless they felt, perhaps because she walked such a tight-rope herself. And so, you see, when she fell off the tight-rope, and it looked like a terrible accident, I wonder if it wasn't what Mummy was there for all along: to show us all that life is very precious and to teach us to use it well.'

It was the longest his father had ever spoken to him and Edwin, unwilling to break the spell of the words, made no audible reply. Instead, he got up from the sofa and crossed the room to where his father was sitting, his fingers joined in the familiar crossed arch.

Outside, a thrush's voice had joined the blackbirds. Edwin, on the arm of the chair, leaned against his father. For a long time they sat there, father and son, watching the westering evening sky over the Shakespeare Garden.

34

The phenomenon of the appearance of the woman they called the Lady Iphigenia at the ancient sanctuary of Artemis Brauronia gathered interest gradually.

At first only the local people came to the shrine where there were sightings. The Lady Iphigenia, it was said, did not appear for those who came in the wrong spirit – with revenge or hatred in their hearts. A woman with terminal cancer had gone fifteen times, seeking her, but to this woman the Lady Iphigenia never appeared. Later it was rumoured that the cancer victim had a vendetta against her daughter-in-law – had made, and was still making, the young woman's life a misery. For the Lady Iphigenia to appear to you, it began to be whispered, you must first cleanse your mind and heart.

A tradition grew up of washing hands or faces in the nearby waters – for the area retains its watery origins. Caroline Nicolaides, who liked to collect tadpoles from the sacred pool, became quite annoyed because too often there were people there now, disturbing the water. But her husband, who had grown quite merry and these days often sang about the house, was more tolerant.

'It is right that they give due reverence,' Spyros opined and Caro knew better than to disagree. He was the poet – he knew about sacred matters.

One day, an English journalist on holiday in the area came also to the site. He was recovering from a nervous collapse and a friend had recommended the restorative effects of Greece.

It was said that the Lady Iphigenia granted him an appearance on more than one occasion. Afterwards he told someone that his breakdown had occurred after the death of the Princess Helena. He had been a tabloid journalist – not, he wanted it to be known, one of the fatal pack on the day of the tragedy but he had been responsible for an article about her which caused him such bitter regret, after her death, he had not been able to write a line since.

The following week a careful article appeared, under his by-line, in the soberest of the British Sunday newspapers. There were no photographs, only a series of well-researched and unsensationally presented accounts of the effects of the visitations on those who had called on the Lady for her aid. About his own experience and subsequent recovery the journalist had been candid. 'It was remorse over what I had done to Princess Helena that caused my breakdown,' he wrote. 'The Lady Iphigenia has healed my mind, in a way Prozac has not been able to do.'

Edwin was reading the Sunday papers with his father over the breakfast table. It was the last full, free week of the Easter holidays. Next Sunday would be the last and he would be packing to return to school the following week. George was coming over later with his new Uncle Henri, who was going to show them some preliminary sketches for Dad's sculpture. George's Uncle Henri had taken a flat nearby and George spent his days-off there, when he wasn't at the stables. Everyone said what a great horseman George was turning out to be.

One day they had corralled Matt who had driven them to the place under the M4 where George had knocked out a brick from the underpass wall. Inside, wrapped in newspaper, was the small silver horse.

Edwin had always been certain that George was right and that the horse had belonged to his mother. Hadn't his own mother always told him that was the sort of thing you knew by instinct? Intuition, Mum would have said. They hadn't been able to trace the body of George's own mother yet. Now there were resources to organize a massive search – but Uncle Henri seemed to think it better not to.

'I think it is not worth upsetting the boy with a useless enquiry,' Edwin had overheard him saying to Dad. 'What happened to his *maman* will emerge when he is ready.'

Dad, who got on with Uncle Henri on account of this thing they both had about art, had agreed. 'Time generally works these matters out for us,' Dad had said. Dad and Uncle Henri had other things in common.

George had met one of his mother's sisters though, who made hats and sounded nice. She had taken George to tea at her flat and showed him lots of photos of his Mum when she was younger. She recognized the silver horse – it turned out that George's mother had been a champion horsewoman and Dad had become tickled with the idea of teaching George polo and then introducing him to Dad's polo club someday.

George hadn't yet decided whether he wanted to meet his grandparents. There was a difficulty because they had chucked George and his Mum out and that was why he had had to be adopted. You could tell George felt pretty angry about this and why he had said 'No way' to meeting his grandparents. So everyone was leaving that alone for the time being, although it was quite funny because it was George's grandmother who Aunt Mary had phoned that day and left her own number – and now George's grandmother kept phoning Aunt Mary, desperate to be buddy-buddies. Aunt Mary, who had points in common with George, had said, 'No way,' too.

It was nice sitting here with Dad reading the papers looking out on to the garden where the statue was going.

'Hey, Dad.'

'Hmm?'

'This article'

'Hmm?' James was reading about an orchestra to which he had recently offered his support. It seemed this government was going to be worse about the arts, if that were possible, than the last.

'Remember that play you took us to, you know, last summer just before Mum . . .'

James recollected. He had taken the boys to a showing given by a theatre company who were reviving Classical theatre.

'*Iphigenia at Tauris*, you mean?'

'Yes. Well, she's back.'

'Who? Damn!' Some marmalade had dropped on to the newspaper; James was trying to scrape it off.

'Iphigenia. They call her the Lady Iphigenia. She keeps appearing to people.'

'But she's a mythical character, Eds – she's not real.'

'Well, read this, then,' said his son.

Edwin was watching the Spice Girls on TV with Hugh, when their father said, 'I've read the article. Like to go there? To Brauron, in Greece?' Helena had always accused him of being unspontaneous.

'You bet, Dad. Hugh, too?'

'I should think so. We've a clear week before you both start back at school. Friend of mine's got a yacht out there. We could fly out and sail down the coast. Get you back in time for school. Might see dolphins.'

Wishing his father good-night, Edwin thought of something. 'Dad, could we take George with us? His Uncle Henri's going back to Paris for a few days and I was going to have George over here quite a bit.'

Seeing agreement in his father's face he hopped back down the stairs and gave him a hug. 'Hey, Dad, thanks. You're cool.'

35

She knew at once that it was them. Even before she saw their faces clearly, James, Edwin and her little Hugh. There was another boy with them – a dark boy whose face she seemed to recall from some part of the old life. Together, the group walked slowly towards the shrine.

She had not been sure if they would recognize her but Edwin had pulled at his father's sleeve when she appeared before them with outstretched hands.

'Dad,' he had said. 'Dad, look . . .'

But it was Hugh who had known. 'Mummy,' he had cried, running down the path into her arms. 'Mummy, Mummy, Mummy.'

A familiar green van had drawn up (rather like a Harrods van, Hugh had said) and taken them all off, the other boy and Angela and Persephone too, to a secluded cove by the sea.

'Mummy,' Hugh had asked, 'can you still play baseball?' And they had played a riotous game, her and the boys on one team, against James, Angela and the boy who was called George. She remembered then where she had met him: at the football match, against the boys' school, where he had scored the winning goal. She and the boys beat the other team at baseball, although George had run them pretty close.

It was Edwin who recognized Angela first.

'You're the nurse,' he said. 'You gave me the message from Mum. And the flowers.'

Red anemones were growing on the slopes down towards the sea. He had seen them from the van.

Angela explained, 'She sent me. She wanted you to know she was safe.'

George was looking at Angela. Suddenly he said, 'You're the lady in the Abbey.'

'The boy who was . . .' she stopped herself. Boys didn't like to be reminded of tears. 'George?'

George looked embarrassed. 'Yeh! I guess I know now what you were trying to tell me. I kind of found my own mum. We think she died when . . .' He gestured towards the couple who were walking away from them along the dunes.

'Will you walk?' James had asked her, and they had walked together along the grassy dunes. She hated leaving the boys for a second but they were playing games in the sea, throwing sticks to Persephone.

For a while they said nothing – each preoccupied and a little shy with each other. Even in the life before, there had been long gaps in their meetings. After a while he stopped her, putting out his arm.

'Do you hate me?'

She looked back. Hugh was doing a silly walk up the beach with Persephone at his heels. Edwin and his friend were having a competition throwing stones at a rock in the sea.

'How could I hate you when we brought those boys into the world together? Besides, I hope I am past hating.'

'Can you tell me what happened?'

The waves of the Aegean were aquamarine under the April sky. Broken reflections of small white clouds danced in the water.

'It's the Greek Easter today. Did you know?' He hadn't. The Orthodox calendar, older than ours, brings the celebration of Christ's resurrection around at a different date. 'Best to say I was moved – from one life to another.'

'They call you Iphigenia?' It was a question as much as a statement. 'Did you know I took the boys to see the play where she is saved from the sacrifice?'

She nodded. 'Eds told me about it.'

'It's an odd coincidence, isn't it? Or do you think it was coincidence?'

Slender, in her yellow gown, she looked to him like a tall daffodil. 'Daffodils, that come before the swallow dares/ And take the winds of March with beauty.' The daffodils in his Shakespeare Garden had been out in splendour when they had left England.

'But *are* you her now?' But to that, too, she made no answer.

They walked on a way until, hardly able to bear it, he said, 'Do you still love me?'

And at this she smiled and her smile was all it ever was.

'I don't know that I ever did love you, James,' He made a sound of protest but she went on. 'I don't think I understood what love was, except for the boys. I *believed* I loved you – I would have sworn, by all that's holy, that I adored you – but I think now it was a picture I had of myself. I wanted to love you – but I had such a limited understanding of love. I didn't love myself. How could I have loved you then?'

He wasn't sure he understood. 'But now, could you love me

now, if we were to start again? I mean, if I could do it, if I could be, well, different?'

Red flowers were growing in the field. A clutch had pushed their way into the sandy grass. Anemones – Aphrodite's flowers.

'What I have learned here, in this life I now inhabit, is that there are many forms of love. One is not necessarily better than another as long as you see it for what it is. The world is very large – there is room for all kinds of love in it.'

'But me, could you love me? I did you wrong.' There were tears in his eyes.

'What you did to me was as much my doing as yours – and it has done me great good. I learnt from it. James, I love you more now than I ever loved you but what does that mean?'

She opened her hands and he grasped one of them.

'Let me stay here with you. I will help you – look after you.'

He meant it. Somehow a life together with her now would make all the wrongs right.

'James, answer me truly, why did you marry me?'

She was looking at him with eyes which demanded nothing less than the truth.

'I thought you were the prettiest thing I'd ever seen.'

'Good,' she patted his shoulder affectionately. 'You see, the reasons were not right in the first place. And I, my dear, married you because you were going to be king and I wanted to help you. Not bad reasons, on either side, but not good enough. Neither of us knew who the other was – how could we really love each other?'

'But it's different now.' He could tell it was hopeless. It was she who was different.

'Listen,' she said, and gently she touched his arm as she spoke, 'we have different paths, you and I. I have no choice about my present life – I am here to help those who need help and are ready to accept it. And you have responsibilities back at home.'

'You mean the boys? Couldn't they come here and be with you too.'

She shook her head. 'It is not possible. They must return to fulfil their own lives. And you have your great task, too. And there is also Jessica to think of.'

Now she really startled him. 'Jessica? You mean you don't mind?'

Again she smiled and he knew then that she had gone far beyond him.

'I used to mind. It filled my waking and my sleeping with bad dreams. But you are with Jessica for a reason. I think, maybe she truly loves you. And you her.'

'It's not the same,' he almost wailed.

'They have a saying here: You can't step into the same river twice. Nothing ever is the same,' she said as she led him back towards the strand where the boys were playing.

She had not seen Dr Asklepios since they had parted company at the Gulf of Corinth all those months ago. She had asked then if they were to meet again and he had been sanguine but vague about the possibility.

'I daresay that Destiny intends for us to meet again. Such good friends are not, as a rule, kept apart. But, as ever, we are in Her hands.'

He had disappeared, off, perhaps, to Epidaurus, he did not say, having delivered her over to a warm, violet-smelling wind, which had whirled her to Brauron.

James and the boys had gone – driven in the green van back to the yacht. She had watched them, from the highest dune, drive away, dwindling into the distance. Of course she had waved until they were quite out of sight.

Dr Asklepios had appeared suddenly at her side.

'Here, a handkerchief. It is Aphrodite's. Silk, I imagine. She

246

dropped it at Ares' place and I must return it to her before that husband of hers finds it is missing. She will be pleased to lend it to you.'

Dear Dr Asklepios continued to talk hard until the tears had stopped coursing down her face and she had wiped it and blown her nose.

'I thought I was supposed to have put all that behind me.'

'Oh, such stuff and nonsense! Emotion never disappears. It is how you take the emotion which alters. It is a matter of taking it gently – the loss, the grief and the joy. This planet of ours is not so old, Iphigenia. There is plenty of time. Do not doubt that you will all meet again.'

'In this life, Dr Asklepios?'

They were walking back, over the sifting sand of the dunes, to where Hermes, having delivered the other party, was waiting for them in the green van. He had taken off his hat and was visible in the front of the van reading a copy of *Hello* magazine. She was glad to see Hermes again.

'In this life I do not know. Who can say?' Dr Asklepios made one of his gestures. 'But there are many lives, Iphigenia, and room for many meetings. Now, I think I take you somewhere nice to eat. Hermes can lend you his hat. Meantime, you sing us again that song you teach us on the way to my home in Epidaurus. "She loves you." We will do the "yeah, yeah, yeahs", Hermes and I. Together we will be – what is it? – your backing group. Yes?'

36

It was half-term. George, whose name had now been altered by due legal process to George Kirk, had been with Edwin to visit the very private place where the Princess Helena had been buried.

'We don't know where your mum is,' Edwin had said, 'so why don't we make this her burial place, too? My mum wouldn't mind.'

They never mentioned the visit to Brauron. Edwin wondered how much memory, if any, his friend had of the event. Hugh, he knew, recalled something. On their return, Hugh had asked if he might have a new puppy and had chosen a black-and-grey spaniel bitch.

'What shall we call her?' Dad had asked and he had seemed pleased when Hugh had said, 'Oh, Persephone, of course.'

Persephone went everywhere with Hugh and even slept on his bed – which Dad seemed quite relaxed about. Dad had certainly changed.

Edwin wasn't sure what Dad remembered. He had seemed sad after they all went back to the yacht. Even the trip to Apollo's island hadn't made much difference. The island was an ancient site where, in the old days, people came to worship the god of the sun. There were tons of ancient remains and effigies there but even these didn't cheer Dad up as much as Edwin had hoped. Dad'd been pretty solemn too since their return. So it was quite a relief when he had said, that afternoon, after they had come back from visiting Mum's family place,

'Look, would you mind terribly if I had Jessica over? Just for tea, you know?'

Edwin was pleased. 'Course, Dad. Look, me and George's going riding.'

'George and I. You don't mind then?'

It was a relief to have Dad correct his English again. He must be cheering up.

Edwin was due to see his grandmother over the half-term. He and Hugh were to have tea with her and they were driven over to her place the following day. Dad stayed behind. Jessica, it seemed, was coming over again – for dinner, this time.

Granny looked a bit worn out but glad to see them.

'I tell you what,' she said, 'what I would really like is a boiled-egg tea. Would you do it for us, Hugh?' And Hugh had been delighted.

As a reward for making them all tea, Hugh had been allowed to watch the Teletubbies on TV.

'The *what*?' Grandpa had asked.

'*Teletubbies*, Grandpa,' Hugh had said, laughing. 'They're the biz!'

Grandpa had gone off to his den to get the racing results and Edwin and his grandmother sat together over their tea.

'You look tired, Granny,' Edwin said. He was fond of his grandmother, who worked hard.

'I'm getting old, Edwin,' she replied. She never called him anything but 'Edwin'.

'Is it tough, being, you know, what you are?'

His grandmother looked at him. A grandmother is not allowed favourites but if she had a favourite it might have been Edwin. He was a gentle boy but brave. Goodness, how firm he had been about his mother's funeral. How silly they had all been then. Poor girl. She missed her.

'You'll find out one day!'

He laughed, pulling a face. 'Don't know that I want to find out.'

'Ah! You know, that sentiment would never have occurred to me. I just knew that it was what I was born for and I expected to have to get on with it.'

Edwin knew this about his grandmother. She had a terrific sense of duty. He felt sorry for her. Suddenly, too, he felt very proud to be her grandson. 'I know,' he said, 'you've done a great job, Granny.'

His grandmother seemed pleased and cut the top off her egg with precision.

'I love a boiled egg,' she confided, 'especially with soldiers.' She ate a buttered toast finger. 'People assume that I enjoy all those banquets and things.' She laughed. 'If they only knew! I long to have macaroni cheese with my slippers on.'

'You should. Why don't you let Dad take over, give you a rest?'

He knew that this was a possibility that was widely discussed.

His grandmother sighed. 'I don't think your father really wants that,' she said. 'We see less of each other, these days, and not always eye to eye. He's not aware of this, but I worry about him. He's really a kind of Renaissance prince, a patron of the arts, you know. Meeting people, state functions – all of that – it's not really his cup of tea.' She sipped her own cup of Earl Grey thoughtfully.

'I'll help you, Granny.'

Suddenly he saw it. It is what Mum had tried to tell him

before they had left her, standing on the dunes by the sea. Before he had climbed into the green van, driven by the man in the winged hat whom no one else seemed to see. His mother had taken him into her arms and whispered, 'Be brave, my darling, and remember who you are.' Like she had on the day he had started school. But this time she didn't only mean he must remember what was important, deep down in his heart. She meant, too, that he must remember what he had been born to be. Granny needed to know that too.

He repeated, 'I'll help you, Granny.'

'Will you, my dear? That's sweet of you.'

'I'll come and visit you. You can tell me all about it – what to do – so that I'll know, you know, when the time comes.'

His grandmother looked at him. He had his mother's eyes. But he also had the character that has the power to change things. He had changed things already. Look at the friend he had made, the lad at Mary's stables, who had turned out, after all (not that her grandson had been at all aware of this at the time) to be related to that Wiltshire family she had known as a gal.

'I hear your new friend's mother was the niece of a friend of mine.'

Did Granny know that George had other origins, more obscure?

'He's not quite what you might be used to, Granny. He's half-black.'

His grandmother smiled, thinking of the old Commonwealth. It was the Empire once. Those days had long passed. If her eldest son and daughter had their ways, she and their father would be riding around on bicycles – although, come to think of it, a bicycle might be fun. 'Dear child, many of my best friends are black.'

'So it's a deal then? We should shake on it Grans – you train

251

me up for when I have to take over, and I'll tell you what I think you need to know – to keep up with things.'

His grandmother glanced over at a calendar on which a photograph of a young foal was displayed. It was 31 May, nine months to the day since the accident. 'Like your mother wanted to do?'

He began to frown and she hastened to correct any false impression. 'No, no, you mustn't mind – I meant it.' He was going to make a first-class king. 'We didn't listen to her soon enough. Maybe I have the chance to listen to her son? Now, tell me about these *Teletubbies* that your brother insists are all the rage. Isn't that what you would call my "keeping up with things"?'

EPILOGUE

Henri Astaffort made the trip to the shrine of Iphigenia, at the ancient site of Artemis Brauronia. His heart had continued to trouble him and he hoped for help there.

He was one of the lucky ones – if luck it was – who were visited by an appearance of the Lady Iphigenia. But he saw, too, another apparition: a young girl who told him the truth about the contents of the coffin that was borne through Westminster Abbey and later buried in that very private place, on an island in the grounds of one of England's great country estates. He told this truth to one other person but the secret remained secure.

Henri's heart ceased to trouble him after the visit. He returned to England where, with the backing of Prince James, he set up a workshop to train young offenders in the art of metalwork sculpture. His own piece, called Hélène, commissioned by Prince James for his private collection, was, many agreed, one of the finest pieces of sculpture of the twentieth century.

George Kirk became a champion jockey. He won the Derby in the year 2000, wearing the Royal colours, when he was just nineteen.

What was known only to a few was that he never raced without carrying on his person a turquoise locket shaped like a heart.

Prince James founded the Royal Society for the Protection of Culture and the Arts. His 'Renaissance Centre', near Shakespeare's birthplace at Stratford-on-Avon, became noted for productions of Ancient Greek drama. Schoolchildren, denied the chance of studying Drama or Classics in the 'new' State education system, were offered bursaries to come and spend their summers at the centre, where they also worked in the famous Shakespeare Garden.

The visitations of the Lady Iphigenia continue to occur. From all over the world the sick and the distressed travel to visit the ancient site of Artemis Brauronia and few who make the journey in the right spirit come away without their troubles lightened.

It is also told, and usually it is a child or a simpleton who tells it – and I am inclined to believe the word of children and simpletons – that a tall woman, dressed in a yellow gown, has been sighted, walking with bare feet by the sea's shores at certain secluded locations along the indented coastlines of Greece, and that on these occasions a tall, fair young man is to be seen at her side. It is said that they walk, these two, arms around each other, deep in talk and that often a younger boy is to be seen along with them, throwing sticks into the sea for a black-and-grey dog. But who am I to know the truth of such observations?

All I know is that I have met her, too, in dreams, the Lady Iphigenia, who some say is but another name for the great goddess Artemis herself. The woman I met, in my dreams, was not a huntress, a bear slayer – nor was she remote, or lofty as goddesses or even princesses are reputed to be. As a matter of fact, she winked at me with one of her remarkable eyes, and told me of the other country, to which she has gone, where things are different, but where, she tells me, they think kindlily of us here and all our myriad and foolish human ways.

AFTERWORD

Handle a large kingdom with as gentle a touch
As if you were cooking small fish.
If you manage people by letting them alone,
Ghosts of the dead shall not haunt you.
Not that there are no ghosts
But that their influence becomes propitious
In the sound existence of the living man:
There is no difference between the quick and the dead,
They are one channel of vitality.

Lao Tzu

Notes

Aphrodite: the goddess of love or, more accurately, lust and desire. Born out of the sea, fathered by Kronos, she is the aunt of **Zeus**, so-called 'father' of the Olympian gods. She was married to the crippled and jealous smith of the gods, **Hephaestus**, but took as her lover **Ares**, god of war. Among her other lovers was the mortal youth, **Adonis**, whom she loved with an unrequited passion. When **Adonis** was killed she was so stricken with grief that Zeus decreed her lover should be reborn each spring, as the anemone which grows wild in Greece and Cyprus.

Apollo: son of Zeus and twin of **Artemis**, was born of Leto on the island of Delos, which acted as a vast sanctuary for the god. He is the god of the sun, and associated with healing. Also with oracular pronouncements – his oracle at Delphi being the most significant in the Ancient world. The father of **Asklepios** he is, like his son, associated with the symbol of the snake – which symbolizes both healing and re-birth.

Artemis: although widely worshipped in Classical Greece she was probably a pre-Hellenistic deity associated with fertility. Daughter of **Zeus** and twin to **Apollo**, she is variously associated with the moon. She is a huntress and 'a lion unto women', with whom she seems to have had a special relationship in matters to do with children and childbirth.

Asklepios or **Asclepius**: the god of healing. His cult was celebrated most famously at Epidaurus, one of the largest therapeutic centres in the ancient world. Therapies included the study of dreams. The Tholos was the round building which housed the sacred snakes. It was counted a mark of the god's favour to be bitten by a sacred snake.

Athena: patron goddess of Athens. In her best-known manifestation she appears in the form of an owl.

Gaia: the child of **Chaos** and the original earth-mother of the planet.

Herakles or **Hercules**: a mythic Greek hero, famous for his mighty labours. He was deified and joined the gods after death.

Hermes: the winged messenger and leader of souls. His winged hat renders him invisible and enables him to move between the worlds of living and dead.

Hestia: one of the most ancient of all the deities of Classical Greece. She became known as the goddess of hearth and home, more emotionally, the goddess of domestic harmony.

Iphigenia: daughter of Agamemnon and Clytemnestra, king and queen of Mycenae, of the doomed house of Atreus. She was sacrificed to **Artemis** by her father, in order to gain a favourable wind to take the Greeks to Troy. In several versions of the myth she is saved from death by the goddess who takes her into her own service. **Iphigenia** is also another name for one of **Artemis**'s manifestations.

Pan: the cloven-hoofed son of Hermes. He can induce panic, especially in groups or among crowds.

Parmenides of Elea: A pre-Socratic philosopher of science and forerunner of modern physics. He argued that nothing in the world changes.

Theseus: a mythic Greek hero. Among his many exploits was the famous slaying of the Minotaur, a monster who lived in the heart of a labyrinth at Knossos in Crete. Theseus found his way in and out of the labyrinth using a ball of thread given him by **Ariadne**.

Zeno of Elea: a philosopher friend of **Parmenides** famous for his arguments based on paradox.

Zeus: although not the oldest of the Olympian gods, Zeus was known as their head or father.